THE 21ST CENTURY CRUSADERS

by

Stan Mason

'Those who fail to learn from
history are forced to relive it.'
George Santayana
(1863-1952)

First published in 1996 by
Gemini-Virgo Publishing,
Tregarron, Mount Ambrose,
Redruth, Cornwall, TR15 1QZ.

Copyright © 1996 Stan Mason

ISBN 0 9528342 0 0

All rights reserved. No part of this book may be reproduced or transmitted in any form or by any means, electronic or mechanical, including photocopying, recording or any information storage or retrieval system, without permission in writing from the Publisher.

Printed and bound in Great Britain for
Gemini-Virgo Publishing
by
Chappell Gardener,
17, Haslemere Road,
Windsor,
Berkshire, SL4 5ET.

To my loving wife, Angela, for all the support she gave me on those many days when I simply disappeared into the world of dreams to write fiction.

PREFACE

Earth....a planet which man strives constantly to master.... where ambitions were limited by mediocre weapons, fewness of troops, and the problems of distance. Such problems exist no more! Nations have proved they can deploy destructive nuclear weapons on land, under the sea, and even in space. Yet the record proves that domination is ephemeral. World powers come and go… irrespective of their strength at the time. History is littered with examples. The Persian Empire, the mighty Roman Empire, Attila the Hun, the Moors who conquered Spain, the Mongol Empire under the Khans, the Ottoman Empire, and even the British Empire. Where are they now? More important is the question……who will be the next major world power, and how violent will it be? Many pundits predict it will be China, but development within that enormous country is slow; it may take a hundred years or more to identify its ambitions. This leaves the field open for Islam in the interim period. Within the next seventy years, Islam will flex its muscles, assemble its vast distributed forces and drive a lance firmly into the ground in Turkey……for that will be the epicentre of the new empire. From that moment on, the echoes of its actions will reverberate throughout the world. It will herald a return to the Crusades ……a thousand years after they first began. The philosopher George Santayana once predicted that "those who fail to learn from history are forced to relive it." The world will come to recognise such wisdom.

CHAPTER ONE

If it wasn't for Primar I would never have become involved at all. The odd fact was that I hardly knew the man. He was a casual person who had crossed my path on holiday. Nothing more! Nonetheless, Primar was the kind of man to cash in on acquaintances......however slender they might be. I had regarded him as a pleasant individual, generous to a fault, always insisting on buying drinks as well as paying for excellent meals. He asked for nothing in return. But I had to admit I didn't care too much for the fellow. He was relatively short, with very dark hair and large dark brown eyes which seemed to look right through you..... almost like laser beams penetrating your mind. All that I could remember was that he told me nothing about himself except that he was in business on his own account. Most of all, however, I disliked his arrogance, but on vacation one tends to ignore most virtues and vices especially when contact entails nothing more than a few games of tennis, some drinks and a couple of meals. When he invaded my life again I was at a low point in relation to my future. He could hardly have improved on the timing of his reappearance.

I left the office at noon on that particular day to visit the old library at Whitechapel in the East End of London. The adjoining hall had become famous as an exhibition centre for lost souls in the world of modern art. I sat on a small bench seat to gaze at the portrait of a young woman standing in the doorway of her bedroom at night, She was so beautiful that as my eyes ran over her body with a strong sense of erotic interest I forgot all about the sandwiches I had brought with me. Suddenly, I heard someone whisper my name softly from the other side of the bench seat. I was about to turn but my action was halted by the imperative tone of his voice. 'Don't look round! Whatever you do, don't look round! I need to talk to you urgently!'

'Who are you?' I whispered. My heart began to drum loudly in my ears in the silence.

'Primar! You remember me. The Costa del Sol last year!'

'Primar!' I uttered sharply, biting my tongue at the outburst. It was extremely difficult to comply with his command. I wanted to swivel round and take a good look at him, however caution held sway. I resisted the impulse and stared straight ahead at the portrait.

'I'll be at your office in half-an-hour. Be there! We have to talk about the 21st Century Crusaders. How's your game of bridge coming along? Haven't seen your name in the winning lists lately.'

There was a slight movement of air and I knew instinctively he had gone. Primar! From the Costa del Sol! He had tracked me down and had followed me into the gallery. What was so clandestine about our meeting that he couldn't be seen to meet me face to face? After thirty seconds had elapsed, I turned my head casually but, as I suspected, no one was there. In that brief span of time he had moved from the seat to vanish from the hall. My mind raced swiftly, trying to fathom the reason why he wanted to talk to me. The only thing I could imagine was that he wanted to trade on our acquaintance and borrow some money in private. He certainly spent it fast enough on holiday! It was only then that I became angry with myself for telling him where I worked. Indeed, on reflection, I had told him far more about myself in that Spanish restaurant than I cared to admit. Why had I been so gullible to reveal so much information about myself to a perfect stranger? It had always been my opinion that holiday friendships died a quick death the moment after the aircraft had taken off on the runway of the foreign shore. Clearly it was different with Primar. He knew exactly how I felt about my appointment with Dandy Advanced Electronics, and the office claustrophobia I detested so much. My God! I had told him it was my earnest desire in the short-term to write a letter of resignation to my employer before walking off into the sunset. He knew my main aim was to remove the shackles and fetters which anchored me to the austere business world. Naturally, I had been spouting with holiday euphoria, wanting to live like a lotus-eater in the hot sunshine for the rest of my life as most tourists desire. On reflection, I had been mad to say all that to a stranger!

After a while, I left the exhibition hall and made my way back through unusually heavily-crowded streets. Once installed in my office on the twenty-third floor I went to the window and stared down below. For most people it was a red-letter day and they were determined to make the most of it. The faint rhythmic sound of a large brass band wafted on the breeze across the City of London as thousands of office workers, tourists and sightseers thronged the pavements. There was an air of excitement as they waited expectantly for the British monarchy to pass along the route. It was the majestic occasion of a royal wedding. One of the younger princes, with little chance of succeeding to the throne, had found the princess of his dreams. Ultimately, a proclamation had been issued declaring that this day was to be set aside for the marriage. The crowd, however, had little concern regarding his potential to the throne: they were interested only in the colourful and happy event of the day. As such, they lingered in the warm sunshine hoping for a brief glimpse of the happy couple and their parents before the ceremony took place. Shortly, the cortege would speed by, with the bride, the bridegroom, and the guests.....all of them dressed in their elegant finery, transported by magnificent coaches, trimmed with red and gold paint, pulled by handsome well-groomed horses. And then, in the span of a few minutes, the grand spectacle would be over. Yet the crowd waited patiently just the same, hardly able to contain their excitement. All the way through the main City streets, large strips of multi-coloured bunting stretched and flapped in the warm breeze against the backcloth of a clear blue sky, while the sunlight glinting on the white flag-poles enhancing the glorious and auspicious occasion. Eventually, one of the brass bands emerged from Poultry and Princes Street, with the reflection of the sun flashing from the silver-coloured instruments, and turned away from the Old Lady of Threadneedle Street to march steadily towards St. Paul's Cathedral. The smart blue uniforms of the military musicians advanced in measured step, with uncanny precision and in perfect harmony, as the people lining the pavements watched amid an incessant babble of noise which persisted above the most tuneful efforts of the band. There had been so many sad days in the City during the winter and in early spring.....at last fortune intended to reward it with a joyous event of national interest that readily touched the hearts of a sentimental public.

I surveyed the scene with indifference, being neither a royalist nor a republican. Such indulgences failed to interest me. Neither did I wish to become involved with the personal lives of people......royal or otherwise. Weddings were a bore! I stared at the multitude of people standing idly below with a complete lack of empathy. It seemed to me there was no justification for any person to wait for an hour or so at the kerbside for the sake of a quick glimpse of royalty in the flesh. Any logical person would watch the incident on television in the evening to obtain a full view of the proceedings in the comfort of their own home.

Fifteen minutes passed before Penny Smith, my attractive secretary, summoned me on the intercom to tell me that Primar had arrived. She ushered him into my office and he sat facing me. 'All rather clandestine, isn't it?' I ventured, giving him a wry smile without offering any greeting at all.

He crossed one leg over the other, clasping his hands together tightly about them, leading me to believe that he was under some tension. 'I'll come straight to the point,' he began. A small edge of nervousness sounded in his voice which was uncharacteristic of him. 'I'm trading on an old friendship but I think you might be interested in a new dimension. I've no intention of outlining the whole scenario in one single broadside. It's far too big for that. So please bear with me and hear me out.'

I stared at him in a bemused way wondering why he was stumbling so badly over the issue, shrugging my shoulders disconsolately without replying.

'When we first met,' he continued, 'I took you to be a sharp energetic individual with a sense of adventure. Someone totally bored with the mundane events of normal life. A person with a great deal of potential which would be lost in a great organisation such as this. Apart from anything else, they don't appreciate what you do for them.'

'Quite an assessment of character during a few games of tennis, drinks in the bar, and dinner on a couple of occasions!'

'Yes......we were only in contact with each other for a short time,' he responded. 'But my opinion has been confirmed over the past two months.'

'What do you mean?' I demanded sharply, seeking an urgent explanation.

'You've been under surveillance during that period.'

Suddenly, it became possible to cut the atmosphere in the office with a knife. My eyes narrowed and I stared directly at him fiercely. 'Would you run that past me again?'

'You've been under surveillance for the last two months,' he repeated, ignoring my reaction.

'What right have you to watch my activities?' I countered furiously, feeling a surge of anger course through my body. 'And for what reason?'

'Calm yourself, my friend,' he continued amiably, hoping to take the sting out of the revelation. 'We have something to offer each other. It will benefit you as much as it will us.'

'Us? Who the hell is us? You mentioned 21st Century Crusaders in the art gallery. Is that who you are? A group of people hell-bent in bringing some cause to the attention of the government or the public, dragging all and sundry into its wake in the hope of scoring political advantage!'

He took a matchstick from his jacket pocket and began to chew on the end of it. 'I'll come to all that shortly. But first, I want to gain your confidence.....and then your support.'

I shook my head in disbelief. 'You must be out of your mind! You march in here with a cock-and-bull story to tell me I've been under surveillance for two months and then say you seek my confidence and support. Primar, I hardly know you!'

He stared at me with a bland expression on his face, seeking to allow the moment to pass in the hope that my attitude would soften, but it didn't. Ultimately, it was his turn to shrug and he reached into the inside pocket of his jacket for a buff envelope which he tossed on the desk in front of me. I opened it slowly, removing a number of photographs which showed a man and a woman in flagrante delicto. The faces of the two people involved were very clear in most of the photographs. I could easily recognise myself making love to my secretary, Penny Smith. It was almost as though we had posed to be filmed in a series of sexual acts from different angles. I dwelt on the possibility that Penny had been bribed to make me a vulnerable target for blackmail. The actions in the photographs were too accomplished, too perfect, to be coincidental. But there was no reason for her to do so. I was an ordinary man. What could she hope to accomplish?

'O.K. Primar, you've got me over a barrel,' I admitted icily, maintaining my temper at an even keel as I pretended to be indifferent to any demands. 'What do you want?'

'I simply want you to join us, Jason,' he invited, looking smug now that he felt he held the upper hand. 'Join us in a quest which has so much adventure and excitement that you couldn't possibly dream about it!'

'Except that you won't tell me anything about it,' I snapped. 'And if you don't, I'm never going to know.' I was beginning to tire at the ham-fisted way he had made his approach.

However, Primar was nothing if not clever. He knew it was unnecessary to rush his fences and he remained silent for a moment to allow the cogs in the wheels of my mind to fall into place. The sound of another brass band could be heard floating on the breeze and a roar went up from the people lining the pavements. I moved out of my chair towards the window to watch one of the open ornate horse-drawn carriages being pulled steadily at a slow trot along the main road. Its occupants looked radiant in their finery, smiling and waving amiably to cheering crowds as they passed through the streets, almost at the end of the journey to the cathedral. In view of the evidence which had just been presented to me by my visitor, my mind was in turmoil and I was unable to appreciate the scene in its full splendour. But it was a tremendous sight, with the sun streaming across the roof-tops of the high-rise office blocks to pave the way for the procession with a warm golden path, adding to the colour and character of the occasion.

'I want you to fly with me to Israel to meet my Commander.' His voice broke the silence and took my attention away from the window.

'Your Commander?'

'He wants to tell you all about it himself.'

I stared at the photographs which lay idly on the desk with chagrin, realising I had little alternative but to do what he asked. It was a case of straightforward blackmail. 'When do you want me to go?'

'We have two hours. A little more if necessary. A private plane is waiting at Stansted Airport right now.'

'You must be joking!' I ridiculed. 'I'm already committed for this evening. Look, what the hell is this all about?'

'We'll talk on the way. Far better to discuss it in private; away from the prying eyes of people in this building. Walls have ears you know.'

I returned to my chair and sat down. 'If you think a handful of embarrassing photographs is enough to make me throw up my job and force me to fly to some distant place at a moment's notice you're wrong. You'd better think again!'

'There's more.'

I paused for a moment to consider what else might have happened to me which could be construed to damage my reputation, my career, or my life. 'More? What more is there to know?'

'At this moment, your secretary is holding a letter for your immediate attention. It will probably alter the trend of your life. Destiny, one might say. Why don't you call her in so that she can give it to you?'

I sat back in my chair and scanned his face, wondering where he had secured the information, then I pressed the intercom and called her. 'Penny, is there a letter out there for me?'

'Yes, Mr. Scott,' she replied. 'It arrived a short while ago, marked "Urgent", but I didn't want to interrupt your meeting.'

'Please bring it in right away.'

There was a long silence as we waited for her to enter. 'By the way,' I ventured unfairly as she came in, not having the decency to question her in private before making the accusation. 'I think you've some explaining to do.' I pushed the photographs across the desk for her to examine, never taking my eyes off her face. As she glanced at the first print, her face turned a pale ashy colour and she almost fainted, her body sagging slightly against the desk on which she leaned for support. I tore open the envelope with a leaden feeling in my bones and removed a single sheet of paper. Primar was not a man who toyed with false threats or irresponsible bluffs. It was all real with him. The contents of the envelope were bound to have a profound effect on my life. It was a letter written to me by my wife. I recognised her handwriting immediately.

Dear Jason,

I know this will come as a shock to you and I'm sorry for the inconvenience, but by the time you receive this letter I'll be many miles away. Since our wedding, I became more disappointed in you as the months went by. You seem to think that life is a constant round of changing jobs, moving house, ending commitments and then starting up all over again. Furthermore, it's impossible to argue with you because of your brutish temper. You seemed also to take great pleasure in leaving me for evenings and weekends to play bridge. I know that bridge is important to you but I have a life to lead as well. Eventually, you started to change my personality although I managed to endure that for a while. But when I learned of the affair with your secretary, that was the last straw. After all the mental punishment in two years of marriage, I was the one cast aside in the end. I don't know what the future has in store. All I know is that you will not be sharing my life again. Oddly enough, once you've mended your pride, I don't think my absence will mean much to you. But that is how you are.

Jan

I allowed the letter to slip from my fingers and stared coldly at Primar. 'You bastard!' I swore. 'You didn't have to tell her about Penny!'

'Me?' he exclaimed, completely taken aback by the allegation. 'I think you owe me an apology for that remark, old boy. I might have been forced in that direction for my next move if you turned me down flat, but I hadn't got that far.'

'If that's true,' I countered, 'how did you know about the letter?'

'By accident,' he related calmly. 'When I arrived your secretary was out of the office. A well-dressed lady entered with this envelope in one hand and a suitcase in the other. She seemed very distressed, threw the envelope on the desk and hurried out. I was curious. The envelope hadn't been sealed, so I read the letter.'

'God.....you must be desperate!' I accused him acidly. 'What on earth is your motivation?' He failed to reply so I turned on my secretary who pushed the photographs back to me with a pained expression on her face. 'Someone's set me up,' I snarled. 'What do you know about it?'

'Nothing!' she blurted out, almost in tears. 'I know nothing about it!' She turned to Primar, her bosom heaving with emotion. 'Who are you? What do you want?'

'None of this concerns you, my dear,' Primar told her smoothly. 'I suggest you get on with your duties and ignore what you've seen here. In fact you'd be wise to forget you ever saw me.

'But this does concern her!' I told him savagely. 'We're in these photographs together. How can she ignore it?'

He bridled for a moment. 'Jason, she doesn't have to get involved. She's not part of the plan. Don't you understand!'

'No!' I shouted. 'You're the one who doesn't understand! Now that my wife has left me, your threat of blackmail is removed altogether. I've nothing to fear from you now.'

Primar released a hollow laugh. 'Blackmail? Why should I want to do that? I came here with a proposition. If I wanted to blackmail you, the threat would be far more effective than to send copies of these photographs to your wife. I would threaten to send them to your employer. But if I did that, you and Miss Smith here would be seeking employment elsewhere which would be counter-productive. Blackmailers usually want money. Those who don't work, don't earn. I showed you the photographs simply to prove you've been under surveillance. Look, Jason, I want you on my side, not against me!'

I dismissed my secretary with a wave of the hand and moved over to the window again. The roar of the crowd below surged into the office, drowning the noise made by the brass band as the monarch came into view. Everyone waved frantically as the raiments worn by royalty glowed with an aura of brilliant technicolour, reflecting the light from a myriad of sparkling jewels which embellished them with majestic splendour. I turned and placed a hand on my wife's letter, as if to blot it out, before returning to Primar. 'What do you want me to do?'

He tossed the old matchstick into the ash-tray, drew a fresh one from his pocket and then started to chew the end of it. 'Let's evaluate your current position! Your wife has left you. Your secretary will treat you like a leper because of the photographs. Your appointment here has prospects....if you're prepared to wait ten or fifteen years. Life is passing you by at a rate of knots, old boy' But I can offer you instant thrills and excitement, an appointment, and greater rewards later on, in the short-term. Trust me!'

'Trust you!' I challenged. 'I meet a man by chance on the Costa del Sol. Some time later he places me under surveillance and wants me to fly to a Middle East country at two hour's notice. Then he says 'trust me!'. You must be crazy!'

'Don't be naive!' he returned coldly. 'I knew all about you long before we met in Spain. You were on my short list of recruits.'

'Recruits!' I guffawed. 'For the 21st Century Crusaders...... whoever they might be!'

'Everything will be revealed to you in good time,' he insisted. 'I suggest you tell your secretary you're taking two weeks' vacation. Then we'll drive to your house where you can pack a bag before flying with me to Israel.'

'What's so important about Israel?'

'It's the first stepping-stone. You'll find out.'

'The first stepping stone of the 21st Century Crusaders?'

He shook his head sagely. 'I told you, all in good time, my friend. You have a certain way with you, Jason. Positive, ruthless, definite. I like that in a man.' His face broke into a smile.

'And Penny Smith comes with me,' I told him, with determination in my voice. 'Wherever I go she comes with me.' The thought of losing my wife and my mistress at the same time was too difficult to bear.

The smile disappeared from his face. 'Not possible!' he replied firmly. 'The faster you detach yourselves from each other the better. This is no adventure for a woman.'

'Then the deal is off,' I replied, equally as firmly. 'If she doesn't go, I won't go!'

He chewed on the matchstick for almost ten seconds and then got to his feet. 'O.K. We all have to make sacrifices. I suppose this one's going to be mine.' He reached the door and turned to face me. 'I've changed my mind about flying tonight. Best make it, say, nine o'clock tomorrow morning at Stansted Airport. I'll be there to meet you and to brief you.'

'Don't you think I ought to know more about your organisation.

You owe me that much.'

'There'll be plenty of time tomorrow, Jason. We'll talk during the flight. That's a promise.'

He departed leaving me in a foul mood. It was the kind of day when nothing seemed to go right. Primar and my wife had turned my world upside down in the space of fifteen minutes. I was a free agent now. Perhaps it was all for the best. Someone once told me that everything that happened in life was written in heaven. Maybe they were right. What had Jan written in the letter? 'I'm sorry for the inconvenience!' How bizarre! Nor was I changing her personality. She was simply growing up....ridding herself of childish ideals. She also claimed I had left her often to play bridge. Well....when we first got married she knew I had reached the Camrose Trials to be selected to play for England. But Jan was always rather short in vision, and with even less foresight. However, she was right about one thing. It wouldn't be long before I nursed my pride back to good health to put her out of my mind. I didn't want to; I had to! It was the only way to safeguard myself from being hurt emotionally, especially after the experience suffered at the end of my first marriage some years earlier.

I pressed the intercom and told Penny to block all calls and visitors to the office. I needed to assess the position more carefully. Although Primar advised me to declare I was taking a two-week vacation, I had a gut feeling that whatever destiny had in store would take a lot longer. I sat at the desk for the best part of an hour, wrestling with my life as I doodled on the blotting pad in front of me. Then I stood up and returned to the window, looking down at the empty streets strewn with litter left by the sightseers who had long departed. By this time, the ceremony at St. Paul's Cathedral would be over and I mused at the affinity which existed between the prince and myself. We were each embarking on a new venture that would alter the trend of our lives.....although our journeys would move in entirely different orbits. Nevertheless, I intended to face the challenge with no regrets at not being the prince: and no doubt the prince, had he even the remotest knowledge of my existence, would have had no desire to change places with me.

❦ ❦ ❦ ❦ ❦

CHAPTER TWO

By the end of the day, when the dust had settled, I left a message with Personnel Division to say that I was taking two weeks' compassionate leave as a result of domestic problems. They would not consider it strange that Penny Smith was also taking her leave entitlement for many senior secretaries took their holidays at the same time as their managers. Penny was obviously upset after Primar's visit. She seemed convinced we were being blackmailed and assumed I was shielding her. I had never donned the mantle of a gallant before, but I did nothing to dissuade her. I recalled she once told me that her father had been a vicar in the north of England before he died. No doubt she had a mother with a high degree of propriety who would take fright if she ever caught sight of the photographs.

I accompanied Penny back to her apartment so that she could pack a suitcase. I had to admit it was not a wise decision to take her with me but we seemed to be involved in this mess together. We gathered her belongings and returned to my house. It seemed cold and empty without Jan there to greet me. Everything was still in its place; none of the furniture, paintings or bric-a-brac had been removed. The repatriation of many of the possessions we shared was likely to come later. The night passed with an uneasy calm, for neither of us could claim to have slept well: in fact it was doubtful whether we slept at all. Consequently, when morning arrived and light entered the bedroom we both felt tired.

Primar failed to meet us at the airport but his absence didn't create a problem. As we proceeded to the reception area, we saw a young man holding a wooden pole bearing a sheet of paper which had my name written in block capitals. He also held a photograph in his hand to enable him to recognise us.

'I'm Chedda!' he announced brightly in a clipped accent as we approached him. 'Primar has been delayed but he asked that you wait for him on board the plane. Come, if you follow me I will take you there.'

He led us across the tarmac towards a strange aircraft I had never seen before. The door was open and he pointed to the steps indicating for us to climb aboard. Chedda's face broke into a smile when he saw the confused expression on my face. 'You know something about aircraft, eh?' he laughed easily. 'But you've never seen one like this before. I'm not surprised. It's a Kfir Junior,' he explained. 'Kfir is the Israeli for Lion. The advantage is it can fly much further than other light aircraft because it has additional fuel tanks fitted to keep it going. You'll learn that the Israelis are great people for ingenuity.'

We ascended the steps into the aircraft and Chedda placed our luggage in a locker located on one side of the cabin. The interior was practically new and very smart, capable of carrying six passengers comfortably. 'How many others are coming with us....apart from Primar?' I asked naively.

'You have star treatment and total privacy today,' he replied. 'In fact, once the door to the pilot's cabin is closed no one can see you at all. You can do anything you wish. The cocktail cabinet is over here and food is in that locker there. Excuse me for a moment. I'll take this opportunity to warm up the engine.'

He left us for a while and we relaxed in the soft, comfortable seats, acclimatising ourselves to the new environment. Primar had thought of everything. There were morning newspapers, the latest magazines, cigarettes, cigars, sweets, drinks, and a variety of food. We were about to travel in style!

It was almost ten minutes before Chedda reappeared. I lowered my newspaper and, at the sight of the expression on his face, sensed he was going to present us with bad news. 'We have a problem,' he advanced in a quiet tone. 'Primar hasn't arrived yet but traffic control has given me clearance to take off. I cannot delay because of airport flight schedules. I'll have to go. Will you secure your safety-belts and prepare for take-off. And, please, no smoking for a while. Yes?'

Before I had a chance to ask questions, he had closed the door and returned to the pilot's cabin. Penny and I glanced at each other uneasily. I shrugged my shoulders in a casual manner but the truth was that Primar hadn't turned up as he had promised!

'How long do you think the journey will take?' she asked apprehensively.

'Just short of four hours, I believe,' I answered. 'It all depends on tail winds. They can make a difference of over half an hour.'

The engines took on a more fortified note as Chedda taxied along the runway and within the span of less than a minute the aircraft had taken off. I smiled amiably at Penny but it was impossible to shift a discomforting sensation that something was very much amiss. After we had gained considerable height, I opened the cocktail cabinet to pour the drinks. What had happened to Primar? Why hadn't he arrived? The only person to answer those questions was the pilot, Chedda, but then it was reasonable to presume he didn't know. For the first time in a long while my nerves started to get the better of me and I had difficulty in sitting still. I managed to find a pack of playing cards and began to play patience to calm myself down while Penny ploughed through a number of magazines. Yet there remained a disturbed silence as neither of us made any effort to communicate. It was almost an hour later when I tired of the cards. I stared out of the port window for a while, gazing dismally at the white clouds floating like cotton-wool below then, impatiently, I got to my feet and knocked on the door of the pilot's cabin. There was no answer so I turned the handle a number of times to discover it was locked.

'Hey, Chedda!' I called out urgently. 'Open the door! I want to speak with you!'

There was silence for a few moments before his voice rang out over the communication system. 'Sorry about all this, Mr. Scott, but I have strict instructions not to communicate with you, or to open the door of this cabin. You can't come in. Those were Primar's specific orders. You have everything you need in there. I suggest you wait until we land when we may both learn something to our advantage.'

'What's going on, Chedda?' I continued. 'What the hell's happening?'

'Don't ask me. I'm just a hired pilot,' he replied calmly. 'I'm just obeying orders. Maybe Primar will contact us on the radio soon and then we shall find out. Eh?'

'You must have known he wasn't coming on this trip when you met us at the airport!'

'What difference does it make? I told you, I'm only the pilot.'

'Let's not play games!' I shouted, turning partly to face Penny who stared at me with concern. 'Open the door! If you don't I'll break it down!'

'Be sensible, Mr. Scott,' advised Chedda unhelpfully. 'There's no good reason for you to come into this cabin. Why not make yourself comfortable until we reach our destination?'

The communication system went dead and I hammered on the door with my fists before realising the futility of my actions. The entrance had been reinforced by a steel sheet, preventing anyone from breaking it down. I returned to my seat angrily. Why should Primar say he wanted me to accompany him to Israel and then fail to turn up? Why should he give the pilot specific orders not to communicate with me, or refuse to let me enter the pilot's cabin? Primar was not the kind of man to issue instructions wantonly. He always had a motive in mind. I regretted having insisted that Penny came on this trip with me. On reflection, it had been a rash and foolhardy idea! My lack of foresight had brought her to the forefront of danger. I sat down again and tried to relax. It was pointless to become agitated in a fight I couldn't win. We were captive passengers trapped in the cabin until the end of the journey.

It was distinctly to our advantage that the tail-winds favoured us that day. We made exceptional headway, reducing the estimated time of arrival substantially. I stared at the face of my wristwatch for about the fortieth time when Chedda's voice rant out over the communication system. 'I hope you haven't been too bored back there. Better fasten your seat-belts please and refrain from smoking. We're coming in to land shortly.'

I finished my drink slowly, determined not to be hurried, but Penny obeyed the request diligently and secured herself tightly into her seat. I glanced out of the starboard window to look at the terrain in the distance. We were still out to sea but approaching the shore very quickly. The pilot warned us again of the imminent landing and I sat down to secure my seat-belt. 'Hold on!' he shouted. 'We're coming in to land now!'

It was the last sentence he ever uttered because there was a tremendous explosion from the cockpit which caused havoc. If the door to the pilot's cabin had not been locked, or if it hadn't been reinforced by a sheet of steel, we would have been blown to pieces at the same time. As soon as the explosion occurred, the aircraft bucked wildly, tipping me back violently towards the tail end. Then it rolled forward onto its nose and hurtled downwards at uncontrollable speed. From my position on the floor, I had no idea of the altitude or how long it would be before the plane hit the sea or land. My mind could focus only on the speed of descent which seemed to be occurring at a remarkable rate. It had all happened so quickly I experienced nothing but panic during those few horrific moments, realising that the span of my life was limited to a matter of a few more seconds. It was not a pleasant thought. However, as luck would have it, an air current caused the aircraft to level out just a fraction. It finished its descent at an angle of forty-five degrees, hitting the trunks of two tall trees simultaneously which shored off both wings at the same time. This event was sufficient to reduce the impact of the crash although the fuselage continued its momentum onwards, like a rocket, to bounce finally into a mound of earth. Fortunately, the fuel tanks had been jettisoned at the time of the explosion, eliminating the danger of fire. Providence caused it that way for neither of us was in a fit state to clamber out of the wreckage to run for our lives. I hadn't worked out the odds for survival on the way down; they would have been extremely slim. Destiny, however, has an effective way of letting you know when your number is up. It wasn't our turn yet! Nonetheless, I was to be punished for my procrastination. The delay in fastening my seat-belt around my girth resulted in some agonising injuries. I had been rocked from one end of the cabin to the other, suffering a painful head and a knee injury, a damaged arm, and a very sore shoulder. Penny, on the other hand, was relatively unhurt having been safely secured in her seat. I was more than grateful to be alive as it had been on the cards that we would both be killed on impact.

It was some time before Penny managed to clear her mind and extricate herself from the wreckage. She pulled me out with strength that seemed far beyond her slender form and I lay against a tree for a while stemming the blood which streamed from my nose. When I had taken full stock of my condition, there were bruises all over my body, my knee was very sore, my head sported a large swelling which throbbed angrily, and my shoulder felt as though it had been wrenched out of its socket. But there were no dislocations and no broken bones. Eventually, Penny helped me to my feet and I went to the pilot's cabin which had been ravaged and torn open by substantial force. The evidence was indisputable. A gaping hole under the dashboard indicated that a bomb had been planted there. On exploding, it had caused serious damage to one of the engines and most of the electrical equipment. Chedda was a mass of dead flesh mutilated beyond recognition, and I turned away quickly trying to resist vomiting at the awful sight.

'A bomb,' I explained to Penny, once I had pulled myself together. 'Someone planted a bomb in the cockpit. It was probably timed to go off when we were somewhere over the Mediterranean....about half an hour before we landed. We were saved by a freak of nature. Those tail-winds allowed us to make fast time, defeating someone's evil object. Otherwise, we would be feeding the fish in the deep blue sea.'

'But why would anyone want to kill us?' she asked. 'Why should Primar make it his business to kill you?'

'I've no idea,' I replied candidly. 'But I'm going to find out. You can bet your bottom dollar on it!' She took a step forward to go towards the pilot's cabin but I grasped her arm firmly. 'No, don't go in there! I's not something you'd want to see!'

I looked round to determine our location. We appeared to be in a valley which had suffered too much from the heat of the sun. I knew from reading one of the travelogues there were many places of this kind in Israel. From the lie of the land, I took a view there was a main road on the horizon.

'I have a hunch there's a highway over there,' I ventured, pointing in an easterly direction. 'I'm going to try for it. Whatever happens, you're not to worry. Stay here. Don't move. I'll be back shortly.'

I started off as quickly as possible, hobbling for the first part, moving along a faint path. It took me nearly fifteen minutes to get to the rise but my hunch was well rewarded. The highway was there as I had predicted. There was also a signpost close at hand with two arrows on the crossbar facing opposite directions. Under one was the name Agios Nikolaos; beneath the other was Rethymon. But facing me from the centre of the post ere the words Iraklion and Knossos. I froze in confusion. This wasn't Israel! We were on the island of Crete! What was Primar playing at? Why the charade and all the nonsense about travelling to Israel when he knew the plane would bring us here? Previously, it mattered little where he wanted us to go, but now the switch had been made there were question which needed answers!

When I returned to Penny, I informed her of our location. She became very tearful, complaining we were simply pawns being pushed around a giant chessboard. The impact of how close we had been to death clearly affected her. Suddenly, I had another hunch. The solution had to be in the pilot's cabin. I didn't like the idea of staring at the remains of Chedda again but I had to search that part of the plane. Avoiding his mutilated body as best I could, holding a handkerchief over my face, I rifled through the wreckage trying to find some evidence which would make sense of our landing in Crete. However, there was nothing to be found. Whatever might have been there was blown into the sky in the explosion. If so, it was lost to us for ever. I started to search the rest of the plane when Penny called out with an element of alarm in her voice.

'Someone's coming!' she shouted. 'I can see a man at eleven hundred hours.'

I stopped searching and hobbled to her side. The man, with a pair of binoculars hanging idly at his chest, wore a sports jacket and grey flannel trousers. He moved swiftly in our direction keeping his hands in his pockets. When he reached us he called out in an amiable manner with an American accent. 'Are you two O.K.? You're damned lucky to be alive.

My God! Look at the state of this aircraft!'

I took him to be an American tourist on holiday having a stroll before lunch. 'Where are we?' I asked innocently.

'You're in Crete. Very close to Heraklion, the capital,' he replied honestly. 'Where were you heading for?'

'Israel,' I replied, wishing I had kept my mouth shut.

He burst into laughter. 'Israel? You must be kidding! That's the best I've heard today. My, you're some way off course. Didn't you use the compass?'

'Can you help us to get to Heraklion?' I asked. 'Do you have a car?'

'Don't worry about that,' he returned slowly, his voice changing to a more menacing tone. 'I'll send you on your way all right, but it won't be where you're thinking. That's the reason I'm here.' He removed his right hand from the pocket of his jacket to show he was holding a revolver. He pointed the gun directly at my head, almost at point-blank range. I froze in my tracks unable to make a move to defend myself.

'Who are you?' I demanded, as fear welled up inside me. 'What the hell do you think you're playing at?'

'Is this man for real?' he laughed, as he glanced towards Penny. 'I'm holding a pistol to his head and he asks what I'm doing.' He turned to look at me again with an ominous expression on his face. 'I'm finishing off the job, you dummy!'

Penny shifted her feet awkwardly as though a stone had crept into her shoe. Before I knew what was happening she bent down and removed the shoe which she raised and hurled at the man's neck with considerable force. The toe-cap struck him in the throat, just below the Adam's apple, and he dropped the gun to clutch at his neck. I moved to reach for the weapon, hampered by the fact that my legs were stiff and sore, but he managed to kick it away and then began to grapple with me. I was no match for him in my injured condition and I knew it would take him little time to overpower me. As soon as he had gained the advantage, he took hold of my throat with both hands and started to squeeze firmly. I couldn't break his grip and soon it became impossible to breathe. A mist started to cloud my eyes and although I could hear Penny's voice calling to me from the distance it became fainter as the life drained from my body.

'Roll clear!' she shouted vehemently. 'Roll clear!'

There was nothing I could do to comply with the order for the man's strength was too much for me. As the life ebbed from me, the mist turned to red before my eyes. I heard the sound of a shot ring out which seemed to echo right across the valley. Then the man's hands loosened on my throat and he collapsed on top of me. I pushed him off and rolled over as Penny allowed the smoking pistol to fall from her hand. 'Oh, my God!' she screamed hysterically. 'I've killed him! I've killed him!'

The man lay at full stretch on the ground with a bullet hole drilled neatly in his temple. It was pointless to test his pulse for there was no doubt he was dead. I clambered into the cabin of the aircraft and emerged with a bottle of brandy, that was still intact, and a blanket. After covering the body with the blanket, I opened the bottle and took a very long pull.

'I had to shoot him,' explained Penny, bursting into tears. 'He would have strangled you.'

'You don't have to convince me of that,' I replied, touching my neck tenderly. 'You were very sharp. That action with the shoe was pretty quick thinking. It's lucky you happened to hit him in the throat. I dread to think what might have happened had you missed.'

She shrugged her shoulders. 'I had to do something. It was all I could think of at the time.'

I nodded and moved to the body. 'You'd better look away while I check his identity,' I advised. She turned her face in the opposite direction as I searched the man's clothing. I removed a wallet and some papers from the inside pocket of his jacket and covered him up again. 'His name's Tomar Duran,' I related, after glancing at his identity card. 'It's all right. I've covered him up. You can turn round.'

She came towards me and stared at the card. 'Who are these people?' she asked quietly. 'Who are they?'

'I wish I had the faintest idea. Perhaps we ought to fly back to London and forget the whole thing. Primar, Chedda, Duran. It's not our business. Anyway, they probably think we're dead.'

'How can you forget all this?' she volleyed with an element of surprise showing in her eyes. 'Two men are dead. Primar might be missing. You've only Chedda's word that Primar didn't turn up. He may be in similar trouble elsewhere. In any case, if we run now, he'll probably turn up to haunt us somewhere else.'

'Look, Penny,' I told her weakly. 'I'm no hero. Who cares about the 21st Century Crusaders! It's not our business. I don't even know what they stand for!'

She pretended not to hear me and took the papers from my hand. 'Nothing here of much importance,' she muttered. 'A few odd notes and a memo from a Commander Spring.'

'Commander?' I echoed. 'Here, let me see that!' I took the memo from her and read it. The sheet of paper bore only two lines. 'The Acropolis Restaurant, Heraklion,' I read out slowly. 'Urgent! Repeat.....Urgent! Commander Spring.' I stared at Penny blankly. 'What do you make of it?'

I pulled a wry face at the thought of pursuing the matter, uncertain whether I should allow Penny to influence me. It wasn't my problem two men had died. Less than twenty-four hours earlier I had been sitting in my office in the City of London with no serious worries. Now, there was conclusive proof of my adultery, my wife had left me, two men were dead, and Primar was missing. In addition, I was physically injured, suffering from a considerable amount of pain, lost in a foreign country, and very displeased with my lot in life. But that wasn't all. My secretary was now pressing me to become involved in someone else's war. I was not amused! We set off for the highway in the hope of hitching a lift and waited for a car to appear, but the traffic was more than scant.

'I reckon that Duran was waiting for us,' said Penny pensively as we reached the main road.

'That's impossible,' I countered. 'If he belonged to the saboteurs he would have expected us to be at the bottom of the Mediterranean. He wouldn't need to be here.'

'He may have been the long-stop, she suggested. 'Chedda knew he was going to land in Crete but he didn't know about the bomb. Someone had to be around in case the bomb failed to explode. If a person positions himself well here, it doesn't take long to reach most parts of this island. Someone monitoring the flight of our plane could have tipped off Duran as to the likely landing spot. He could have driven close to the point before we came down. The main road runs straight across the north here, so I reckon his car can't be far away.'

I wasn't certain of the logic but there was nothing to lose and we wandered off in a westerly direction. Shortly we came across an old Volkswagen parked in a lay-by. The driver was absent and there was no one else about. Penny searched the car in an attempt to connect it with the dead man so that she could be sure we weren't stealing someone else's vehicle, but it was a hired car devoid of anything which might help us. However, the keys hung neatly in the ignition lock which was the most important factor of all. I drove to Heraklion and after searching the streets parked the car near the Acropolis Restaurant. We entered naively knowing nothing except the name of the Commander. I had the feeling we were putting our necks in a noose. We sat at a table and stared at the menu. Very shortly, a waiter with a stained tea-towel draped over one arm hurried across the room towards us.

'Meester Scott!' he whispered urgently. 'You shouldn't be out here with the customers. Come queekly before you are recognised!'

I stared at him with incredulity. I had just entered a restaurant I never knew existed, in a town I had never seen, on an island I had never visited before, to be approached by a local waiter who had never met me, and he called me by my name. It was uncanny! Almost mesmerised, I followed him to the back of the room through an open doorway across which hung long strands of brown beads. He led the way down a series of steps into the basement, leaving us there before returning upstairs to his duties. I adjusted my eyes to the gloom and noticed a television monitor fixed to the wall. I pressed a button to switch it on and, as it glowed into life, a man's face appeared on the screen.

'Commander Spring?' I asked inquisitively, wondering how it was all going to end.

'Stop playing games, Scott!' he admonished, with irritation in his voice. 'You've got to learn to temper the fun side of your personality. It's just not on! Who's there with you?'

'Penny Smith, my secretary,' I replied woodenly.

He stared at us more deeply, scanning our faces as we stood in that dank area. 'That's an excellent likeness!' he continued, brightening up considerably. 'My apologies. You're to be commended on the choice. You'd better come down.'

The picture faded from the screen and a door opened mechanically in the wall of the basement to provide us with a small lift. We entered and the doors closed sleekly before the elevator went on its downward path. When the doors opened, we walked into a room filled with television monitors and electronic equipment. The Commander, dressed smartly in a brown uniform, faced us with a broad smile on his face. My attention was taken up with the two other men seated at monitors. They also wore brown uniforms and carried holsters containing ominous-looking revolvers. The Commander held up a photograph and compared it with Penny's face.

'An exceedingly good likeness!' he congratulated. 'It really looks like her! Does she speak English?'

'Of course she speaks English!' I snapped.

'Marvellous!' He glanced at the photograph again. 'I wonder if she has a mole on her right..........'

'That's enough, Spring!' I interrupted. 'You'd better tell me what you have in mind!'

He looked at me strangely. 'Quite frankly, I wish they'd picked someone else for your job instead of you,' he returned testily. 'You're too much to take sometimes! If you weren't so good at bridge, a hundred others could have taken your place. Just look at the state of your face and clothes! You look as though you've been pulled through a hedge backwards. I honestly don't know what to make of you!'

'Bridge?' I thought. He wasn't making any sense at all. 'What has bridge got to do with it?' I asked.

'Oh, do stop fooling around!' he cautioned, staring hard at Penny. 'We'll have to wait until Duran returns before we proceed to the next stage.'

'Duran is dead,' I told him, putting my head even further into the noose. 'The plane landed about a mile south of Heraklion. The pilot was killed and Duran was shot.'

'Shot?' he echoed. 'Who shot him?'

'Never mind that now. I want to know what's going on!'

'Cut the crap, Scott!' He was becoming angry. 'All the information is on a 'need to know' basis and you don't need to know. You're here to do a job. All you have to do is follow orders. Is that understood?' He turned to one of the telephones on a desk and dialled a number. 'Tell Commander Brook in the European Area that Phase One Code B is completed. We're still awaiting news on Code A.' He paused to listen to the person at the other end of the line for a few moments. 'My information tells me it exploded just before landing. The timing device was set too late. Either that or the tail-winds were too strong. I've a man out there examining the wreckage but I'm told he was shot. We'll recce and report later.' He replaced the receiver into its cradle and stared at us thoughtfully. 'How do you know Duran was shot?'

'When it comes to 'needing to know',' I retorted cheekily, 'you don't need to know.'

'I warn you!' cautioned the Commander. 'You'd better stop playing games for your own sake. Now listen carefully! You leave tomorrow morning. Be here at seven hundred hours sharp! Do you think you can manage that Mr. Scott, or are we interfering with your personal arrangements?'

He ushered us into the lift and, before we knew what was happening, we found ourselves back in the restaurant. As we left the premises, I noticed a man with the same facial structure and physique as myself. He was wearing a similar suit and strolled casually towards the restaurant.

On his arm was a young woman who faintly resembled Penny. I changed direction and moved towards them, determined to challenge them. 'Don't we know each other, old man?' I began. 'Trinity College!'

He seemed startled for a moment but recovered well. 'What a coincidence meeting you in Crete,' he said smoothly, in a voice not dissimilar to my own. He smiled easily although I could not understand why he failed to recognise me. 'Forgive me, old boy, if I can't recall your name for the moment. I'm Jason Scott, and this is my secretary, Penny Smith!'

CHAPTER THREE

The unforeseen event of coming face to face with oneself is not a practice to be recommended. It does something strange to the mind beyond giving it a short, sharp unexpected shock. The impact is even greater with the realisation that a conspiracy is taking place. To add to the intrigue, the imposter was holding the arm of a woman whom he passed off as my secretary. In a way it was all rather flattering. I had always considered my personal role in the grand design of life was singularly unimportant: yet someone had taken the trouble to arrange for me to have a double, and here he was talking to me in the street! In the confusion that followed, the effect of the confrontation caused me to become lost for words. To my surprise, however, Penny picked up the baton swiftly which led to the next development.

'Commander Spring wants you to come with us to meet Tomar Duran in the valley south east of here,' she informed them, issuing a statement which was totally untrue. 'There's no need to confer with him. He said it was urgent. We haven't any time to lose.'

The bogus Jason Scott stared at her suspiciously. 'What's this all about?' he enquired. 'I thought the Commander wanted to brief us on the flight arrangements tomorrow.'

'You'll understand when we get there,' continued Penny in a firm tone that was not to be denied.

The man pursed his lips for a moment in deep thought. 'That's odd!' he muttered. 'I thought Duran was covering our tracks. In case of need.' He shrugged his shoulders. 'It's too bad! They never tell us what we want to know. Well, if that's what the Commander desires, so be it!'

We led them to the small Volkswagen and clambered inside before driving back along the highway to the path leading to the wreckage. I had no idea what was to happen when we got there.

'I understand you play bridge,' I ventured, testing him out. I had never seen him playing in any major competitions, nor had anyone else for they would surely have mistaken him for me and mentioned it in due course.

'Yes,' he replied easily. 'I used to play duplicate in the north of England. Then I left for the United States and took part in a lot of tournaments there. Recently, I worked for the management of a couple of clubs....gambling clubs. You know, playing for the house.'

'Which system do you use?'

'Quite a few. Acol, Precision Club, American Standard, and a few others. If you're interested we might be able to get up a foursome.'

I could understand why Commander Spring was so concerned. My double was far too amicable and much too casual. He needed more tutoring in my mannerisms and the way I spoke. It baffled me why he failed to recognise me as the original Jason Scott. 'What's your view of the Vienna Coup?' I pressed on relentlessly.

'Great!' he responded breezily. 'One of my favourites, on the right hand of course. I love it when there's a squeeze!'

'And the opening of four no trumps in Acol?'

'Asking for aces of course! I say, you seem to know your game. Are you looking for a partner?'

He obviously knew his stuff when it came to playing bridge, but why was that the criterion? And why did they choose to replace me? At that moment we arrived at the spot where we had picked up the car. 'We'll have to walk from here,' I told them, stopping the vehicle in the same lay-by. I tried to fathom a reason why we had returned to this place but without success. 'It's only a fifteen minute stroll.'

He rubbed his eyes as he left the vehicle and blinked a number of times before starting to walk down with us. 'I've got these strange contact lenses,' he related. 'My eyes are grey and the Commander insists they should be brown. They provided a special pair of brown-coloured contact lenses but they blur my vision. I'm afraid they'll have to go back to the drawing-board. And this woman's no help. She may look like Penny Smith but she doesn't speak a word of English!'

So that was the reason he hadn't recognised me, and why the woman had said nothing. I was grateful to the Commander for small mercies. The four of us continued down the track, accompanied by the constant prattle of the other man as he rambled on for what seemed to be an eternity about the island. He may have looked like me but he was not like me at all!

'Do you know there are one thousand five hundred varieties of wild flowers on Crete, and three thousand caves and grottoes,' he ranted liberally. 'One could come to the island and live rent free simply by becoming a cave dweller. I'm sure you'll agree with me that any place which attracts sunshine for three hundred days a year deserves a vote for a place where one could retire at leisure. It's known as the crossroads between Europe, Africa and Asia, and it's the fifth largest island in the Mediterranean. By the way,' he paused, staring directly into my eyes, 'you didn't tell me your name.'

It was a game we could play no longer, but I had no idea how to end it. But I didn't need to worry because Penny had an immediate answer. 'It isn't necessary for you to know,' she countered icily, producing a revolver from her handbag. 'Step aside, Jason!'

The last time I recalled seeing Duran's gun was at the moment Penny let it fall from her hand after she had shot him. In the aftermath of the crash, the fight with Duran, the pains in my body, and the throbbing in my head, it had slipped my mind entirely. Penny must have picked it up before we left. I could only imagine she saw it as some kind of useful insurance if we ever got into serious trouble. Now she chose to use it to threaten two other people. I wasn't sure of her intention but the opportunity to extract further information was too good to lose. 'All right!' I snarled, determined to take the advantage. 'What's going on? Why are you pretending to be Jason Scott and Penny Smith?'

'You'll have to discuss that with the Commander,' he replied flippantly, causing me to believe that nothing had been divulged to him yet. He peered at me and recognition began to appear on his face. 'But first you ought to tell me why the Commander arranged for another set of people to look like us. I thought one set would be enough. Perhaps he thinks we're all dispensable. I wouldn't be surprised.'

He moved slightly, starting to withdraw his right hand from his pocket and, without warning, Penny fired the gun. The imposter clutched at the area of his heart before collapsing to the ground. The other woman screamed and turned to run away. As she did so, Penny fired again. My feet turned to clay as I stood on the same spot horrified at the sight of the two bodies laying on the ground. I knelt down painfully to examine them. Both had been shot neatly through the heart. Whoever they were, they hardly deserved to be the victims of such wanton killing!

'Why did you do that?' I gasped, looking up at my secretary who was still holding the gun out in front of her in case either of them moved.

The pained expression on her face indicated she was confused. 'I thought he was going to pull a gun from his pocket,' she explained almost in a whisper as her eyes filled with tears. 'I thought he was going to kill us.'

I drew the man's hand from his pocket to exhibit a large white handkerchief. 'All he was going to do was to wipe the tears in his eyes caused by the contact lenses!' I told her angrily. 'My God! This is turning out to be a nightmare! What on earth possessed you to pull the trigger? And why did you have to kill the woman?'

She started to cry and I pulled an unhappy face deciding not to continue with the inquisition. It was possible to accept that Penny's nerves were so stretched and taut she imagined death to be imminent from every source. After all, she was a petite, innocent secretary who ostensibly would never hurt a fly. Yet, on reflection, she had been responsible for killing three people by her own hand within the span of an hour!

'Let's get out of here fast!" I urged, taking the gun from her hand and placing it in my pocket. I pulled at her arm and led her along the path until we reached the highway again. As we approached our vehicle, two police cars scorched along the road to pull up beside us with their tyres screeching. Four policemen emerged swiftly from the cars and raced across the road towards us. Two of them grabbed me roughly and pushed me face down onto the bonnet of the Volkswagen, pinning my arms behind me. Pain seared through my body like red-hot pokers and I groaned loudly, almost falling into a faint. They propped me up as I slid sideways, while one of them ran his hands over my body, reaching into my pocket to discover the revolver. Another one uttered something in Greek which in any language would have translated into: 'You are under arrest!' Then I was handcuffed before being thrust into the rear seat of one of the police cars like a common criminal. They drove back to the police station at tremendous speed, with the siren on the roof of the car wailing like a lonesome banshee, as we raced through the streets of Heraklion.

I had expected someone to read out a charge on my arrival and then to be interrogated after contacting the British Embassy or a lawyer who spoke English. I was very much mistaken. There was no communication, no questions, and no explanation for my arrest. Rough hands grasped my upper arms and I was pushed down a short flight of steps before being tossed into a filthy cell. It was an awful place. The only furniture available was a flea-infested mattress which lay on the floor, covering nearly half the space, and an old stench-ridden bucket with flies darting to and fro above it. The sides of the cell were damp and covered with fungi, while high on the wall, near the fifteen-feet high ceiling, was a barred window from which streamed a narrow shaft of light. After the cell door was locked, I sat on the mattress and struck it with my fist several times in frustration. Eventually, I calmed down to evaluate the situation. There was no doubt that the police would link the gun with the three dead bodies in the valley. They were well aware a capital crime had been committed. Someone must have contacted them with the information otherwise I would not have been arrested. As a result of the prima facie evidence of three bodies and the murder weapon, which I had taken from Penny and placed in my pocket, I was the prime suspect. I was the only suspect! Nothing I could say or do would change their minds. I wasn't sure whether the authorities in Crete jailed murderers for life or whether they executed them.

I lay down on the mattress to ease the pains in my legs, and to rest my throbbing head. There was a chance I had fractured my skull in the crash. If so, a medical examiner might be able to prove I was out of my mind when the murders were committed.... even though I hadn't carried them out. The sentence might be commuted to ten years, or maybe less. Primar had become angry when I insisted that Penny Smith had to accompany me on this adventure. She was my secretary, with whom I was having a sexual affair....a diminutive, young, attractive woman who took dictation, ran the outer office efficiently, served me with coffee during the day, and looked after all my business activities. Her recruitment at Dandy Advanced Electronics had taken place about seven years earlier, nearly five of which had been spent as my secretary. During the past year we had become lovers, involved in an affair we both enjoyed. There was nothing extraordinary to report concerning her office or leisure activities, yet she had executed three people with considerable ease, seemingly without very much remorse. Admittedly, each time she had burst into tears, playing the innocent, but it was too much to believe the events were coincidental. At the back of my mind there was something else that kept trying to trigger the answer, but it just wouldn't come. Yes....there was a phrase she had used which caused a ripple in my brain at the time. I tried to squeeze it from my mind by concentrating my thoughts but nothing sensible emerged. It was about an hour later when the piece of the jig-saw fell into place. I had run through the events at the time of the crash in minute detail to recall something she had shouted that made me leave the pilot's cabin when I was searching for documents. 'Someone's coming!' she had called out. 'I can see a man at eleven hundred hours!' A phrase like that was adopted only by the military. Only women employed in the armed forces would ever express a direction in such a manner. When I employed her as my secretary, I took great care to examine her records. There was no mention of any service in the armed forces. Now that I had time to think it through, there was evidently far more to Miss Penny Smith than met the eye.

In addition to my current dilemma, there were two acute problems which concerned me. Someone had tried to replace us with duplicate people. Why did they want to do that? Surely it had nothing to do with bridge although, apparently, that activity was a criterion. The only other possibility was my employment with Dandy Advanced Electronics. I needed more time to consider that prospect in depth. Primar knew of my indifference to the company and my lack of loyalty. I never made any pretence of it. No doubt someone would enlighten me of the true reason at a later date. The other problem was more immediate. What would happen when Commander Spring discovered that the false Jason Scott and the woman masquerading as Penny Smith were dead? Somebody had taken a lot of trouble to employ a person to pretend he was me. It seemed likely that the bomb on the plane was intended to eliminate Penny and myself to make way for the other two. That assumption blew holes in my previous theory. If Penny was on their side, whoever they might be, why did they want to kill her? None of it made sense!

A little later I fell asleep. Throughout the night I twisted and turned on the flimsy straw mattress until the morning light began to filter through the bars of the tiny window. The noise made by the warder, as he slid the breakfast tray noisily across the stone floor of the cell, awoke me. I rubbed the stubble on my chin, moved my legs sideways, wincing at the pain, and rose to walk stiffly to the door. At least the throbbing in my head had stopped. As I bent down to pick up the tray, which contained a cup of ugly-looking liquid and a hunk of stale brown bread, I noticed the cell door was slightly ajar. I shook my head to clear my sleepy mind and pushed it gently with my right hand to make sure my eyes did not deceive me. It was definitely open! Within seconds, I discarded the evil breakfast and hobbled stiffly into the corridor, making my way stealthily towards the steps. I crept up the short staircase only to find the duty sergeant absent. In fact it appeared there was no one in the police station at all. I had a golden opportunity to escape unnoticed. But was it a trap so that they could shoot me and save embarrassment on an international scale? There was quite a lot of pressure placed on foreign governments when trials of subjects were reported in the Press. Perhaps the Cretan method was simply to eliminate the problem by shooting 'escaping' prisoners. In the face of trial for murder, I really had no option. I had to take the chance! Outside the jail, I took a deep breath of fresh air and walked at a casual pace to the end of the street trying very hard not to hurry. A sign displayed the name Dikeosinis, and I smiled to myself as a silly pun formed in my tired mind ....it was all Greek to me! From there on, I turned right into the Platia El Venizuelou, through Platia Kelergon, until I reached Parko El Greco. I sat on the grass in the park for a while considering how I could make contact with the British Consul to ask for assistance. As soon as he made enquiries, however, the Cretan authorities would identify me as a wanted criminal....a man responsible for three murders. And they had the murder weapon to prove it! I would be handed over to the police as a formality to avoid an international incident. No....I would not get sanctuary with the British Consul. On the contrary, all hell would break loose! I sat there feeling sorry for myself for the best part of ten minutes when I heard footsteps approaching quickly. I looked up to see Penny Smith walking towards me, dressed in a brown uniform similar to that worn by Commander Spring.

'Kali mera!' she called out brightly. 'Ti kanete?'

I nodded my head slowly, considering I now knew the true answer.

'Well, you certainly fooled me,' I admitted candidly. 'You were one of them all the time.'

'I don't think you should assume anything until you know what's going on!' she countered sharply. 'If you do, the odds are you'll arrive at the wrong answers and all the wrong conclusions.'

'I'm sure I would,' I answered drily, deciding to prove she was not as clever as she thought. 'There was one phrase which gave you away. Or, as they say, blew your cover. When I was searching for documents in Chedda's cabin after the crash, you told me you could see a man at eleven hundred hours. It was a dead giveaway! The only people who use such terms are those trained by the military.'

'Come!' she returned with a certain amount of urgency, ignoring my remark. 'I have a car to take you to safety.'

'To safety? What does that mean?'

'You don't think you escaped from prison by pure luck, do you? The police will soon start a murder hunt for the killer who got away. They have three dead bodies on their hands. Someone's got to answer for such a terrible crime. I'm afraid you're very much in demand.'

It was paradoxical that, having committed those murders herself, she was offering to protect me from being punished for them. I struggled to my feet and walked with her to the park exit. Before we reached the road, however, a police car sounding its siren screamed to a halt. All the doors opened as four policemen emerged. I was convinced they hadn't seen me but I was in such a panic I started to run from the scene. Fortunately, Penny had a stronger will and greater intuition in this kind of situation and she held my arm tightly to prevent me from being recaptured. She walked over to a refuse bin, withdrew the large plastic bag inside and motioned me to climb inside. It was partly filled with litter left by visitors to the park and smelled vile. Penny pressed her thumbs through the sides of the bag to provide two small holes to allow me to breathe. After I had climbed inside, she advised me to fall to my knees and crouch down. Then she took the ribbon which tied back her hair to secure the top of the bag, making it appear to be ready for the refuse collector. She walked off to avoid drawing attention to the spot while I remained perfectly still, holding my breath for long periods to reduce inhaling the nauseous stench of the rubbish in which I knelt. To my dismay, the police took their time to interrogate every person in the park and to look behind every tree and bush before deciding to give chase elsewhere. When Penny returned to undo the bow at the top of the bag, it was a great relief. I struggled up from my aching knees and climbed out, shaking my head slowly.

'Someone had better make sense of all this!' I muttered angrily. 'It's starting to get on my nerves!'

She laughed and took me by my arm to the Volkswagen. This time she sat at the wheel. 'I'm taking you to a neutral place. A safe house. Just as a precaution. There are some crossed wires that need to be unravelled, but they'll be sorted out soon enough.'

She started the motor and drove off. It was all I could do to resist the temptation of inundating her with questions. Shortly, we arrived at a small house on Kalonadon Street where she ushered me inside. It was sparsely furnished and I sat down in a small chair, snorting to try to rid myself of the persistent stench which hung on my clothes. Penny poured two drinks from a bottle and handed one to me.

'You'll have gathered by now I was planted as your secretary nearly five years ago,' she explained. 'Shortly before that I joined the 21st Century Crusaders. You weren't particularly high in the pecking order in the company in those days but my superiors recognised your potential.'

'Before you go on,' I broke in, slowly sipping my drink, 'there are two questions I have to ask. Firstly, I'd like to know the reason I've been chosen. Why me? I've nothing to offer your group. I've never supported or belonged to any cause in my life. Secondly, I feel sick at the thought that our intimate relationship was just flim-flam to you. A way of doing your job for the cause. I thought you felt real affection for me. Did you make love solely for the benefit of the cause?'

She smiled at me as a mother would to a child. 'With regard to the second question I'll bounce it back to you. Do you think I was faking affection for you over the past year? Over the whole year? If you don't know the answer to that one you know nothing about women.'

I shrugged my shoulders indifferently. 'I never had any doubts yesterday.'

'Then don't have any today,' she replied. 'I didn't need to make love to you if I didn't want to. I could have served the cause just as well without becoming emotionally involved. But putting our personal relationship aside for the moment, I'll tell you something about the 21st Century Crusaders. For the last hundred years, the political doctrines in the world of extreme right-wing and left-wing attitudes have been translated broadly into Communism and Fascism. Somewhere in between lies Democracy, except that few people know what it means any more. As a result, there's always friction which culminates into wars, as well as changes of political control in different parts of the world. There are two major issues which cause war, death and suffering....politics and religion. Everyone is willing to tackle the political problem. They're all scared of the religious one. For example, Vietnam was a typical political confrontation. Thousands of soldiers, innocent men, women and children were slaughtered. Such misery can never be expressed in its reality to the rest of the world. Politicians of major powers have a lot to answer for. Although religious war isn't new, it's important to note it has developed in recent years, changing the emphasis to include an additional extremist ideal. Certain religious factions have forced their way into government in the Middle East as the advanced guard, intending to start the change of the balance of world power. There will be a resurgence of the Holy Wars which the world once challenged in the Crusades if nothing is done. This time they will be well-organised. We'll face a structural oligarchy of Ayatollahs, Mullahs, and the like. We're not talking about people with whom we can reason with, or to whom we can talk logically. They're fanatics, martyrs, kamikaze believers willing to die by their hundreds of thousands for the holy cause. They regard us as the heathen. Logic and reason through diplomatic channels will have no effect. You can't get through to such people. Therefore, alternative action is necessary. We're repeating an element of history which started nearly a thousand years ago....the Crusaders against the Rest in the Holy War. But now the threat has grown because of the wider spread of Islam and the use of modern weapons. This time it's nuclear weapons.'

'Who are you actually taking on?' I asked, somewhat overwhelmed by her declaration.

'We're taking action against the religious powers which have overthrown democratic control in certain Middle East countries, and against others where religious fanaticism could affect the stability of the world. We want to prevent an adverse shift in the balance of power to prevent the institution of an empire that will rape the Earth, referring its laws back by thousands of years. Islam will rise, assemble, and impress itself upon the world. Our aim is to prevent that from happening.'

'Fine words, but what can a small, unknown group accomplish against a new empire?' I challenged.

'You'd be surprised how many people have rallied to our cause. It's an action replay of the first Crusades, with modern weapons. Those who can't be with us support physically by means of their cheque books, but if you follow history you'll note that knights volunteered without pay or reward in the first Crusades. Just because certain people wage war in the name of religion doesn't mean they're right.'

I sat back and stared at the ceiling for a moment to gather my thoughts. 'Quite frankly,' I uttered softly. 'I think that you and your friends have taken on something far larger than you could ever swallow.'

She paused without being daunted by my criticism. 'In answer to your first question,' she continued, 'you were selected for three reasons. One: you work for an international conglomerate specialising in weaponry and defence systems. Two: you achieved a key position there over the years but it does not provide the motivation in life you seek. Three: you play bridge at international level.'

'I don't understand why those features make me a candidate for your cause.'

'You will, Jason, in due course. As far as bridge is concerned, you can visit any country to play in regular international tournaments without anyone raising an eyebrow. You can cross borders with all the freedom you wish, in order to play in those tournaments.'

'Tosh!' I countered sharply. 'The leaders of Islamic countries don't recognise any form of gambling. It's not allowed. So what use is my ability to play bridge on an international scale?'

'You'll have to think more laterally,' she responded, and I felt angry that my secretary had the nerve to talk to me in such a fashion. 'But that's not our immediate problem. We have trouble within our own ranks. Primar was my section leader and we began to establish an organisation in Britain. Other officers have been developing cells in different countries throughout the world....even in one of the countries intending to wage the Holy War. Recently, someone has tried to take control of some parts of our organisation. No one knows their identity but it's created serious problems. Their plan was to dispose of us by planting a bomb on board our aircraft. That much is clear. We were very lucky to come out of it alive. Then we found ourselves facing our doubles. That was quite a shock, to say the least. Duran let me in on that one.'

'Duran!' I cut in, with surprise. 'But you shot him!'

'He came over to the aircraft when you went to the highway to find out where we were. He warned me there was another Jason Scott and said he would spare my life if I said nothing to you when you returned. He wanted to eliminate you near the wreckage, place you in the cockpit and then set fire to the plane. You would simply disappear and the police would believe that the pilot of the plane was killed when he crashed. When you returned, Duran was hiding in the trees nearby.'

'You took one hell of a chance with my life, didn't you!'

'He would have killed me too. You can be certain of that. I'm not sure about Commander Spring. But when we caught up with the false Jason Scott and Penny Smith it was impossible to let them roam free. I had to eliminate them.'

'So now,' I said logically, 'we can masquerade as the false Jason Scott and Penny Smith as well as being the real ones.'

'That's right! You're getting the picture. We're actually standing in for our own doubles!'

I blew out my cheeks wondering where this was going to lead us when my thoughts were interrupted by a siren. A police car pulled up outside and the siren stopped. I leapt to my feet and stood by the window, shielded by a flimsy curtain. 'Damn!' I growled irritably. 'They've found me! Someone in your organisation must have told them about this place!'

'The car,' returned Penny calmly. 'They tracked down the car.'

'Well?' I asked miserably. 'You're the one with all the bright ideas here What do we do now?'

She smiled at me sweetly. 'It makes a nice change,' she laughed. 'You're the important executive at Dandy Advanced Electronics but I'm in charge here. Follow me!'

She led me to another room and knelt down by a Persian rug. Then she pulled a small ring hidden in the pattern of the carpet, releasing a catch. A section of the floorboard covered by the rug was raised to reveal a set of steps leading downwards. We descended and Penny closed the hatch behind us.

'They won't find this place,' she told me confidently, producing a torch as she led me through a long tunnel.

We climbed a further set of steps to emerge in a shed belonging to another house in the next street, and left without haste to make our escape. After the police had gone, we returned to the Volkswagen and she drove me to a field where an aircraft was waiting for us. This time it was not a Kfir Junior but something slightly smaller. We clambered aboard as the pilot started the engine.

'Where are we off to now?' I asked quietly.

'To see Commander Yasood near the Gaza strip in Israel. At least we can trust him!'

I shook my head slowly at the need to trot around the globe in this fashion. The cause seemed to have a remarkable lack of control of its activities and personnel. But then such foolish fancies of absolute power often develop in organisations which comprise no more than small groups of vigilantes. It was that way with the 11th Century Crusaders....it hadn't changed with the 21st Century Crusaders!

CHAPTER FOUR

We arrived outside the Gaza Strip in Israel later that day. It was a complete mystery to me, and a credit to the pilot's navigational skill, that he was able to find a suitable place to land the aircraft safely in a sea of sand. This time I was delighted to be set down by the conventional method of flying, instead of risking my neck as had been the case in Crete. Apart from the terrifying ordeal in which I believed my end had been imminent, the recollection of Chedda's mutilated body was enough to give me nightmares for the rest of my life. As we alighted from the aircraft, a military jeep could be seen approaching from the distance and we did not have to wait long to meet Commander Yasood. If necessary, I could have picked him out of a crowd of people for he was exactly as I had imagined him to be. A tall, slender man, with dark hair, a tanned skin and a slightly curved nose. He wore a light-weight brown uniform with flashes on the upper arms portraying a crusader in shining armour riding a black horse. Around his waist circled a broad belt from which hung a packed gun-holster.

'Welcome to Gaza!' he greeted, in a slightly clipped tone. 'I trust your journey was reasonably comfortable.' He scanned my face closely as I shielded my eyes from the sun.

'There's an awful lot of desert around here,' I commented, surveying the scene.

'The Gaza Strip is over one hundred and forty-six square miles, mostly sandy and flat,' he informed me. 'Gaza itself has long been an important centre of the Islamic tradition. It declined during the Crusades and never regained its former importance. Saladin defeated the Crusaders here at the Battle of Hattin in 1187 and the city reverted to Muslim control, passing to the Ottoman Turks in the sixteenth century.' He walked back to the jeep. 'Come, I'll drive you to our base!'

The Commander was a mine of information. I climbed into the back seat of the jeep slowly as my limbs were still feeling stiff and sore. Penny followed suit. However, instead of driving towards the sea where the city lay, Yasood headed out into the wide-open desert. After travelling over the barren terrain for ten minutes, we came to an enormous rock and, to my surprise, he stopped the vehicle. Following the events which had occurred during the past twenty-four hours, I began to entertain foolish fancies and horrid visions of being pushed against a wall to face death by a one-man firing squad, but fate did not have that in store. Yasood produced a small remote control unit from his breast pocket, aimed it at the rock, and pressed a button. There was a smooth humming sound as a door in the rock-face slid open. He drove the vehicle inside and started to laugh when he saw the perplexed expression on my face.

'Don't be concerned,' he chuckled. 'this is a very remote area. No one comes out here. In any case, you could lean against the rock outside and not even know there was an entrance. We employ some excellent craftsmen. The door was designed to fit into the contours of the rock.'

He turned and pressed the remote control so that the door closed behind us and then drove into an underground car park in which there were about twenty vehicles. He motioned us to alight and we walked along a corridor where our footsteps echoed on the flagstone floor. There were fluorescent lights fitted to the ceiling which guided us on our way.

Yasood could see I was inquisitive and provided further information on his own accord. He seemed to be delighted to offer details about the headquarters. 'All our light and power is obtained from solar panels placed strategically. It's very efficient in this part of the world where we have so much sunshine.'

We continued walking on a little further before arriving at a set of double doors. Yasood opened them and we found ourselves in a large auditorium. On one side there was a dais backed by an enormous blackboard, and also a screen for displaying films as well as an overhead projector. The rest of the room was filled with seats, most of which were occupied by people I had never seen before. It was noticeable that the atmosphere was air-conditioned, smelling fresh and clean. I was fascinated and impressed that a cause comprising so few people had drilled into a rock in the desert to establish a conference base for itself. At the same time, as a businessman, I was aware of the gigantic cost of such an operation. No doubt there had been a large cave in the rock and someone had the vision to encourage the development. I was certain that the auditorium was only part of a complex which probably included offices, lounges, a large dining-room, a sizeable kitchen, many bedrooms, plus all the facilities required. I wondered how they managed to get water to the place before realising they had probably drilled a well. The Commander pointed to two seats, indicating where we should sit, and then moved towards the rostrum. He stood on the dais in front of a lectern, pausing for effect, and then introduced himself. As soon as he began to speak, his tone and attitude led me to believe that his vocation had once been a teacher or a lecturer.

'The reason you've been brought here may already be known to some of you; the rest will soon discover why. And there will be counselling for some of you,' he began. 'However, I'm sure you'll all be interested in our briefing today. Thereafter, you may discuss the matter amongst yourselves, enjoy the refreshment and stay for the night, or leave to fulfil any arrangements you have already made. We're fortunate to have over a hundred bedrooms here. Consider this place a hotel. Not the Hilton....but a hotel! Fine! We start off with the words "Petroleum....Oil". A commodity essential to the running of the Western world, not only for use in vehicles for travel and the distribution of goods, but also in factories. And who controls a large proportion of the oil delivered throughout the western world? OPEC....the Oil Petroleum Exporting Countries, comprised mainly of Kuwait, Iraq, Iran and Saudi Arabia. This is not surprising when you learn that the Middle East has sixty-six per cent of the world's petroleum reserves. Over the past thirty years, the oil moguls have accumulated enormous wealth by exporting oil but they've made little use of the revenues. They've built a few townships, made some roads, provided certain facilities for their people, and eliminated taxes, but at the end of the day they have sat back and enjoyed the income, depending almost solely on oil production, rather than establish factories or manufacture goods to compete in world markets. Oil is their sole economy. Everything would be fine if this planet had unlimited stocks of it but those reserves will eventually become exhausted. At that time, the members of OPEC will wring their hands and wail misfortune. When will this happen? Well, it will probably occur somewhere towards the third quarter of the 21st century. But what will they do when the oil runs out? You tell me! They don't have the ability or commitment to compete in world markets against the superior manufacturing production of Japan, the United States, Germany, Hong Kong, South Korea or Taiwan. In any case, they're unwilling to stump up the investment or train the vast numbers of workers required to produce the necessary skills. Joint ventures with other countries would accelerate development plans but their past record of attitudes towards joint ventures has been appalling. Their views of 'foreigners' are almost xenophobic. Western countries have learned their lesson. They will not be duped again! So where does that leave OPEC in, say, the year 2030. Oil starts to peter out. The rich sheiks disappear to other countries taking their fortunes with them. Middle East countries become impoverished, seeking help from the West who may resent and resist such aid. There could be chaos, famine, disease, looting and murder. Is it any surprise they are taking action now in the only way they know? The Holy War! The Jihad! The unification of Islam in the Middle East as a new empire or world power within the next hundred years. And we're talking of a world power. Islam is the youngest of the world's major religions. It is also one of the largest and fastest-growing and is dominant in the Middle East and Africa. Currently, it has one thousand two hundred million followers. Yes, my friends. One thousand two hundred million! Today large areas of India are Muslim and it is estimated that there are some forty million Chinese. After the death of the Prophet Mohammad in 632 a.d. there were Arab conquests in Egypt, Persia and the Levant. At that time, a dispute arose between two of the leading families of Mecca....the Hashemites and the Umaiyids. They argued who should succeed to the leadership of the Moslem community. The Hashemites were the Prophet's own family and they claimed that succession should go to a relative of Mohammed. The Umaiyids claimed, in accordance with the tradition of the Arabs....the Sunna....that it should go to the most suited person to be the Caliph. The Umaiyids, established in Damascus, won the argument in the end. The Hashemites continued to press their claim, gaining the support of those in the God-fearing and puritan Arab armies who resented the extravagance and nepotism characterising Umaiyid rule. They became known as the Shias from the term Shia Ali, the Party of Ali. In terms of percentages, the Sunnis comprise some eighty-five per cent of all Muslims, the Shias about fifteen per cent. To date, Islam is predominant in Iraq, Iran, Syria, Lebanon, Egypt and parts of Israel, North Africa, Indonesia, Bangladesh, Pakistan, parts of India and the Soviet Union, the Eastern part of Turkey, and Albania, and even China. Nearly two million pilgrims go to Mecca each year. Are there any questions?

'Although there are many Muslims in the world,' called out one man at the back of the hall, 'they are spread fairly widely over the globe. They have no organisation or leadership and their past record indicates that they spend most of their time fighting each other. What possesses you to believe they will change their attitude towards each other to become a major power within the next hundred years?'

'The once great Muslim empires no longer exist but Muslims are united by the faith of Islam which forms a common bond between them.

The main differences between Shias and Sunnis is the succession to the Caliphate after the death of Mohammed. To change from a Shia to a Sunni all one has to do is to revise his opinion in the privacy of his conscience about the right to that succession. The major differences beyond that are matters of custom, ceremony and the superstition that tends to be grafted on to most religions. Shias invest leaders with a spiritual authority taking them closer to Allah than ordinary people. Sunni jurists are distinguished by their superior learning. However, the Shias have messianic notions of a Mahdi....a God-guided deliverer. And that is the key to their future.'

'Do the Sunnis agree about the Mahdi?' asked a smart young woman seated in the centre of the auditorium.

'No, they don't,' answered Yasood calmly. 'But when the chips are down, and the oil starts to run out, someone is likely to emerge as their leader. A person with charisma, aura....call it what you like. And when he comes, the Shias and the Sunnis will look to him as their saviour. Once those in power throw their weight behind such a man, the rest will follow very quickly because many of them are fanatics.'

'Or perhaps a woman?' countered the smart young woman.

'The role of women in Islam is low. Mohammed did not raise their status to that of men although he did improve it significantly. The practice of murdering female babies was forbidden and the number of wives a Muslim could have was limited to four....provided a man could afford them. Women in Islam are still regarded as inferior to men. The Mahdi will not be a woman.'

'When is the Mahdi supposed to come?' asked another man.

'They say that everyone will know when he arrives. This year, next year, in twenty years' time....who knows? But he will need to arrive within the next thirty or forty years. He may not come from the desert or be a camel driver, like Mohammed. He'll probably be reading at Oxford, Cambridge or Harvard. What I'm saying is that the Mahdi will not be a wild, rough, illiterate person but well-educated and knowledgeable about logic and the strategy of war. He will also be adept at making alliances and funding the Jihad with adequate finance. We must not underestimate the situation. The most dangerous feature, however, is that sectarian differences between Muslims hardly count when compared with political differences between the revolutionary Islamic government in Iran, the monarchy in Saudi Arabia, or the secular regime in Iraq. Like families, there will always be arguments between them, but when push comes to shove they will unite under the Mahdi, and the forces of Islam will be unleashed on an unsuspecting world.'

'I don't understand how they can do that,' ventured a man towards the left of the room. 'How can they become a world power? They have nothing to offer. All they have is oil. If that runs out they're finished.'

'That's exactly my point,' related Yasood to a hushed audience. 'By the year 2050 they'll probably be able to boast about two billion followers. Maybe more. Who will stand up against them in the Middle East, in Europe, in Africa, in India, and perhaps even in China? Their roots in Indonesia, the Philippines, and in other Pacific areas will help them encompass the world. They will be formidable! The core is already there, laying dormant, waiting to be awakened.'

'Why haven't the developed countries in the West recognised this danger?' asked another man.

'They're too busy trying to establish stability within their own confines. Western powers are famous for looking in the other direction when crises occur.' He paused for a moment. 'I would like to talk to you later about the 21st Century Crusaders but I recognise that many of you have travelled long distances to get here without a break. If you take the double doors to your left you'll come to the refectory where you can enjoy some refreshments. This is not a secret society. Please feel free to discuss anything you wish with your colleagues.'

I got to my feet amid the hubbub as Penny Smith took my arm and led me out of the auditorium. A buffet lunch was waiting for us and I had the chance to take a deep breath and assess the situation. About a hundred people had been invited although I had no idea from which countries they came. Some of them spoke in different languages. I could detect French and German but most of them spoke English. Before we could help ourselves to the aperitifs which were set out on a table, Commander Yasood moved towards me.

'Sorry about all the rush, Jason,' he apologised. 'A great deal of activity is going on at present. Look, I want you to go on from here to Tel Aviv tonight. I have a house in Arlosoroff Road which you can use. The key to the front door is in this envelope together with another address in Jaffa. I want you to see a man there by the name of Menel.'

'Menel,' I repeated woodenly. 'Who's he?'

'He'll tell you all about his role in the organisation when you meet.'

'Is anyone else here going to see him?' I asked quietly.

'Jason,' returned the Commander. 'We all have different parts to play. It's horses for courses.'

'So why am I here? The only thing I do really well is to play bridge.

How's that going to help you?'

'You'll find out when you meet Menel. Now, enjoy the food. It all has to be eaten, otherwise the staff will have it for breakfast for the rest of next week.' He pressed the envelope with the door-key into my hand and laughed at his own joke as he walked away.

'What's he talking about?' I asked Penny. 'You must know.'

'It's best left for Menel,' she replied. 'But seeing him has nothing to do with playing bridge. I assure you of that.'

I became angry with her for not confiding in me but, in the presence of a hundred strangers, I was forced to remain silent. Penny had created havoc with my life and now kept her distance when it came to important information which I needed to know. I had no doubt that, like Primar, she would soon be asking me to trust her. After the refreshments, we returned to the auditorium to listen to Commander Yasood once more.

'You now have advance warning of the war to be waged within the next hundred years,' he began to his captive audience. 'It will become known in the history books as World War Three. What is amazing is the fact that history tends to repeat itself. On two occasions in the 20th century, the Allies were caught out at the beginning of hostilities with their pants down. Despite advance information at the start of both World Wars they were totally unprepared. It will be the same again except for our intervention but this time any country caught on the hop will be unable to recover in the face of nuclear attack. Let's look briefly at the Crusades....the Western invasions of the Holy Land between 1097 and 1191 a.d. against the Muslim powers....to see what lessons can be learned. The Seljuq Turks had embraced Islam and moved south and west into Iran and beyond. The concept of the Crusades was to provide aid to fellow Christians in the east although some historians identify them as a result of social, economic and institutional growth in Western Europe. The prime goal was not to become involved in battle but to establish the successful defence of fortified positions. Open battle was a very uncertain and risky business in those days. The number of manoeuvre campaigns which ended without a major battle or siege far outweighed the number of actual battles. Not only that, but war was seasonal. Once winter set in, field armies generally dispersed. However, such was Europe's fear of Muslim power that the concept of Crusades persisted well into the 17th century. Fortunately, in spite of the rhetoric about the Holy War, the Jihad, it made little difference to the average peasant whether his ruler was Christian or Muslim. The forces of Islam were unorganised, without a real military campaign, and they used brute force, courage and martyrdom in place of useful weaponry and strategic and tactical planning. You see, on the Christian side there were never more than two thousand knights and twenty thousand foot soldiers. Furthermore, it was impossible to gather them all together. In rural areas the Crusaders lacked numbers to alter the pattern of government seriously. It will be different this time. So too will be the weaponry. In the first Crusades, mailed knights on horseback used lances and swords but the primary weapon used by soldiers was the crossbow. In the 21st century, the forces of Islam will threaten with weapons bearing nuclear warheads. Every country, every government, every person in many countries will live in fear.'

'If what you say is correct,' demanded the man at the back of the hall who had asked a question earlier, 'what happened with Iraq and Saddam Hussein? He had nuclear weapons which were destroyed by Israel. He also waged a vicious war with Iran before committing himself to the acquisition of Kuwait.'

Yasood's face broke into a smile. 'In every organisation there are mavericks....people with illusions of world domination and those who make bad tactical errors. They are often forced to undertake desperate deeds to cover up the mistakes. Saddam Hussein is no different. He almost made Iraq bankrupt by pursuing and all-out war with Iran borrowing the finance for that war from Kuwait. When the conflict ended, he demanded that Kuwait cancel the loans granted to support him in that war. When they refused, he invaded them to wipe out all the debts and capture the oil wells. Every organisation has such problems....people trying to attain high levels of rank and power and treading on others to get there. Allied units in some countries have taken the initiative too early. We have seen evidence of that in Yugoslavia where Muslims were at one time the main target. Such zeal is less than helpful to the cause. It fails to contribute to our aims because the actions are sporadic, singular and too ineffective to stop the Third World War. If we fail to prevent such a war, the number of deaths will be counted in hundreds of millions, or mankind may even destroy life itself on this planet. Are there any more questions?'

The room remained silent and sombre for a few moments as the audience digested the information. Commander Yasood wasted few words and little time.

'What can we do to prevent a nuclear invasion?' asked a young woman. 'We may be able to get information from countries like Iran but it's impossible to penetrate them. They're prohibited to visitors or foreigners.'

'We have a man in this room today who may well be able to avert the danger with a weapon that has more a devastating effect than nuclear warheads.'

A ripple of comment spread across the group and I looked round to see whether anyone was going to own up to this remarkable admission. Then Penny touched my arm briefly. 'It's you,' she uttered softly. 'They're talking about you!'

I stared at her in amazement. 'Me? What are you talking about? I don't know anything about weapons!'

'That's why you're seeing Menel tomorrow.'

I gave her an old-fashioned look because I had no idea what she meant. The Commander continued to ramble on about the Crusades, Islam and World War Three and then the lecture came to an end. I opened the envelope he had given me to find a door-key and the addresses for Arlosoroff Road in Tel Aviv and Menel in Jaffa. 'How do we get to Tel Aviv from here?' I asked my secretary.

'We take a plane to Ben Gurion Airport. It's necessary to come in by that route, otherwise we might get shot down by Israeli artillery as a suspected invader. You can't be too careful out here, you know.'

'Why not?' I advanced flippantly. 'Everything else has happened since Primar came on the scene. Why not get shot down this time?'

Commander Yasood came towards us to bid farewell. He took me aside to whisper discreetly in my ear. 'Between you, me and these rock walls,' he advised softly, 'take care! We expect a lot from you. And watch out for Primar! I have strong suspicions in that quarter. Be very, very careful!'

As we departed, Penny could hardly contain her curiosity. 'What did he say to you?' she asked sweetly.

'You'll find out in due course,' I riposted, taking revenge for her reluctance to answer my earlier question. 'In due course!'

Within an hour we were back in the air again. I sat at the window of the aircraft staring down at the desert. Strangely enough, I was wondering where Jan was at that moment and with whom she might be. It was probably a reaction from being angry at Penny for rebuffing me earlier. Either that or I wasn't anything as hard-hearted as Jan had described me. If that had been the case, I would have been able to exorcise her existence from my mind altogether by now....but I couldn't!

'A penny for your thoughts,' offered my secretary, bringing me back to the real world again.

'I daren't open my mind to thoughts,' I replied. 'Islam, the Crusades, World War Three. I won't even be around when it all happens.'

'That's not the point,' she countered. 'It's your duty to do something!'

'Do what? I don't take sides. I've never taken sides! God help the people who worry about the starving millions in Africa and Asia, who collect money for charities, who would give their last pennies to widows and orphans! I tell you straight, this 21st Century Crusaders thing is not for me! Who knows? Maybe Islam is the right course and we're wrong! It's not my business!'

'It's money, isn't it! Money is the only thing you're interested in!' The disappointment stemming from my remarks showed in her face.

'Look, there are three things important to me in life. Me, you and playing bridge. Money doesn't come into it!'

'If you feel anything for me at all you'll co-operate.'

I shrugged my shoulders. 'Sure....I'll co-operate. I said me, you and playing bridge. I wouldn't let you down. Just don't expect me to have the same feeling for your cause.

After touching down at Ben Gurion Airport, we passed through immigration and hired a taxi to take us to Tel Aviv. The journey lasted about twenty minutes and allowed me to take my first view of a country which for so long had been a battleground in a war of attrition. As we travelled along the well-built road, I considered it to be a far cry from the references in the Bible. Although there were still large tracts of desert, I was surprised to note fertile areas and modern concrete establishments among the barren terrain. There were also scattered farmlands on either side of the highway. Many fields were cultivated and occasionally the vehicle passed close to a village sheltered by a hill adorned with cypresses, old pines and casuarina trees. For a while we passed some citrus orchards and then arrived at Tel Aviv itself. The city consisted of a mixture of young and old. New buildings and developments indicated the dynamism to expand. On the other hand, a great deal of care had been taken to ensure that no feature of history, biblical or mediaeval, was damaged. I noticed that many ancient sites had been preserved in an effort to restore the national heritage.

'Where to now?' asked the taxi-driver, in a New York accent.

'Arlosoroff Road,' I informed him.

'Your first time in Tel Aviv, eh?' he asked sagely, turning the vehicle in the right direction.

'Yes. The first time. What's that great square tower?' I pointed through the open window of the car.

The driver didn't need to follow the direction of my hand. 'In English it's known as the Tower of the Forty, after the forty followers of Mohammed. It was built in the early thirteen hundreds by the Egyptian Mameluke sultans.'

'But they were Arabs, weren't they?' I continued, puzzled by his reply. 'How is it possible that the Jews who are bitter enemies of the Arabs protect a monument which embodies part of the spirit of the other religion?'

'You know very little about us,' he responded. 'The Jews and Arabs are both of the Semitic race. Brothers under the skin. We're the clever ones: they're the lucky ones.'

'Why lucky?' I asked naively.

'Why lucky? If Moses had turned right instead of left when he fled from Egypt we would have had the oil as well. But then you can't have everything in life. We're passing King Solomon Road. You've heard of King Solomon, eh? It's not far now. We turn off here to Arlosoroff Road. Say, while you're in the cab, do you want a quick tour of the city or a cruise along the sea front? It's the Mediterranean, you know.'

'No thanks,' I refused wearily. The travelling and the heat were having an unpleasant effect on me and I could hardly wait to relax with a cool drink in my hand.

We arrived at our destination and paid off the taxi-driver. The place was far from satisfactory. The designer ingeniously had used every millimetre of available space fitting out the accommodation with a tiny kitchen, a small bathroom, a few cupboards, and living quarters. I opened the shuttered windows to let in some fresh air and flooded the room with sunlight.

'I'm going to have a drink and then walk round the town,' I told Penny. 'My bones ache like hell and so does my head but there's a lot I want to get out of my system. Walking is the only way I can do it.'

'Don't you ever get tired?' she asked.

'Let's say there's an itinerant bug running round in my bloodstream. It keeps me on the move.'

'Well I'm bushed,' she yawned, pulling the settee so that it unfolded into a bed. 'When you go out close the shutters, will you? The noise of the traffic might keep me awake but at least I can control the sunshine.'

I found Tel Aviv fascinating mainly because the city was so young and alive. It had developed at a tremendous pace with the port of Jaffa by its side. I learned later that when the cornerstone was laid at Jaffa, its founders sought to create a quiet residential suburb on the golden sands of the Mediterranean. No one believed it would grow into a city overshadowing the original port. I wandered along the straight streets with their new houses designed in modern architectural vogue. There were numerous museums, theatre companies and night-clubs of every description. The place had a character of its own. After walking along the sea front for a while towards Jaffa, I retraced my steps and found my way back to our humble abode. To my surprise, Penny was still awake, sitting up on the bed with a magazine in her hand. 'Couldn't you sleep?'

'I've had my sleep. An hour is enough for me to catch up during the day. You were gone for ages. Find anything interesting?'

'Nothing much.'

'By the way, we received a call while you were out. Just as I got my head down the 'phone rang. A Schmuel Musaphia is staying at the King David Hotel and would like us to join him there for breakfast.'

'Who's he? And is he on our side or the other side?'

She shrugged her shoulders. 'The only way to find out is to meet him there tomorrow morning.

I was getting very tired of this cat-and-mouse game as well as my inability to control the situation. No longer did I make any arrangements myself: they were dealt with by others. Either I was instructed to meet someone at a certain place at a particular time, or I was invited to meet them at their convenience. I seemed to be a pawn in someone else's game of chess....and I didn't like it! I didn't like it at all!

CHAPTER FIVE

Although the King David Hotel was exalted in many high-quality travel brochures, any form of prose could hardly do it justice. But it had to be said that the hotel, being exquisite in every sense of the word, had no conscience in setting its tariff at an eminent level. For most people, spending a day at the hotel might cost as much as a fortnight at home, but no one ever complained it wasn't worth it. There was a multitude of well-dressed hotel staff available to attend to one's bidding at a moment's notice, a menu that could hardly be challenged, luxury at every turn, and a highly-sophisticated atmosphere. We arrived there quite early and the head waiter led us to the open verandah where Musaphia was sitting.

'Jason Scott and Penny Smith,' I announced, as we reached his table. 'You rang us yesterday to invite us for breakfast.'

'Welcome to my table,' he replied in a shrill voice, without moving from his chair. 'Sit down.' He stared at Penny for a few moments to admire her dress. 'You look very pretty, my dear,' he complimented. 'I love having pretty ladies around me wearing lovely clothes. It makes one feel young again!'

She smiled at him pleasantly as we sat down and I scanned him clinically. He was very thin, with a wizened tanned face, and wore a spotless white suit, a white shirt and a neat red bow-tie. He sported a pointed beard which was very grey, although his hair was dark with white streaks reaching back from the temples, giving the impression that he used hair-dye regularly. A large Cuban cigar was held firmly between his lips which remained in the same position whenever he spoke. He waved his hand without looking round and a waiter approached to stand hovering at the edge of the table in anticipation of his instructions.

'What would you like for breakfast?' asked Musaphia. 'Don't worry about the cost. It's on me!'

'I'll have some eggs and bacon, with toast and coffee, if that's all right,' I ventured.

'No it's not all right,' replied our host, with a smile touching the corners of his mouth. 'No one here eats of the pig.'

I became extremely embarrassed and apologised for my ignorance, modifying the order to a Continental breakfast as I waited to find out what he wanted to discuss.

He examined me closely before breaking the ice. 'You look in pretty poor shape,' he began as though concerned about my welfare. 'Bruises on the face, and no doubt on your body too. I gave up all that stuff a long time ago. Life's too short to suffer from fisticuffs. I always thought it unnecessary but some people enjoy violence. I'd better lay my cards on the table. Normally, you'd never have met me. I don't usually deal with small fish. If I did I wouldn't be able to stay at this hotel. I'd be relegated to an area like Arlosoroff Road.' He laughed briefly at his own comment in a shrill thin voice. 'I deal in diamonds. Industrial diamonds. And with certain types of jewels. But, for the moment, that's beside the point. The concept of the 21st Century Crusaders is the subject of discussion. It makes a lot of sense. And I'm always right. If I wasn't always right I wouldn't be rich.' He stared directly into my eyes. 'Tell me, what do you think of the organisation?'

'I've seen nothing of it yet, except for the trip to Gaza. Commander Yasood offered a generic view but it was very brief. Having said that, I suppose it's possible someone will stir things up among the Arabs when they realise the oil is going to run out. Who wouldn't if they knew there was going to be nothing more than poverty to look forward to in the future?'

'Possible!' he said vehemently. 'It's more than possible! It's going to happen! That's why I've invited you here today to find out what you intend to do about it. But I wish to make one point clear. We're not talking about Arabs but Islam. There are many non-Arabs who follow the Islamic faith.'

'Before we go any further,' I returned, feeling my temper rising, 'can we get a few things straight! In my present state of mind, and in my present condition, I have no intention of doing anything. I don't belong to your organisation. I don't want to belong to any cause. Am I making myself clear?'

'That information has already been passed to me, Mr. Scott. I know how you feel. I also know the reason why you're here.....'

'Look!' I interrupted angrily, 'it's a very long story I don't care to tell at this time, but if the truth is known I'm trying to find out a number of things for myself. Not least the identity of the person who tried to kill us.'

At that moment the waiter came bearing my breakfast on a silver tray. 'Come,' invited Musaphia, completely ignoring my minor tantrum, 'eat before the adrenalin causes rise for indigestion.' He paused until the waiter had poured the coffee before continuing. 'You tell me you wage a vendetta with a person or persons unknown. That's all very well but you continue to risk your life while you fish in these waters. Let me give you some friendly advice. There are spies and assassins everywhere in the Middle East. They breed here like flies. If you happen to say the wrong thing to the wrong people, or even do something that makes them suspicious, your life won't be worth a fig. Treachery is a common cause. And let's face it, as a foreigner, you stand out in this region like a sore thumb. I've had a lot of experience. Experience you would never believe possible.'

'Buying bags of diamonds and carting them from here to there!' I riposted rudely. 'I'm not particularly interested in your experiences, Mr. Musaphia!'

He took a small gun from his pocket and pointed it at my head. I felt the blood run cold in my veins. Surely he wasn't going to shoot me at the King David Hotel! But then stranger things had happened to us in the past two days. He pressed the trigger slowly and a small flame spurted from the top of the gun which he used to light the end of his cigar. As I relaxed, I felt as though the blood had just drained out of my body. 'If life were that simple,' retaliated the old man, starting to philosophise. 'You're still young. You don't understand. How old do you think I am. Sixty-five? Seventy? Seventy-five? Don't bother to answer! I'm eighty-four and still in the run of things. I attended coronations you would have to read about in books. Why should I look so young? I don't know, especially after being caught up in a war so horrifying you'd never dream it could happen in civilised society. I'm talking about the holocaust. The Second World War in which six million Jews were singled out for torture, experiments and mass annihilation. I was in Germany. I know what it was like.'

'Mr. Musaphia,' I reminded him. 'We came out here at your invitation expecting to hear something which might be important to us. All these reminiscences............'

'All these reminiscences!' he hissed angrily, his beard bristling as he raged with anger. 'All these reminiscences! Will you young people never learn from history, or the teachings of your elders?' His face took on a menacing look. 'You will listen to me and not interrupt or I'll have you thrown out of this hotel! Why is it that young people always want to sweep history under the carpet before falling into the same trap again? I'm trying to open your eyes but you insist on being blind! The world is waiting for an accident to happen right now. It's totally unprepared for the millions of Muslims ready to unleash themselves from all quarters of the globe. Surely Yasood made you realise what's going to happen....and the reasons why! It's no use turning round afterwards and saying you should have taken the advice. Hindsight is a waste of time! The world is full of poor people and losers wailing in hindsight! Don't make the same mistake!' He paused for a few seconds and his manner altered swiftly as he searched for information. 'To change the subject a little, I'm interested in any details you can give me about Primar. Do you know where I can contact him?'

I shrugged my shoulders. 'I'd like to find him myself.' I waved a hand towards Penny. 'Miss Smith might be able to give you a pointer. After all, she started the British end of the organisation with him.'

Musaphia stared hard at Penny. 'I don't think that's correct, my dear, is it? Neither you nor Primar were charged with that task.'

I looked at Penny waiting to find out how she was going to respond to the allegation. She countered quickly and effectively. 'Who are you, Mr. Musaphia?' she asked. 'Who are you really? I can't imagine the organisation recruiting a man who's eighty-four years old for any kind of reason. I'm highly suspicious of this meeting and of the questions you ask. And if you want to throw us out of the hotel it's your prerogative to do so. Nothing will be lost from my point of view!'

Musaphia's face creased into a smile. He paused for a moment to puff on his cigar and then turned to me. 'I like her,' he mused. 'She has spirit and fire, and she's full of life. If I were in your place I would never let her go.'

'You never answered the question,' I said to Penny. 'Why did you say you formed the British end of the organisation if you didn't?'

'We'll discuss that later,' she returned sharply, ostensibly nursing hurt feelings.

'She's right, you know,' I told our host, as I considered her argument. 'You're eighty-four. What interest could you possibly have in something that might happen in the next century?'

We sat calmly on the terrace. Musaphia had a glazed look in his eyes as my words faded into the fragrance of flowers on the sea breeze. 'Do you imagine things happen so slowly, Mr. Scott? It took Hitler only seven years to become ready for war after he became the Chancellor of Germany. Only seven years to take a nation on its knees to become a power determined to capture Europe, Africa, India, and eventually the world. And he had only fifty million men, women and children with which to do it. I'm told that Islam already has one thousand two hundred million followers at present. How long will it take them to find a leader and become a fighting nation? Five years? Ten years? Twenty-five years?'

A small cog in the wheels of my mind clicked suddenly. 'I'd like to go back on something you said earlier. You mentioned you knew the reason why I was here. What did you mean by that?'

'To find your wife of course. That's why you've come.'

'To find my wife! What do you know about her?'

'I know she was kidnapped a few days ago. I thought that was why you came out here. The reason why you were willing to co-operate with the organisation. Am I wrong?'

I looked at Penny who shrugged her shoulders. 'It's all news to us,' she related. 'We were never told she was abducted. Do you have any details?'

Musaphia shook his head. I heard she was kidnapped that's why I invited you here. I'm always concerned when personal problems interfere with business. I have contacts everywhere. Everywhere.'

'But I received a letter from her saying she'd left me.' I turned to Penny for confirmation. 'You saw the letter. Primar said that a woman answering Jan's description came into the office and left the letter there.'

'Ah, Primar again,' muttered our host. 'His name seems to turn up all over the place. Too many times for my liking. You realise now the letter was false.'

'It was in Jan's handwriting. I'm certain of that.'

'Of course it was. They made her write it.'

'Then why didn't they tell me she'd been kidnapped in the first place? If they wanted me to come out here why not say so?'

Musaphia bit harder on his cigar. 'Because she may have been kidnapped for another reason. Who's to know? Don't imagine she was taken by the organisation. We're not interested in tactics of that kind.'

'No, of course not,' I replied sarcastically, trying to keep my voice and temper at reasonable levels. 'The bomb on the plane. The police in Crete. Commander Spring and our doubles. Tomar Duran. The alleged kidnapping of my wife. None of it's your fault. Anyone with half a brain could see that!'

He nodded sagely. 'Take it easy, Mr. Scott. We're on your side....remember!'

'Oh, you're on my side! Well tell me who's taken my wife and where she can be found! You tell me that!'

'Please lower your voice,' advised the old man firmly. 'we don't need to draw unnecessary attention to ourselves. I'll try to find out some details. It was my understanding she was brought to Israel but the source was not reliable.'

'How do you know she was brought here?'

'I told you. I have contacts everywhere.' An expression of surprise appeared on his face as I got to my feet. 'Why are you leaving? What about your breakfast? They're very sensitive about guests leaving their food here. It reflects on the cook and the reputation of the hotel.'

'To hell with their reputation!' I shouted. 'Look, Musaphia! I want my wife back! You find out where she is! You telephone me tomorrow and tell me where she is!' After that outburst, I stormed out of the hotel leaving Penny to follow behind.

She caught up with me on the pavement. 'Hey!' she chided. 'You were a bit rough on the old man, weren't you? He didn't mean you any harm. In fact he could be quite useful.'

'Oh, really! He didn't mean any harm! Then how come he knows Jan was kidnapped? Why didn't anyone else happen to mention such a minor, unimportant matter to me? Dammit, I am her husband! And you....you have a lot of questions to answer! I'm getting fed up being pushed around. Now it's going to be my turn to do some shoving!'

'You're upset, Jason. But be careful. Some of the things Musaphia told us were true. This is not a game. It's all for real.'

'You got me into this, Penny, you get me out! I don't care about your 21st Century Crusaders! Just get me out!'

I expected her to sulk at my rudeness but she took my hand and led me to the shore. We walked along the beach enjoying the cool sea breeze and then doubled back to return to Arlosoroff Road. As we reached one of the quieter streets we stood at the edge of the pavement ready to cross the road. It was then I noticed a large black car moving in our direction from the middle distance, approaching at a steady rate, smoothly, easily, intently....like a great predatory cat cruising towards its prey. The car seemed to surge forward suddenly and within seconds its near-side wheels shot across the pavement where we were standing. We leapt back in alarm as it missed us but the margin was very slim. Gathering our wits, we started to race across the road. However, the car turned within a very short distance and made its way back relentlessly. I tried to determine the face of the driver but my effort was frustrated because the windows of the vehicle were made of darkened glass. The decision to cross the road left us extremely exposed. I felt like an inadequate toreador in a giant bull-ring. I put my arm firmly around Penny's waist as the car moved in our direction. Now that we were two-thirds of the way across the road, the driver would assume we would sprint for the pavement on that side. It was the logical thing to do. But, as the car approached at speed, I feinted as though intending to continue to the pavement and then turned sharply the other way, pulling Penny with me. The ploy worked admirably because the car raced past us without causing any harm. From then on we reached safe ground and watched the vehicle cruise off into the distance.

'Who would want to kill us here?' I asked. 'I mean, no one knows who we are!'

'Maybe it's something to do with Mr. Musaphia. Any man with a lot of contacts also has a lot of enemies. Someone may have been watching.'

'I think we ought to buy a gun to protect ourselves,' I suggested. 'It's time we fought back at these assassins!'

We continued on our way until arriving back at the house. As I fumbled for the key, I noticed that the front door was slightly ajar. I pushed it open slowly but the shutters were closed causing the room to be shrouded in darkness. As we entered I closed the door and switched on the light. To my astonishment, I found myself staring into the face of an enormous Arab dressed in a wealth of dark rags which smelled abominably.

'What in heaven's name.......!' I began, staring at the giant, and turned to find another man laying full length on the bed-settee with his hands behind his head in a relaxed pose. 'Primar!' I exclaimed. 'So....you finally turned up!'

'I'm always turning up, Jason,' he laughed. 'Often in the right places at the wrong time. But I'm very disappointed in you. You let me down once. I trust it won't happen again!'

'Let you down!' I exclaimed furiously. 'What are you talking about? You were the one who let us down!'

'No, no, no! Let's get the story straight, Jason! I waited for you at Stansted Airport. You didn't turn up!'

'Oh, come on, Primar!' I snarled. 'We were there early in the morning. Chedda picked us up.'

'Chedda? Who the hell is Chedda?'

'The pilot you sent to meet us.'

'You've got it all wrong. I sent no pilot.'

'Yes you did. He rushed us into a Kfir Junior aircraft and we took off right away.'

He shook his head slowly. 'Are you mad? In a Kfir Junior? Why would I use an Israeli aircraft?'

'To take us to Israel as you planned.'

He sat up sharply. 'Look, the last thing I want to do is to wave the Israeli flag all over the place to alert everyone. We keep a very low profile. Our plane is an ordinary Cessna.'

I calmed down a little. 'Chedda led us to believe he was working for you. He said his orders came directly from you.'

'Well he was lying. I waited but you never turned up.'

Penny moved forward to add to the conversation. 'I think there's more to this than meets the eye, Jason. What Primar's saying is that he was responsible for placing the bomb on the Kfir Junior. No doubt he intended to kill someone important. We took their place on the wrong plane and nearly died as a result.

'I don't believe a word of it,' I challenged. 'Chedda had our photographs in his hand.'

'It makes no odds who's right or wrong,' returned Primar.

'Oh doesn't it!' I told him fiercely. 'I ought to take you apart!'

He laughed. 'What....for being on the wrong plane?'

I dropped the subject and started on a new tack. 'What the hell are you doing here? This is private property!'

'My dear old chap,' he laughed. 'I came to welcome you. I couldn't bear the thought of an old acquaintance arriving in Tel Aviv without a proper welcome.'

'All right, Primar,' I growled. 'The time for playing games is over. I don't believe you wanted to kill someone else on that aircraft. You tried to kill us. You murdered Chedda! And where's my wife? I've just been told she was kidnapped!'

'Easy! Easy!' he replied, pushing the bed back so that it became a settee once again. 'You're fraught with allegations and problems. Who said I tried to kill you? How do I know your wife has been kidnapped? You read the letter she left you. If she was abducted where's the ransom note....the telephone calls demanding money....the threats on her life? You mustn't listen to the prattle of old men in their dotage. Men, pretending to be Gods, who have nothing more to do in life than play games with people from high-class hotels.'

I started to lose my temper and advanced towards him menacingly. The giant Arab moved at tremendous speed to cut off my approach, holding me tightly around the neck and forcing my right arm behind my back.

'Oh, forgive me,' continued Primar insincerely. 'I forgot to introduce you to my very good friend Kemal. He's taken an interest in my welfare and volunteered to act as my protector. You can't be too careful in foreign parts, can you? Some people entertain evil thoughts and evil intentions.' He made a sign to Kemal who released me.

'How did you know where we were staying?' asked Penny, seemingly unperturbed at my predicament.

Primar ignored her as though she wasn't there. 'I want you to join me in a little venture, Jason. I'm setting it up in the Middle East. There's a place some many miles distant from here ....a group of mountains to be exact. My fortress. I intend to make it my headquarters for a while anyway. Modern methods of surveillance are so superior that one always has to keep on the move.'

I turned to Penny. 'Did you know about this....venture?' She shook her head slowly and I faced the intruder again. 'Why me, Primar? I'm not interested in politics or causes.'

'How would fifty million pounds in sterling suit you?' he replied. 'Or a hundred million United States dollars? The figures don't really matter.'

'I'm not worth it. I could never be worth fifty million pounds to you or anyone else.'

Primar laughed again. 'Such innocence! Such modesty! I'm willing to offer you a deal that will set you up for life.'

'Why should you bother to offer me anything? What have I got that's so important?'

Primar looked towards Penny. 'My God! Haven't you told him yet?' She shook her head and he turned back to me. 'I thought you were a businessman, Jason. How long does it take the penny to drop? Like everyone else, we're extremely interested in Project Bull's Eye!'

'In what?' I had no idea what he was talking about.

'Project Bull's Eye! Oh, don't come the old soldier with me! You work for Dandy Advanced Electronics! You must know all about it!'

'Dandy's an international company with many operations. I work on the domestic side of computer engineering. No one's privy to information outside his own division. Even the executives only learn about specific divisional activities from the Chairman's Report and the Annual Accounts.'

'Well then let me tell you something about the organisation in which you work. They have an advanced weaponry division. You must know that....surely!'

'Well of course I know that!'

'Then you know as well as I do about the plans concerning the new laser gun for use in warfare. Apparently everyone knows of it except you. It can destabilise weaponry or armoured vehicles within a range of three miles and can be handled by two men on a transportable unit. It may even be able to reduce armoured tanks to dust. A very powerful weapon against all kinds of ground troops and possibly aircraft.'

'It may be common knowledge to you, but no one has appraised me of such facts.'

Primar moved his hand as a signal and the giant Arab placed an arm round my neck restricting my breathing. 'He could kill you within five seconds if necessary.'

'It wouldn't help your cause,' I hissed, gasping for breath as I tried to ease the pressure on my windpipe.

'Listen, Jason, and listen carefully. I want the plans of that laser gun and you're going to get them for me!' He motioned to Kemal to release me and came close. 'I'll keep my end of the bargain concerning the rewards. You'll be a very rich man.'

'You're out of your mind,' I told him. 'There's no way I can get those plans. The security at Dandy is so tight you can hear it squeak. It's a mission impossible! There's no point in trying!'

He looked extremely disappointed. 'Oh, we can't have negative thoughts like that!' He made a sideways movement of his head to the bodyguard who took hold of me by the shoulders and dragged me roughly into the kitchen. When we arrived at the sink, he turned on the cold water, holding my head in a fixed position under the tap for what seemed to be a lifetime. The Arab then let me go and threw a towel across the room. I caught it, wondering whether it was a measure of good faith, realising shortly that it was to prepare me for the next stage. Before I could feel sorry for myself, I was propelled back into the other room and pushed forcefully into a chair.

'Well,' suggested Primar, brushing imaginary dandruff off his lapels delicately. 'Shall we continue?'

Kemal grabbed me by the hair with one hand and lifted me about two inches off the seat of the chair. After a few seconds, Primar removed his hand from his jacket pocket, holding an object which remained hidden. Without warning, he took Penny's arm and thrust it behind her back, at the same time pressing the button on a flick-knife. The smooth-steel blade sprang from the shaft of the handle to its limit, with its point resting on the skin at the side of her neck close to her jugular vein. 'O.K.' he said menacingly. 'If you won't co-operate perhaps a little persuasion is necessary. What do you say, Miss Smith?'

Penny started to become panic-stricken as he pressed the point of the knife to her throat, drawing a small amount of blood. 'Tell him you'll do it, Jason! Please! Tell him you'll do it!' Her face had turned red and her mouth was open and gasping for breath.

'Leave her out of this!' I warned. 'My decision has nothing to do with her!'

'Do I get a 'yes' or a 'no'?' He wasn't going to let her off the hook and seemed willing to kill her in cold blood to prove his point.

'All right, Primar, cut it out!' I told him, realising I was the one who held the whip hand. 'Let her go or you won't get your plans....ever! And that's a promise!'

Primar pushed Penny on to the settee and nodded to Kemal to free me. 'Be very careful my friend,' he snarled. 'Violence will always win in the end if one is prepared to use it. You may delay in getting the plans....that's up to you....but if you deny me you won't live long enough to tell anyone about it! And that's a promise!' To make an impression, he swung the knife across the settee slicing a long gash in the material. 'Hm, these knives are really sharp, aren't they? Imagine what they would do to a pretty throat if one had the mind!'

I swallowed hard. The man was right. The meek would never inherit the earth....it would fall to the revolutionaries, the dictators, the tyrants and the despots, and anyone else who used violence. What was the old adage? Kill a single man and they hang you: kill ten thousand and they pin a medal on your chest!

'I'll give you seven days,' he said in a parting shot. 'I advise you not to let me down!'

The two men left the premises quickly and I locked the door behind them before turning on my secretary. 'You knew all about this right from the beginning, didn't you?'

She picked up the towel and started to dry my hair. 'That's what Dandy Advanced Electronics is all about. But it wasn't supposed to happen this way. Primar had instructions to get the plans, but they were to be given to the organisation.... not to be used for his own purposes. I asked you to trust me and I still do. I'll get everything sorted out, even the mystery concerning your wife.'

'What do you suggest we do now?'

She threw the towel into a corner of the room. 'I'm glad you asked that,' she responded warmly, starting to undress. 'Now is the time to make love.'

'You're nuts!' I told her. 'It's not even ten o'clock in the morning and, anyway, my bones still ache. My God, we were both at death's door only a few minutes ago!'

'I know,' she replied. 'That's what makes it all the more exciting. Just hold me tightly and I'll make sure all your aches go away!' She opened the settee into a bed again and pulled me down on it before starting to undo my shirt.

'By the way,' I ventured. 'I didn't ask you before but you came here in a uniform. Where did you get that dress?'

'In the wardrobe,' she countered smoothly. 'There's a whole rail of dresses in there.'

'And they all fit you, I suppose. They're all your size.'

She smiled sweetly. 'As it happens they are.' She rolled on top of me and began to laugh. 'You asked for eggs and bacon,' she chortled. 'In Israel! Eggs and bacon! Oh, I'm so crazy about you! Her lips found mine and I became lost in sensation!

CHAPTER SIX

Jaffa is unusual in its geography in that the coast line to the north regresses to form a knee-shaped bend. This peculiar characteristic, protected by numerous coastal rocks, enables small ships to cast anchor in the bay, presenting a squadron of sea vessels of all different shapes and sizes as part of the panorama. It was not difficult to understand the reason why Jaffa had played such an important role in history, originally serving as the port for Jerusalem. Its sheltered harbour, above which the city looms on a rocky hill, made the settlement an easily fortified seaport and commercial centre. The harbour is quite small, however, so that larger vessels must cast anchor out into the Mediterranean, close to the Rock of Andromeda, and unload with the aid of boats and rafts. At night, one can see lights moving along the shore as the fishermen land their catches of sardines.

It was a blistering hot day. The sun blazed like a torch in the sky bleaching walls, baking earth, and sapping human energy. Penny was dressed in a light blouse and slacks and we travelled directly to the harbour in Jaffa, keeping as close to the sea as possible to gain the benefit of any breeze that might be available. We arrived at the port at a leisurely pace and gazed at one of the tourist attractions. It was a mosaic floor, evidently the paving of an early synagogue, which had been set there in the Byzantine period, about the 6th century a.d., depicting King David playing the harp dressed as Orpheus, the Greek hero. We left the dock area to push our way through the tightly-crowded flea-market in Jaffa. It was a most unpleasant experience. The jostling of bodies as they pressed and nudged each other moving in different directions between the stalls, the shouting by the traders and buyers as they haggled over prices, and the babble of the crowd which made so much din that it became too much to bear in the oppressive heat. We took flight from the bazaar with haste to break away from the multitude, retreating down a rugged street which had an uneven surface and no pavement at all. It was a slum area with rubble and decaying matter resting incongruously against the walls of houses, lying inert below inscrutable shuttered windows. A stench of unknown origin pervaded the air with an odious aroma which was not only foul but remained ubiquitously persistent.

There was no escape from its repulsive presence. It took us a while to find the house we wanted. By then, within the confines of small alleys which were protected from the sea breeze, the effect of the heat was intolerable. When we finally arrived at the place, the house of Menel wore a facade that seemed centuries old; its state was deplorable. The property was terraced, although it was only fair to say that the whole street, from start to finish, was terraced. Every house conformed to time-honoured architecture, each one exhibiting rough ochre-coloured walls, baked hard by the constant rays of the sun. These were off-set by dull green or brown shutters, the paint having been stripped off by austere weather conditions in the effluxion of time. The hovel seemed inconsistent with the cause of the 21st Century Crusaders but that was not our affair! Penny and I glanced at each other for a few moments and then I hammered on the door with my fist, there being no other means to attract attention. After a short while, a tall bearded Arab answered and stared at us with a fierce expression on his face. I was immediately reminded of Kemal but thrust the image of that giant to the back of my mind. The man bade us enter with a sweep of his hand and we shuffled into the dark hallway unable to see anything at all after the door closed behind us, for the pupils of our eyes were contracted, still accustomed to the brilliant sunshine outside. The Arab moved past us and we stumbled behind him blindly into a room where a man sat behind a large table.

'Good morning!' he greeted in excellent English, although his accent was slightly clipped. 'I am Menel. I welcome you to my humble home where we shall enjoy some refreshments and discuss matters relevant to both of us. Please sit down.'

We relaxed in comfortable chairs as Menel studied us closely in the dim light. He was a dapper man, dressed smartly in a black pin-striped suit. Despite the fact that the temperature inside the room was about a hundred degrees, he still wore a white shirt and a tie knotted up to his Adam's Apple. It was difficult to determine whether he was an Arab or a Jew, not that it mattered, for he was probably a mixture of both anyway. His brown face had a slightly longer appearance as a result of the absence of hair on his head, and he sported the smallest of moustaches which fitted neatly on the central ridge below his nose. Menel had two obvious nervous habits. The first was to rub the middle finger of his right hand over his tiny moustache. The second involved jutting out his jaw and moving his lips over the front of his false teeth before releasing them in a kind of spasm. Yet, despite these nervous traits, he carried an air of authority which commanded respect, and his manner, although curt, was pleasant. It soon became apparent that Menel was in no hurry to launch the meeting, and he scanned us closely in his own time. Then he clapped his hands together twice and the bearded man, swathed in white clothing, brought a small tray containing cups of dark liquid which he offered us.

'Please accept my humble hospitality,' begged our host meekly. 'The hot coffee will cool you down but you may be surprised by its taste. If you require any other refreshments....falafel, peanuts, pumpkin seeds....they are yours for the asking.'

'Falafel?' I asked with interest.

'Falafel are little balls of ground peas fried in oil, wrapped in pita....a king of bread spiced with hot pepper. We have many delicacies if you would care to try them.'

'No thank you,' I replied, regretting having asked the question as my stomach began to feel unsettled. 'I'll stay with the coffee, if you don't mind.'

'You're not used to our way of life,' he continued amiably. 'We have customs which may seem strange to you. You will learn to love us though.... if you live that long!'

'What do you mean by that?' I asked with alarm.

Menel jutted out his jaw and moved his lips over his teeth. 'Information of the sensitive kind brings its own danger. The more sensitive, the more dangerous. We live in troubled times where the emphasis on intelligence becomes more imperative each year. You see, more wars are in progress in the offices of secret service agencies in most countries than are ever fought on the battlefield. You are amateurs and I can only assume you like to live dangerously.'

'You don't believe in pulling punches, do you?' I muttered, swallowing hard.

'It depends on how much you value your life.'

The air was hot and absolutely still, while the stench emerging from inadequate plumbing and the cooking of spicy foods in the kitchen was quite nauseating. In addition, there were numerous flies which enjoyed tormenting us, landing briefly but regularly on hands, arms and faces. Menel had found a tried and tested solution for such problems. He waved a fan, shaped like a large table-tennis bat, in front of his face every twenty seconds with an automatic sweep of his hand.

'O.K.,' he continued. 'Let's get down to business. I'm an arms dealer. The top man in this country.'

'The top man!' I repeated unbelievingly. 'If you're so successful why do you live in a dump like this?'

A smile flickered across his face. 'Does the Chief Executive of the Bank of England in London have to live at the Savoy Hotel? This is my place of work....my office. We have no need of filing cabinets, documentation, computer systems or the like. In my profession, all the information is up here!' He tapped his forehead with the first two fingers of his right hand. 'Clearly, you're not aware that this row of houses is a fortress. Shock-proof, sound-proof, bullet-proof and bomb-proof. I am, as you say, as 'safe as houses'.

I rued the fact that it wasn't odour-proof as well.

'As you know,' he continued, 'the Strategic Arms Limitation Talks, known as the SALT I and II treaties, imposed limits on the numbers of nuclear weapons to be held by Russia and the United States. Inevitably, it meant that some of this weaponry was certain to find its way into the hands of other countries. The Americans possessed two major missiles....the Cruise and the Pershing 2. The Russians had four....the SS-20, the SS-4, the SS-23 and the SS-12/22. The last three were too short in range and very ancient. So seven hundred Soviet missiles had to be destroyed. But human nature is such that people do not always follow the rules. Not all of them were destroyed. Some are in foreign hands. Worse still is the fact that those controlled by the major powers are placed in so many countries there is doubt as to who actually controls them. There are three categories of nuclear or 'dual-capable' weapons which exist. Dual-capable artillery pieces are guns with ranges of nine to eighteen miles. Within the NATO Guidelines Area they are deployed by Britain, the United States, Belgium, Holland, Luxembourg, Germany, Czechoslovakia, Russia and Poland. Some three thousand of them! The Dual-capable aircraft, mainly NATO's F-111 and Tornado, and the old Warsaw Pact's Su-7, Su-20, Mig-23 and Su-24 total over one thousand two hundred, and they have a range of nearly three thousand miles. They too are located in numerous European countries. Battlefield nuclear weapons comprise NATO's Lance missile with a range of almost seventy miles. Additionally, there are the Frog/SS-21 and SCUD missiles. If one nation were to occupy another nation by force very quickly it would automatically acquire a whole armoury of nuclear weapons.

I held up my hands for him to stop. 'All this is extremely interesting but what has it got to do with me? I'm no weaponry expert. I deal with domestic computers.'

Menel shrugged, jutting out his lower jaw and playing his lips over his teeth. 'I'm well aware of that but you work for Dandy Advance Electronics. They've been successful in producing a laser gun for military purpose. I'm told it's far superior to the American prototypes which were supposed to be used in the Star Wars programme.'

I sipped at the coffee, trying not to show my distaste for the ugly liquid. 'Let me guess,' I told him contemptuously. 'You want me to get the plans for you.'

'Indeed. But first let me explain the situation. When Islam starts to assemble its troops for World War Three, it will have in its possession a whole array of nuclear weapons.'

'But so will we!' I countered.

He flapped the fan forwards and backwards in front of his face. 'That's correct. So will we. But what do we do with them when Islam takes over a host of countries in its advance? The main advantage of a nuclear weapon is that it acts as a deterrent. It can never be employed as an operational weapon. If it did the planet would be wiped out. In essence, it's not a weapon but a threat. An enemy could invade a continent claiming it has an arsenal of such weapons and no one could do much about it. You see, if one side decides to press the button there will be retaliation. So weapons of this kind can only be considered as a deterrent. If we became too frightened to retaliate we would be unable to defend ourselves. Therefore, it's essential we find a new weapon far superior to nuclear missiles to give us control. In that way, we could ensure that the enemy was contained.'

'And you believe this laser gun will do the trick.'

'Without any doubt whatsoever,' he responded calmly. 'The laser beam produces such intense heat it dissolves metal and kills people instantly. It can be made to be a death ray. Islam could threaten us with nuclear power but we would dissolve their rockets and planes before they reached us, as well as their guns, and their tanks. We would also be able to wipe out their soldiers in the field with great accuracy. World War Three would never be able to get under way.'

'What's your role in all this?' I asked, going onto the attack. 'I mean, you're an arms dealer. What are you going to do with the laser plans, if you get them? Sell them to all and sundry for a huge profit?'

His eyes seemed to penetrate me as though I had offended him, and then he looked away slightly before replying. 'Mr. Scott, I'm a top-class arms dealer. I've made more money in the last decade than you would make if you lived to be a thousand years old. Profit no longer interests me. My role, as you would call it, is the appointment of Chief Arms

Adviser to the 21st Century Crusaders. I have laid my life on the line for them.'

'For what reason?' I asked suspiciously. 'You don't have to take risks like that.'

He clapped his hands once for the cups to be removed but, instead of the Arab who had appeared earlier, a young woman entered the room. 'Let me present to you my daughter, Davina!'

She smiled at us and began to clear away the crockery. She was a slender, beautiful young woman with long black hair that almost reached down to her waist. Her face was distinctly Eurasian, with jet black eyes and high cheekbones. I was stunned by her natural beauty forgetting, in that instant, my feelings for Penny. Even when she had left the room, the outline of her delicate features and her lithe body lingered in my mind like a haunting refrain.

'She is the reason for my interest,' explained Menel. 'I have all I want for myself. It's my responsibility to ensure my family can enjoy freedom for the next thousand years. I speak not only for her but for millions of young people like her.'

'Why don't you present your case to the Chairman of Dandy Advanced Electronics? You might be able to persuade him to do some kind of deal.'

'It cannot happen that way. As a commercial organisation your company does the Research and Development to make large profits on innovation. In any case, the British Government has provided funds for the development of the weapon and retains tight control.'

'Then if what you say will happen....the rise of Islam....the British Government could use its power to stop it.'

'Peace in our time! Isn't that what Chamberlain said in 1939 when he returned from a visit to Hitler. After that, more than fifteen million people died in the Second World War. We cannot trust any government. They may not feel inclined to act at all. The United Nations would be useless too because many Arab states would use the veto on actions related to force. War would be inevitable. The only way to resolve the problem is for you to obtain a copy of the plans. Will you do that for us?'

'I'm going to give a lot of thought to all this before I get involved,' I told him unhappily. 'A lot of thought!'

'Good!' he replied, as though I had agreed. He removed a buff envelope from the inside pocket of his jacket. 'This is a microfilm of plans which appear to relate to a laser gun. They are spurious but you may need to substitute them for the originals.' He rubbed his moustache with the middle finger of his right hand before passing the envelope to me. Then he clapped his hands together twice and the tall bearded Arab reappeared. Menel conveyed an order to him in Arabic, after which we found ourselves shepherded out into the street trying to adjust our eyes to the bright sunlight.

We left the house and started off down the narrow street with Menel's words buzzing in our ears. Then something caused me to turn and I saw the black car coming towards us at speed. It was the same vehicle which had tried to run us down before. I touched Penny's arm in alarm and we both began to run towards the cross-roads at the end of the street. The black car reached the point at the same time and skidded to a halt in a one hundred-and-eighty degree turn. The two front doors opened and a man and woman slid out of the seats to crouch defensively behind the doors. 'Stay exactly where you are!' shouted the man through a megaphone. 'Do not attempt to move! We will come to you!'

'Run!' urged Penny, giving me a push in the back to start me off.

Before I knew what was happening, my legs were pounding the rough pavement towards an unknown destination. It was obvious our pursuers were not the police....but who were they? I didn't know and I had no intention of staying to find out! They were the hunters; I was the prey! I couldn't remember how long I kept running. When I stopped, my body was soaked with perspiration and I could scarcely breathe through exhaustion. I hesitated for a moment before hiding in the shadow of a strange door and then closed my eyes. This was a nightmare! But I was living it therefore I couldn't afford to rest....not even for a moment....in case they were close behind me. The seconds were too precious to waste: I had to move on! My face felt as though it was on fire, my head throbbed with an agonising pain, and the saliva in my mouth tasted strangely of blood. A sense of urgency passed through my tired body as the echoing of footsteps hammering on the rough pavements could be heard only a short distance away. It seemed that whatever direction I took they were bound to catch me. I had no idea what had happened to Penny. It was my belief she was safe because all the footsteps appeared to be heading towards me. It sounded as though they were covering every street and alley to prevent me from making my escape.

The footsteps came nearer but it was difficult to determine their precise location. The only advice I could offer myself was to run like the devil for as long as possible. As I was about to drag my weary limbs a little further, I heard the faint noise of an approaching motor car. If I could get a lift I would be able to clear the area before anyone knew I had gone. The vehicle came into sight some distance away. It was a red car racing at a fast rate down the small street. I stepped off the kerb into the road waving my arms wildly in an attempt to make the driver stop. There was a loud squeal of brakes as the car swerved dangerously, tacking its way along the road until it came to a halt. The driver leaned out of the window to hurl a torrent of abuse at me but before I could reach it he had restarted the engine to race down the road out of reach. Dispiritedly, I returned to the comfort of the darkened doorway. They would soon be closing in! I ran down the next street and turned into an alley, leaning against the wall as my lungs heaved painfully in my chest. The voices of the hunters sounded very close and I pressed on to find myself confronted by a wall some ten feet in height. At its peak, there were long slivers of glass embedded in cement to deter intruders. As the man and the woman loomed out of the sunlight behind me, a voice called out my name from above. Penny held a large rock in her hands which she dropped on the glass slivers, smashing them to pieces. Then she quickly laid a discarded rug across the broken glass and leaned out over the wall, extending her arms. I glanced at the dangerous edges of the nearby slivers and hesitated for a moment.

'Now!' she called out imperatively. 'It must be now!'

My fear of the known was less than the fear of the unknown. Instinctively, I grabbed her arms, trying to run up the wall. Penny wedged her feet at the top and pulled me up until I could scramble over the barrier. Then we both ran like the devil to another part of the dock area. The left leg of my trousers was torn and my knee was bleeding badly. We stopped for a moment while she used my handkerchief to stem the blood and continued at a more manageable pace. But life wasn't going to be that simple. Less than five minutes later, the black car appeared in front of us again and, once more, Penny and I set off in different directions. My decision proved to be poor. Not knowing the geography of the area, I hurried off in a westerly direction which led me to a line of warehouses at the edge of the docks. It wasn't long before I discovered that the warehouses were locked. The only protection afforded me were the cranes on the wharf. I chose a derrick with a jib, hoping it would maximise protection but, to my dismay, a gunshot rang out as I began to climb the iron giant. This was followed by further shots which ricochetted off the metalwork. I had no means of escaping from my dilemma this time. Climbing the derrick was no mean feat but it was only a matter of time before they gunned me down.

Then I heard the sound of a motor car approaching the area. My heart sank as I recognised the black car again. Then despair rose to elation as it drove menacingly towards the first assailant. The man tried to race for the refuge of the nearest warehouse but his attempt was denied. The nearside bumper caught him behind the legs in mid-flight and he was mowed down without mercy a long way short of sanctuary. The car turned and sped towards the woman. She decided not to move and concentrated her efforts by holding her gun with both hands at shoulder height and aiming it at the driver. She fired four shots in quick succession until being struck by the vehicle with such force that her body flew through the air like a missile to disappear into the sea.

The door of the black car opened slowly and Penny climbed out. 'Some people are really stupid, you know,' she called out coolly, as though nothing serious had happened. 'They left the keys in the ignition. Not only that but she knew the windscreen was bullet-proof yet she still went on firing instead of running. She could have dived over the side into the sea and still been alive.'

I climbed down from the derrick trembling like a leaf. I reckoned I had lost a few pounds in weight during the chase, not only from the effort of running but from fear itself!

'Come on!' she continued. 'Climb in and I'll drive us home in style. I'm not pushing the car into the sea when we can make used of it.'

When we reached Arlosoroff Road, the telephone was ringing. I took my time to open the door and it was clear that the caller intended to wait indefinitely for an answer. I picked up the receiver and grunted into the mouthpiece. The voice was imperative.

'Jason! You mustn't let Miss Smith know who's ringing! Just keep listening and say nothing! This is Davina....Menel's daughter. We have to meet. I'll be at the "New York, New York" restaurant in Tel Aviv in twenty minutes. I have information about your wife. You must come alone and not tell anyone about this conversation. Just say O.K. if it's all right.'

'O.K.' I answered quietly.

'Good!' she replied. 'Twenty minutes! And say nothing to Miss Smith!'

The line went dead and I replaced the receiver in its cradle

'Who was that?' asked Penny.

'Look,' I told her. 'I have to go out for a while. I'll tell you all about it when I get back.'

A look of surprise appeared on her face as I walked out, but I couldn't afford to take chances. I hailed a taxi and sat at a table in the "New York, New York" restaurant waiting for Davina to show up, thinking about her hair, her dark eyes and those lovely high cheekbones. After a while I started to look into the distance in anticipation, but she was nowhere to be seen. Foolishly, I began to make excuses for her; however, there was little comfort in such deception. Thirty minutes passed by which turned into an hour, then an hour-and-a-half. I wanted the information about Jan desperately but it seemed unlikely I would get it. Eventually, I settled the bill and started to walk away. I had hardly taken a dozen steps when she appeared and took hold of my arm.

'Davina!' I whispered, staring at her beautiful face. 'Where have you been?'

'I'm sorry! It wasn't possible to get here earlier,' she explained briefly. 'I couldn't contact you. There are too many eyes....too many ears! Let's walk and talk.'

There was clearly an affinity between us. I felt strongly attracted towards her and, from the look in her eyes, she felt the same way about me. I took her hand and we strolled for a short distance without speaking. Then I stopped and faced her squarely, rubbing my hand gently across her cheek with affection. She leaned her faced into it to indicate her feelings. 'You're so beautiful.........' I began passionately.

She placed the tips of her fingers to my lips to silence me. 'Don't say anything. Please! This is merely a fleeting moment of our time....a single second spent in eternity. Let's carry it in our personal thoughts for the rest of our days as a cherished moment of our lives!'

I stared at her with a puzzled expression on my face, unable to follow her train of thought. 'What are you trying to say?' I asked.

There was no immediate reply and we turned to walk on a little further. 'In my world,' she began, 'our customs are ancient, our beliefs profound, and faith is total. In your world, love is important, pleasure ranks high, freedom is paramount. What I'm trying to tell you is that you can fall in love with me but I'm not allowed to fall in love with you. You see, my father betrothed me at birth to the son of one of his friends and that's a promise which cannot be broken. I must honour my father's wishes.'

'Do you love the man? The one to whom you're betrothed.'

'It makes no difference whether I love him or not. Those are the facts.'

'The facts!' I echoed with chagrin. 'What are the facts? That one evening over a few drinks many years ago your father and his friend made a foolish drunken promise designed to end in misery for their children! Is that what you're saying?'

'Believe me, nothing can change the situation!'

'And what if I invited you back to England?'

She laughed for a moment and then sadness filled her eyes. 'I must fulfil my father's promise. It's a bond that cannot be broken. The stars will record for eternity that Davina fulfilled her father's promise to marry Musaph. The stars live on for ever: emotions of love or hate exist only for a brief span of years. But let us talk of your wife! My father has news of Jan....if that is her name. She's being held in the East End of London at St. Katherine's Dock near Tower Hill. I hope I pronounced it correctly.' She handed me a sheet of paper. 'Here are the details!' I took it and she clutched my hand firmly. 'You're a very handsome man, Jason Scott! Perhaps in another time, in another world, in another life!' She kissed my hand tenderly and then darted away to become lost in the crowd.

I stood for a long time in the same spot thinking about her. I had a feeling I would never see her again. The responsibility of her father's promise was greater than any love I could offer. If she transgressed, she would be filled with guilt for the rest of her life for failing her father and her religion. It was an invisible barrier which could not be overcome. Mankind had built many of them to mock at civilisation itself. And at the end of it all was the fact that I had no right even to think about her. I was not only married but I had a mistress as well. I walked all the way back to Arlosoroff Road trying to exorcise the image of Davina from my mind.

Penny met me with an inquisitive look in her eyes. I could hardly blame her. 'We have to get back to England,' I related as soon as I returned. 'I know the address where they've taken Jan.'

'Who gave you that information?' she asked suspiciously.

I passed the sheet of paper to her. 'Menel's daughter. She was the one who telephoned. She insisted I met her alone and told no one about it.'

'Why couldn't she give you the information over the telephone?'

'You'll have to ask her the answer to that one,' I retorted.

'I'd like to,' replied Penny in annoyance, 'seeing you were gone the best part of three hours.' She waved the sheet of paper in her hand. 'Was this the total message?'

'Yes it was.'

'And it took nearly three hours to deliver it!' She moved towards me jealously until her face was only a few inches away. 'What do you take me for, Jason?'

I put my arms round her body and pulled her close. 'What do I take you for? I take you for everything! My love, my heart, my life!' I kissed her firmly on the lips.

Her body went limp for a few moments and then she broke away. 'Jason Scott, you're the biggest rogue I've ever known!'

'Then that makes two of us, Miss Smith!' I retaliated. 'I thought you were an innocent secretary a few days ago. But you told me nothing of the truth. And you've killed five people!' My attitude mollified at the sight of her expression. 'Mind you, I'm certainly glad about the last two.' I moved towards her and held her in my arms again. 'Thank you for saving my life,' I told her gratefully.

She kissed me tenderly. 'One day you may have to return the favour. I hope you don't forget.'

I thought about her comment for some time wondering what she meant. No doubt the future would reveal the truth!

🌿 🌿 🌿 🌿 🌿

CHAPTER SEVEN

It was late in the evening when we arrived at Ben Gurion Airport. Penny decided to circulate while I bought our airline tickets. It was a busy night and I had to stand at the end of a queue of people with the same purpose in mind. When it was my turn, I began to provide personal details which the ticket operator started to commit to the computer. However, as soon as I mentioned my full name she pressed a button on the desk and raised her arm in the air. Within seconds, two security officers rushed to the scene. Before I knew what was happening, they took me by my arms and whisked me away down a corridor.

'What the hell is going on?' I demanded, as they ushered me firmly towards an office.

'You'd be wise to keep a still tongue until we're alone!' advised one of the security men. 'Don't concern yourself. You won't be harmed.'

They guided me to a small room which smelled strongly of stale cigarette smoke, and one of them motioned me towards a chair.

'Please sit down,' invited the younger of the two officers pleasantly. 'I'm sorry we had to go through that charade out there but it was advisable to remove you quickly from the main area. But first, tell me the name of the Commander you saw recently.'

'You mean Commander Yasood?' I asked.

'And where did he meet you?' He lit a cigarette with an elegant lighter and puffed smoke towards the ceiling.

'In the Gaza Strip. Look, what's this all about? Why did you have to pull me out of the main area?'

'We know unofficially of your mission,' related the older man taking off his jacket so that I could witness the revolver he carried in a holster. 'It's essential you recognise its importance as well.'

'What does that mean?'

He adjusted the holster slightly to make it more comfortable. 'Our information tells us you are like the reluctant bride, unwilling to go to the altar. Is that how you see it too?'

'If you'd been through what I've been through over the last few days you'd also feel miffed,' I replied. 'The whole thing's been handled very badly. I've almost been killed four times as well as spending a night in some lousy jail in Crete! If that's how you recruit people to your organisation, forget it!'

The younger man puffed smoke towards the ceiling once more. 'Organisation? We don't have an organisation! We know of your mission. That's all! However, we're always interested in adding a new military weapon to our armoury....especially if it's a superior weapon!'

'Where's my secretary, Penny Smith?'

'She's O.K.' replied the elder officer. 'You don't need to worry about her.'

'Tell me,' I continued. 'Am I being arrested?'

The younger man laughed and drew on his cigarette again. 'Arrested? What for? You're a V.I.P. Didn't you know that? In fact we've even paid your fare back to England. Let's just say it's a payment on account.' He reached into his inside pocket and handed me an envelope.

'On account that you're going to get the plans of a certain weapon,' the elder man commented. 'Look, you've met a few people here and you've learned a little about the future of the world. We'd like to make sure you keep everything confidential. There's a lot at stake here. We don't want some fink shouting his head off to the newspapers. If someone did that, he would have to be silenced. You understand.' He ran the index finger of his right hand across his throat to indicate I would have my throat cut if I stepped out of line. 'On the other hand, we know how to treat our friends.'

'Well, I'm glad I'm not regarded as one of your enemies,' I told him, opening the envelope. It contained a single airline ticket on an El Al plane to London. 'Hey! There's only one ticket here!'

'That's right,' declared the elder officer. 'You're only one person, aren't you? O.K. We'll take you to the plane now.' He motioned me to get to my feet and led me down the corridor, through the exit lounge, and out on to the tarmac. It was the first time I had ever been escorted to an aeroplane. It made me feel as though I was being deported. Within two minutes, I was aboard the aircraft sitting in the next seat to Penny.

'I was getting worried about you,' I told her, breathing a sigh of relief. 'They gave me only one ticket.'

'They gave me only one ticket too,' she responded with a very lovely smile.

'I also received a warning to keep my mouth shut about all that's happened. I presume they said the same to you. What are our plans when we get back?'

'Over the past four years I've collected quite a lot of material about the weaponry division of Dandy Advanced Electronics. It's all stored in a cupboard in my apartment. I suggest we go there and take a good look at it before deciding what to do next.'

I stared at her with a certain amount of dismay. 'If it wasn't for Jan's abduction I would let the whole thing drop. This is not really my game. I know nothing about the 21st Century Crusaders....let alone risk my life for them.'

'They want the plans. Nothing more,' said Penny. 'If you get them the matter will end as far as you're concerned.'

'And if I don't?'

'We could have another world war. One more horrifying than all the wars in history put together. And you may never see Jan again. I don't think you want either of those things on your conscience, do you?'

I fell silent for a long time, fighting the battle in my mind. Should I continue to risk life and limb, or would it be more expedient not to help anyone? Was it worth risking my appointment at Dandy Advanced Electronics by becoming an industrial spy, or would it be more sensible to resign from the company and disappear deep into the country away from it all? I wanted to ensure that no one would take any further interest in me. But then, what would happen to Jan? Penny was right. It would remain forever on my conscience!

As soon as we landed, Penny headed for a telephone booth. 'I have to make a call to my mother. She never stops worrying about me, you know.' I nodded and hovered at the exit for a while waiting for her to complete the call. As soon as she rejoined me, we made our way to her apartment. As we entered, I had a strange sensation that someone had been there during the past few days. The staleness that exists when a place is left unoccupied for a few days was absent. I helped myself to a drink and sat on a settee before Penny brought a large cardboard box into the lounge from the bedroom, leaving the door open behind her. 'Much of the information is general,' she began, lifting the lid to show that the box was almost full of papers, 'but together it offers a reasonable account of the weaponry division and its operations.' She took an armful of papers and started to segment them into piles on the carpet.

'You'll be disappointed when I tell you I know nothing about lasers,' I told her. 'My field is commercial computers, and for the rest of the time I concentrate on bridge. I focus my mind only on those things in which I'm successful. Everything else gets blotted out.'

She looked at me as though I had commented casually about the weather. 'That's fine,' she said quietly. 'We'll go through all this together.

It should be interesting to say the least. As you know, the Head of the division is John Packman. The company allows directors three years tenure in the weaponry division for security reasons. He's been there for that period of time and is due to move very shortly. Why don't you contact him for lunch? Even better, arrange to visit the weaponry division. You'll have to obtain a pass-card for access. Why don't you contact Packman on some pretext....that you're working on a new idea for commercial computers to be manufactured by lasers beams, or of some technical development involving lasers which would benefit your division?'

'So, in addition to stealing the plans, you want me to lie in order to get them.'

'We're dealing with World War Three here, Jason. It's not what I want you to do....it's a matter of saving millions of lives! And you can do it. As the clown says in Twelfth Night, "Some men are born great, some achieve greatness, some have greatness thrust upon them". You've been chosen for this role. Be it angel or devil! You don't have a choice, especially where Jan's concerned.

She wasn't pulling any punches either and, in my mind's eye, I could see her dressed in that brown uniform. Her views were biased but I appreciated the arguments. 'All right,' I conceded, 'tell me all about this laser business!'

She picked up the first pile of papers and raised them to reading height. 'A laser is a device that strengthens light. It can burn a hole in a diamond or carry signals of numerous television pictures at the same time. Unlike other forms of light, laser light travels in one direction only. Lasers are used in communications such as radio and television, in industry for cutting and inspection, in medicine for use in surgical operations, in scientific research, and in military operations. In the past, laser beams have measured the distance and speed of enemy planes and ships. They've guided bombs or shells to their targets and have been used as navigational devices. Military research has been under way for many years to develop high-energy lasers that could destroy enemy aircraft, tanks and missiles. Such development would also include the destruction of ground troops. A number of organisations in the United States have been working on military research for the past decade for the Star Wars programme which put such fear into the Soviet Union when it was a major world power. The idea was to threaten everyone on Earth from satellites in space, but no one seems to have emerged with a satisfactory solution. British ingenuity has come to the fore again at

Dandy's weaponry division. Such a weapon is under manufacture there, albeit it's imperfect and somewhat erratic.'

I held up my hands to stop her. 'Hold on! If it's imperfect and erratic why should Commander Yasood and the rest of the gang want it? After all, if Penny Smith knows it doesn't work properly, they must know it too.'

'I think that's where Schmuel Musaphia and Menel come in,' she answered.

'Really?' I retorted, showing surprise. 'Where the hell do they fit in?'

'There are many kinds of lasers but the one we're dealing with is called a crystal laser. It employs a fluorescent crystal such as a ruby as its light amplifying substance. The power for a ruby laser comes from a flash tube, often coiled round the crystal. The flash tube excites a large number of chromium ions, which are electrically charged atoms, in the ruby allowing it to melt hard materials. Such streams of light can burn a hole through thin steel in one burst. That's really the problem. A ruby laser can only produce light in short bursts because the flash tube generates such intense heat in the ruby. There's a garnet called neodymium yttrium aluminium which produces a continuous beam of light. This occurs because it uses less power to operate than a ruby laser, and it can be cooled by water. It's used generally as a drill. The first laser was built in 1960 and people have been researching laser guns since that time all over the world. But they still haven't come up with the death-ray machine everyone's after.'

'Do you realise what would happen if such a laser fell into the wrong hands?' I ventured. 'Imagine if someone like Menel decided to sell it to a number of different bidders!'

'He told you he wanted to preserve a decent life for his children, grandchildren and their families.'

'That's what he said. But can anyone believe him. It sounded very much like bull-shit to me!'

'We haven't any choice.'

I shook my head. 'Without the plans of the laser weapon it hardly matters whether we have a choice or not. I can understand where Menel fits in as the chief advisor on weaponry but you haven't explained Musaphia. What has the old man got to do with all this?'

'He's an expert on diamonds and jewels. Rubies are used in lasers. Perhaps he has some good expertise in that field.'

'I'm not convinced about that,' I grunted.

'I'm sure we'll meet him again,' she forecast, lowering the papers.

'Not in the King David Hotel I hope,' I responded sharply. 'I don't want to go through all that again!' I yawned and rose from the settee, walking towards the bedroom. I did not intend to look inside but the door was partly open. Beside the bed were a pair of two-tone black and white shoes of the kind that Jan used to wear. Very few women wore two-tone colour shoes. They were not in fashion. As Penny sorted out some of the papers, I slipped inside to examine them. They were size five. Jan's size!

'By the way, ' I asked, keeping my voice on an even keel when I returned to the lounge, 'what size shoes do you take?'

She looked up at me with a surprised expression. 'Five. Why? Are you going to buy me shoes for my birthday?'

I shook my head and made a feeble excuse but I refused to accept her reply as the truth. It was too much of a coincidence that both Jan and Penny wore two-tone black and white shoes, size five. But it was something I had to push to the back of my mind for a while. 'I'm going to visit John Packman at the weaponry division,' I told her. 'Theory is one thing. Practical knowledge is another. I must see this weapon for myself.'

'Then you'll need to know the rules and the layout of the division,' she advised.

'Rules?' I echoed. 'What rules?'

'You won't get past the main gate without a pass. You'll have to get that from Packman. Then there's a procedure before you can get to the area you want to go. The laser gun is very well guarded, as you'll find out.'

'I'm not interested in the gun itself. Where are the plans kept?'

'There are two sets on microfilm. One of them is in the Chairman's office, the other is in a safe at the factory.'

I looked at her icily. 'and you know the combination of the safe I suppose.'

'No I don't. The plans are also on the computer system but access is restricted and it also requires a double password. Packman holds one of the passwords. I have no idea who knows the other one. There's also another problem. You might find a way into the main computer system but, for the purposes of security, the weaponry division has a separate computer independent of the main system. To work on that one, in order to crack the codes and passwords, you'll have to break into the security zone.'

'That's great!' I muttered in annoyance. 'Two sets of plans in safes fitted with alarms, and one on a separate computer system with barred access and dual passwords in a security zone. We can't get to any of them!'

She stared at me coolly. 'There is a way. I know a computer expert who's first class at breaking passwords and codes. He lives and breathes computers. 'He could help you do it.'

'Is he a 21st Century Crusader?'

'He's just been released from jail. He got three years for computer hacking.'

'Oh, brilliant! Brilliant! A jailbird to break into a security zone with me!'

'The problem is entry into the weaponry division.'

'I can get Packman to let me have a pass to gain access to the plant.'

'If everything were that simple! The pass is a sensitised plastic card. Once placed into the machine, a security device makes certain it can't be used again for twenty-four hours. You'll need two passes. One for yourself and one for Chris Devon.'

'Packman won't give me two passes,' I growled. 'We'll just have to copy the damn thing!'

'That won't work either,' persisted Penny, ostensibly destroying every suggestion I made. 'The card is designed not to be copied. It will corrupt if you try to do so. But there is technology to overcome the problem.'

I sighed loudly to show my dissatisfaction. 'It's not on,' Penny,' I insisted. 'Third parties will have access to the weaponry division. They could enter the premises whenever they wanted.'

'It's the only way. You'll have to trust me.'

'Don't keep saying that!' I felt the blood surge through my veins as anger built up inside me. 'The risks are too great. I can't do it!' I walked to the door and opened it. 'I'm going to the East End. St. Katherine's Dock. I have to check whether Jan is there.'

'Very well,' she nodded, 'but it's essential we see Chris Devon, my computer expert, as soon as possible. I'll meet you at Leyton underground station in, say, two hours' time.'

I glanced at my wristwatch to note the time. 'If we have to. Two hours. But then I must get some sleep. I feel I've been awake for a thousand years.'

She came to the door and kissed me sweetly. 'We'll see it through,' she told me, brushing my hair back gently. 'See you in two hours.'

The area leading down to St. Katherine's Dock comprised a maze of ancient warehouses. The place was dingy and dirty, and the air was polluted with wisps of wool imported from Australia which had been stacked in many of the warehouses. There was a strong smell of coffee, and the delicate aroma of musk, peppers, and a whole host of other spices. I read the address on the sheet of paper Davina had given me. It was a warehouse down one of the narrow lanes leading to the docks. The door was slightly open when I arrived and I peered inside. When my eyes became accustomed to the darkness I entered. 'Is anyone there?' I called out foolishly, for if this were a trap I had walked straight into it with my eyes open. 'Jan? Can you hear me?' My words echoed throughout the empty warehouse. 'Jan! Are you there?' I sat down on a sack which appeared to contain sugar and waited for a while but nothing happened. Eventually, I got to my feet and was about to leave when I noticed a long table near a tiny barred window at the end of the room. I walked towards it hesitantly to find out what was laying there. It appeared to be a body. I touched it with horror to discover it was Jan's coat filled with two bundles of hay to make me believe it was her corpse. Someone was playing a very sick game! Unfortunately, such antics did little to help me find my wife. Where was she? In England....in Israel? I could only hope she wasn't suffering!

I sat on the table with my back against the wall for a while in anticipation that someone might turn up to find out whether I had discovered the 'mock' corpse but no one did. Then, fatigue overcame me and I fell asleep. When I awoke, over an hour-and-a-half had passed. I hurried out of the docks area to keep the appointment with Penny. When I got to Leyton Station she was waiting for me patiently.

'It's not far from here,' she said, walking on so that I was forced to follow her. 'Chris Devon's a real expert with computers. I met him years ago at evening classes. I got as far as word-processing: Chris went on to better things.'

'Or worse things, if you take his prison sentence into account,' I corrected.

'Maybe,' she replied, 'but no one can take his talent away from him. He's brilliant!'

I shrugged my shoulders as we arrived at a terraced house in a seedy area of London. For a moment it reminded me of the time we had stood outside Menel's hovel in Jaffa. Penny lifted the large knocker on the front door and brought it down three times. Shortly, the sound of footsteps clattered on the stairs and the door opened. Chris Devon was someone to whom I took an instant dislike. He was as thin as a rake and wore a gummy smile because all his front teeth had eroded. His long black hair was tied in a pony tail at the back of his head and he sported an ugly beard which had grown entirely out of shape. In each lobe of his ears there were three ear-rings, and he had a mock-diamond pin through one side of his nose. He wore a dirty shirt and stained trousers and I was not enchanted with the foul odour that followed him wherever he went.

'Come upstairs,' he invited. 'Hope you don't mind the mess. Wasn't expecting you!' We followed him up the narrow stairway and I hit my head on the well of the stairs which hung extremely low. 'By the way,' he called out tardily. 'Mind your head!'

We entered a small room which sported a profusion of television monitors, electronic equipment, and shelves of computer books. As Penny had told me, Devon lived, ate and breathed computers. The only evidence of normal life were a tiny table, a skinny chair, a kettle on a single gas-ring, a bottle of milk, and half a loaf of bread.

'So you're the computer expert!' I offered in a contemptuous manner.

'Sorry there's no other chairs. Never need them. Don't get any visitors normally. Er....there's a half bottle of beer somewhere if you can find it.' He pressed a button on one of the computers and a video game appeared.

'It's all right,' Penny told him. 'We're not staying long. We have something that might interest you.'

'Oh, yeh?' His mind was a million miles away as he started playing the video game. 'What's it all about?'

'Hold it there for a minute!' I shouted angrily. 'Just hold it there!'

He stopped the game and stared at me non-plussed. 'Did I miss something? I thought I got all the invaders.'

'Not the game, you idiot!' I snarled. 'We've come here to offer you a job. A very important job! I don't want to have to talk to you while you're playing a damned computer game!'

'Man,' he explained, 'you don't understand. I can do two things at once. I can listen to you while I play the game.'

'Not while I'm talking to you!' I told him point-blank. 'You either listen or we find someone else!'

Reluctantly, he stopped the game and closed it down. 'O.K. man, what's on your mind?'

'Before we discuss the matter, I want to swear you to secrecy. Do you understand what I'm saying?'

Devon looked towards Penny with an old-fashioned expression on his face. 'Is this guy for real? I mean who's he with? The C.I.A. or something. Swear to secrecy? That's rich! Wait 'til I tell that one to the guys!'

'That's exactly what you can't do, damn you!' I swore. 'You can't tell anyone. Not even your mother!'

'I don't have a mother,' he returned calmly.

I threw my hands into the air in despair and turned to Penny. 'Is this the best we can do? Is this really the best?'

'He's the right man for the job,' she replied, trying to hide the smile on her face relating to the personality clash.

'This conversation must be kept entirely confidential. Is that understood?'

'If you say so, man. You know, this is getting to be boring. Isn't it time you told me what it's all about?' He shifted his position and sneezed, ostensibly into his beard.

'The target is an international conglomerate making military weapons,' I explained.

'Oh, Dandy Advanced Electronics,' he returned, cutting across my diplomatic approach like a hot knife through butter.

'What makes you think that?' I demanded.

'Well, there's only two major companies in the field and you wouldn't dare to break into either of their computer systems. Anyway, Miss Smith works for Dandy.'

'All right, I continued, with irritation. 'You know it's Dandy. I need some information from their computer but I don't know how to do it.'

'No sweat! Lead me to the system and I'll crack it. When do you want to go?'

'It's not as easy as that. We have to break into the plant to get to the computer system. You can't just walk in there with a front-door key.'

'The other problem,' cut in Penny, 'is that the information is access barred and there are two passwords required to get into the system.'

Devon shrugged his shoulders. 'It takes a bit longer, that's all.'

'I'll come clean with you,' I admitted. 'The weaponry division runs off a separate computer system. We would have to get past a number of security checks before we even got to it.'

'What information are you looking for, man?' he asked casually.

'Why do you have to know that now?'

'Are we searching hundreds of files or is it something simple ....like a set of plans?'

The computer expert had a disarming way of reducing important matters to mere trivia. 'It's a set of plans. Will you do it?'

He smiled in an ugly fashion at Penny. 'For this lady I'd do anything....anything! You just say when you need me. I'll come running. I presume there's a fat fee for all this.'

'Just leave that to me,' my secretary told him. 'You'll be contacted within the next few days.'

A cold chill passed through my body as her words echoed in my mind. I had already witnessed how Penny Smith took care of people. Often it was effected by a bullet through the head or the heart. At other times she ran them down in a motor car. In my opinion, Chris Devon should have been far more concerned about my secretary than he was about his probation.

He switched on his computer game again and started manipulating the buttons on the console. 'Is there anything else we have to talk about, man?' he asked.

'Just one thing before we go,' I challenged. 'Everyone tells me how good you are, but how good are you really?'

'Man,' he replied, without moving his eyes from the television monitor. 'I'm the best! I can get to Level Eight in this game with no sweat!'

'If you're so good, how come you were sent to jail?'

'That's the reason why, man! You see I'm the only person in the world who broke through a scrambler 'phone system. A scrambler device lets people talk secretly over the telephone. It's unbreakable. But I found a way. I made a small gismo which I fitted to the computer and it worked.'

'And who's telephone did you unscramble?' My mind sought an answer to the question before he responded. Who could it be? A government department? MI5? A military establishment? Perhaps the Bank of England? It had to be someone elevated for him to be sent to prison.

He paused for a while to eradicate a number of space invaders falling out of the sky. 'It was stupid really. I shouldn't have done it but it did wonders for my ego. I tapped into a conversation between the President of the United States and the President of Iraq.'

'Was this about the time of the Gulf War?' I ventured.

'Don't ask me, man, I'm not interested in politics. Only computers. But they were talking together like real good buddies.'

My mind was reeling when we left him. He had opened a window to world politics I never knew existed. People often believed that treachery occurs at high levels. Even the media were kept in the dark. Now I understood why governments placed limitations on the release of information claiming that to reveal it was against the public interest. Sometimes those dates stretched as long as a hundred years so that anyone involved would no longer be alive. Of one thing I was certain....the quicker this task was completed, the faster I would be rid of that awful person, Chris Devon!

CHAPTER EIGHT

Penny and I arrived at our offices at Dandy Advanced Electronics at nine o'clock the next morning but I had no intention of starting work. I put an early call through to John Packman, the director of the weaponry division. He wasn't there at the time and I left a message. It was almost an hour when he returned my call.

'Sorry, Jason,' he apologised. 'I had to see the Chief Executive. We had a few problems over the weekend. Some idiot tried to break into the weaponry area. Every time that happens we have to tighten up security. What can I do for you?'

Tighten up security! I could have cheerfully throttled the fool who tried to break in. He didn't help my cause one little bit! 'Someone's come up with an idea for laser welding to improve domestic computer production,' I lied. 'I'm pretty naive about lasers and I thought you might be able to fill in the gaps if I came to look at the equipment in your division.'

'We have lasers,' he replied reluctantly, 'but the research relates to military capability.'

'I've never seen one at work so it might be useful to get a worm's eye view. Anyway, it's about time I went on a tour of your division to find out what goes on there.'

He hesitated for a moment at the other end of the line as though weighing up the pros and cons. 'All right,' he said eventually. 'If you want to come over, you'd better do it right away. I'll have to get Personnel Division to transmit your photograph and curriculum vitae to the computer terminal in the security block otherwise you won't be able to gain access to the compound. We have one of the best security systems in the country, you know.'

I replaced the receiver slowly after the conversation had ended. So far, so good! Within a short while I would be inside the weaponry division to familiarise myself with the layout and security.

'Well done!' commended Penny, when I told her the news. 'Stage One is now operational.'

'Operational!' I grunted. 'I don't think that's the right word. I can't seem to get the spectre of your computer man out of my mind. I'm sure he's bad news!'

'Then you'll be surprised when the time for action comes along,' she countered.

I left the building and drove out of the city. Before long, the car was cruising across a derelict suburban area. The establishment was easily recognised, surrounded by stout concrete fencing, safeguarded by miles of ominous-looking barbed wire. Large signs alerted visitors to the fact that the fence was electrified. It was further protected by two groups of uniformed guards, some carrying rifles while others handled savage Alsatian dogs. I pressed a button which lowered the side window and showed my company card bearing my photograph to the sentry. He scanned the information, checked that the photograph was like me and then took it to a computer in the station to compare it with information which appeared on a screen. He returned to the car shortly and handed the card back to me. However, before raising the barrier, I was asked to open the doors, the boot, and the bonnet to allow him to inspect the vehicle thoroughly. Thereafter, I cruised into the compound and stopped in front of a small dismal building. Outside was an armed guard and I walked past him uneasily until reaching a reception area. An elderly officer dressed in army uniform, with the rank of Brigadier, sat behind a desk. As I arrived, he laid down his pen and looked up at me with a bland expression on his face. 'Mr. Jason Scott?' he asked.

'That's right,' I replied. 'I must admit I'm impressed with your security.'

'There's a triple check on everyone who visits us, Mr. Scott. Mr. Packman sent a message directly to this computer terminal alerting me of your imminent visit, the front gate confirmed your arrival via a computer message, and I've just checked that you're the same person. We have to be on alert for twenty-four hours of the day.'

'Do you keep the same number of guards both day and night?' I asked, following the conversation with vested interest.

'Not as many. The alarm equipment assists at night time. We tend to rely on electronic sensors. But they can't be used during the day or we'd be tripping over them all the time setting off the alarms.' He picked up a baton, put on a peaked cap, and started out of the building. 'Follow me!' he commanded.

I leapt to my feet and charged after him, and we climbed into a waiting jeep. He drove to a building about a mile south. There were a number of tanks spaced at regular intervals to represent a conventional theatre of war and I presumed that tests took place here when no visitors were present. We entered the porchway of the building and stopped at a computer terminal. 'I prepared this card for you when the director told me you were coming,' he said gruffly. He handed me a plastic card before placing a similar one into the machine. A door opened which closed behind him swiftly after he had passed through. I ignored the machine and tried to push the door open but it was made of solid steel. I was forced to retreat and emulate the actions of my guide to join him inside.

'You can't get past that machine without identification,' he told me. 'The bad news for any intruder is that a card can be inserted in a computer terminal only once in each twenty-four hours. It's done to ensure maximum security. The good news is that you don't need a card to get out of the place. Ah, here's Mr. Packman!' He saluted as the director came to meet us.

'Jason!' Packman called out. 'I can give you thirty minutes, then I'll have to pass you back into the hands of the Brigadier. You can wait here, Brigadier, while I show Mr. Scott around.' He took my arm gently and led me further into the building. 'We have an upstairs and a downstairs. Both are considerably large. All the secret stuff is located below, divided into non-nuclear, nuclear, lasers, armour structure for vehicles, tanks and ships, and general research.'

'Armour structure?'

'Yes. Do you know that in 1987 a new anti-tank rocket was provided for the British army after ten years of development. By that time the Soviets had moved on to reactive armour, so the anti-tank rocket was ineffective. It was a shoulder-launched LAW80. The Ministry of Defence claimed that the tracks of a tank were the traditional part attacked. As the tracks of the Russian tanks were not made of reactive armour they were still vulnerable. How some civil servants will defend budgets even when they know it to be wrong. Unfortunately, we're in the hands of politicians who keep whining that public money must be used for services such as health, education, transport, housing, and a variety of other needs in preference to defence. What they don't understand is that the world is not a Garden of Eden with only the snake to concern us. Every country must have protection. The worrying factor is the accelerating level of weaponry. Where does it all end? It's a pity we don't manufacture crystal balls to allow us to look into the future. I'd be the first in the queue to buy one!'

'I heard about your laser weapon. The most advanced lethal weapon of its kind in the world.'

He stopped dead in his tracks. 'Where did you hear that?'

I paused for a moment realising I had said too much. 'At a Board meeting, I believe. I overheard someone mention it in the background.'

His face showed that he was annoyed. 'Well they're very naughty to have done so. Dangerous talk costs lives. It's an illusion to believe we live with a world of human beings in civilisation on this planet, Jason. Half of them are animals. Wild animals. They'll lie and cheat and kill for power....for greed....for causes! Come, I'll take you downstairs to the laser area, but you must promise that what you see will remain a secret.'

I placed my hand over my heart. 'Everything will be kept entirely secret, I assure you.' He was right in his philosophy on people. I was already becoming one of those wild animals!

He led me down a corridor with a sloping floor until we came to a dead end. Another computer terminal was located by the side of the wall. 'Ah,' I said knowingly, ' I can't use this card for at least another twenty-four hours. That's what the Brigadier told me.'

'He was quite correct. All cards can be used only once during that period. But this is a different security check. The machine will answer only to one of two sets of handprints.... that of the supervisor of this area and mine.' He placed his hand on a glass plate and a light glowed. Suddenly, the wall at the end of the corridor slid open with a gentle hum and we passed into a large room. There were five men working on different projects as the director took me on a brief tour. 'In many cases, laser light works only in short bursts. Where continuous beams of light are available, the power source is insufficient to produce the kind of energy force we need. We experiment with glass lasers with flash tubes, solid lasers which use crystals and produce strong sources of power, gas lasers where gas is installed in glass tubes measuring up to thirty feet in length, and also liquid lasers.'

I looked round the room focussing my eyes on the weapon everyone was so eager to possess. 'I presume that's the secret military weapon of the 21st century,' I ventured, pointing my finger in its direction.

'There are five companies trying to manufacture the same weapon in the United States for Star Wars. No one knows who's ahead at the present time. Frankly, as Rhett Butler said In "Gone With the Wind", I don't give a damn! There's a company rule which states that, for security reasons, directors are not allowed to extend their appointment in this division for longer than three years. Well, my term's up now so I shan't be here for very much longer. What's it like in commercial computers? Maybe it's on the cards we'll exchange places.'

I smiled but continued to stare at the laser weapon. 'I should imagine the plans for that monster are well tucked away. I wouldn't like to think someone could steal them.'

He walked over to a bank of computers and placed his hand on one of them. 'They're well protected. The computer is access- barred to delivering such sensitive information. It won't work unless it has two pass-words. Most passwords contain four digits each, ours comprise five. We've made it as tough as possible for any potential hacker. I have one set of the pass-words; the Chief Executive has the other. I don't know his; he doesn't know mine. The system's foolproof!'

'Thank heaven's for that!' I responded falsely, pretending to be relieved at his comments.

'You say you want to use laser beam applications for commercial computers. I thought all our manufacture was farmed out to other companies on a sub-contract basis.'

'It is,' I confirmed. 'But we may consider acquiring a computer manufacturer or an assembly company. If so, I want to be ahead of the competition. We can't beat the Far East countries in terms of the cost of manufacture because wage levels out there are so low, so we have to find other methods. Robotics interconnected with laser beam operation might be the answer.'

He thought about it for a moment and shifted his feet uneasily. 'Hm. I hope they don't have a project of that kind in mind for me when I move from here. It sounds too damned complicated for my liking!'

'Well, these matters are all tentative. It could take months, or years, to come about.' I took in as much of the room as I could at one visit. There were television cameras located near the ceiling in every corner which probably operated by day and night. They offered the security staff a view of every part of the complex on an array of monitors in a central zone located elsewhere. 'I'm glad you have security cameras installed for night work.'

'Both night and day,' revealed Packman. 'We call the security staff the "television crew".'

'Where are they located?'

'They're the boys in "B" Block. Worth their weight in gold! I couldn't sit watching eight television screens for hours on end. It would drive me crackers!'

My eyes drifted from the machinery as I began to stare at the workers undertaking research. They seemed the normal group of men employed in any establishment of this kind, dressed in white coats, but there was one man in particular who caught my attention. I moved to a different position in the room to examine his face more carefully, trying not to arouse suspicion. Then I became positive in my identification. It was Tomar Duran. The man who had approached the aircraft in Crete and had threatened to shoot me. I scanned his face. Yes! There was a cut above his eye which probably happened as we fought. But Penny shot him with his own gun! 'What's the name of that man over there?' I asked. 'The one with number five on the back of his white coat.'

Packman picked up a clip-board on the table next to the computer and glanced at it. 'Number five. That's a man called Tomar Duran.'

'Has be been absent recently?'

The director tapped into the computer system. 'Yes, he took three days off. Why do you ask?'

'I presumed he's been cleared by your security.'

'Of course. We take the most stringent measures to ensure that everyone here is whiter than white.'

'I'd like to see his curriculum vitae.'

'Impossible!' returned Packman. 'Personnel Division never release records unless recruitment or promotion is at hand. He's been with this division for over two years.'

'I'd like to ask him a few questions if I may. Do you mind?'

The director shrugged his shoulders. 'It's not up to me. It depends on him whether he wants to answer your questions.'

We walked over to number five and he turned to face us. It was definitely Tomar Duran. 'You took a few days off recently,' I began, staring directly into his eyes. 'Can you tell me where you went?'

'Of course,' he replied, in an English accent, keeping his voice on an even keel. 'I went to Crete. It was a family funeral.'

'Did anything unusual happen when you were there?'

He lifted his hands with the palms upwards as a token of innocence. 'They buried my uncle and I came home.'

'Where did you stay in Crete?'

'In Heraklion. My family owns a restaurant there. The Acropolis Restaurant.'

'Do you know a Commander Spring?'

'Commander Spring.' He pursed his lips as though thinking very hard. 'No, I don't know anyone of that name.'

The conversation ended there and Packman and I walked towards the door. It opened automatically from the inside and we left the building by the main exit where the Brigadier was still waiting.

'What was that all about?' asked Packman.

'I used to know someone who looked just like him but he was killed recently.'

'Well Mr. Duran is very much alive,' he laughed. 'at least I hope he hasn't come back from the dead to haunt us. If so, he could waltz through the walls and we wouldn't be able to pick him up on the security screens.' He glanced at his wristwatch and shook his head. 'Hm. I would have like to show you more but time is against us. I'm due for the monthly meeting with a committee from the Ministry of Defence. They're no fun, I assure you. Everyone thinks this job is a dream. Don't believe it! I have to fight budgets, cuts in financial aid and grants, political ambitions, and a host of irrational decisions. Look after him, Brigadier! See him off the premises!' He moved towards a large black saloon and drove off smartly, leaving me in the charge of the security officer.

'He's a good man,' commended the Brigadier. 'His term of office expires soon, so he's in the danger period.'

'The danger period?'

'Three of the last four directors of this division experienced the same problem. Someone tried to break in to steal something during the last thirty days of their reign. But technology is so advanced these days it's unlikely anyone could get past the main gate.'

'Why, Brigadier,' I smiled. 'You sound as though you're looking for a challenge.'

'Naturally,' he replied gruffly. 'Technology advances at such a pace no one knows whether anything really works as effectively as they hoped. It took the Falklands War to prove that exocet missiles were exceptional weapons at sea, while the Gulf War allowed us to test devices to scuttle the SCUD missiles and also gain more experience with laser targeting. By that means, one aircraft could identify a target, send down a laser beam onto it, while a following aircraft would drop a bomb along that beam. Without challenges we couldn't test our new weaponry. The same relates to security. I wouldn't mind the system being tested by the fine mind of a highly-professional burglar. We need such challenges!'

'Do you know anything about Tomar Duran?' I asked, as we walked towards the jeep.

'Number five,' he commented. 'Not allowed to discuss matters concerning staff. How do you know about him?'

We climbed into the vehicle. 'I know him because I found him dead recently.'

His hands froze on the steering wheel and he turned to face me. 'What do you mean....you found him dead? Explain!'

'He got into a fight in Crete and someone shot him. When I saw him he was dead.'

'How long ago was this?'

'A few days ago. If he was the same man he should have a lump on his head the size of an ostrich egg, apart from the bullet wound.'

In an instant, he lifted the telephone receiver in the jeep and pressed a button on the instrument before speaking into the microphone. 'Security! This is the Brigadier! I want a double check on Tomar Duran for security reasons. Ignore the current file. Find out the truth! Report to me as soon as you discover anything. And check him physically before he leaves the division today. I want to know every bump and birthmark on his body!' He replaced the receiver and turned to me again. 'You can never be too careful in security. We'll find out the truth.'

'What happens when you find that someone's cracked your security system?' I asked. 'I mean, enough to get into the compound.'

He started the motor and drove off. 'It happens precious few times, thank heavens! We deal with such intruders in our own way. Can't afford any publicity or someone shooting their mouth off. Not with the Ministry of Defence putting up a lot of the money for research and development.'

'So how do you deal with them?'

'Anyone caught breaking in will find out to their cost. Do you realise what would happen if any of our plans found their way into the hands of a third party? They'd be hawked round the world to the highest bidders for profit, and then everyone would have them. Small wars would break out in insignificant countries and some mad, ambition bastard would set the world in his sights and go for it.'

'Then why keep designing new weapons?'

The jeep pulled up sharply outside the small dismal building which housed the Brigadier. 'It's been a pleasure to meet you, sir,' he declared, climbing out of the jeep before saluting me smartly. 'By the way, I have a nephew who's very keen on computers. Do you think you could arrange a visit to your division for him?'

'I'd be delighted, Brigadier. Tell him to contact my secretary. She'll make all the arrangements.'

I got into my car and drove to the main gate. The sentry waved me to stop, examined my identity card again, once more comparing me with my photograph. Then he search the interior of the car, the boot, and the bonnet before waiving to his colleague to raise the boom. I drove away from the weaponry division feeling as though I had just escaped from a maximum security prison. I dared not think how it would feel when I tried to break in.

I stopped the car a short distance away and looked back. The complex seemed to be impregnable from the outside. Woe betide any unauthorised person who actually managed to intrude past the sentry gate to the interior, for that was where the security system really came into its own. However, it was Penny Smith and Tomar Duran who captured my thoughts at that moment. Had she killed him in Crete or was she playing some kind of game? If Duran's gun was filled with blanks, it was likely that our doubles were still alive as well. If so, the police in Crete would have discovered only one body in that field....Chedda, the pilot! It would have been assumed he had crashed on a solo flight. Why should anyone think otherwise? Therefore, someone must have alerted the police in Crete to the bodies in the field for me to be arrested. When the corpses "disappeared", I was left to escape. Yet they had hunted for me later on!

When I returned, Penny seemed to be very agitated. 'You have a visitor but I'm not sure you want to see him. It's Primar.'

I entered my office and sat down. Primar had been waiting for me patiently, chewing on the end of a matchstick. 'What's the matter?' I asked. 'Have you plucked up enough courage to do business without Kemal?'

He smiled easily. 'This is England, Jason,' he replied. 'That sort of thing doesn't happen here. We're all decent fellows, don't you know.'

'Who's side are you on, Primar? That's what I want to know. And what do you know about Jan's abduction?'

'Why does everyone have to take sides? People always do so when they watch two football teams playing, or for a particular horse in a race, or one side of a cause. Why do they feel so strongly about choosing a winner, or being on one side?'

'Only you would know,' I told him. 'Only you would know. But I want to know what's happened to Jan.' I picked up a paperweight on my desk and held it at though ready to throw it at his head.

'Oh, come on, Jason!' He almost laughed at the threat. 'We're not really going to indulge in histrionics, are we? Not in your office! I'll explain what's happened to your wife in a moment. My information tells me she's perfectly all right.'

I lay the paperweight down on the desk. 'You want something from me or you wouldn't be here.'

He took a deep breath, almost a sigh of frustration. 'You know what I'm after. You were almost beaten up for it in Israel.'

'How can I have obtained the plans?' I remonstrated. 'I've only been back in the country a matter of hours!'

'But you've been to the weaponry division. I know that because everyone else knows it. Even your secretary.'

I stood up and walked towards the window, staring down at the city streets. 'What's it all about, Primar? You've got to come clean and tell me what's going on!'

'I thought Commander Yasood would have given you all the information you need.'

'Oh, he told me all about the cause and his opinion of the future of the world. What bugs me are the other matters you seem reluctant to discuss. Let's talk about Chedda!'

'I've never heard of anyone called Chedda.' He flicked a used matchstick neatly into the ash-tray and felt in his pocket for another one.

'We both know you're lying!' I snapped. 'Let's have the truth for a change. Then I might be able to help you.'

He looked at me for what seemed to be a long time, chewing on the end of the matchstick, before conceding. 'O.K.' he began. 'Perhaps we can do a deal. You give me the plans and I'll tell you about Chedda.'

'Chedda first!'

He sat back with his legs stretched to the full and his hands behind his head. 'Chedda is my cousin. We were brought up together. Like Esau and Jacob in the Bible. We were always at loggerheads. There was never any brotherly love lost between us. He knew I belonged to the 21st Century Crusaders and put every obstacle he could find in my way. I was originally chosen to form the British end of the cause and recruited Penny Smith to help me. Chedda drove a wedge into that one. He found out the name of the Commander and declared I was unfit for the job. He pulled all the skeletons out of the family closet as evidence of his claim. So someone else got the promotion.'

'Well, that rings true,' I intervened. 'Schmuel Musaphia denied you'd formed the British end.'

He chewed on the matchstick a while longer. 'Chedda found out you were important to me. I think he diverted you at Stansted Airport that morning and took a bomb with him on the plane. He intended to parachute into Crete leaving the plane on automatic pilot for Israel with the bomb aboard. Before you reached Israel it would have exploded.

Chedda would then have laughed at me for losing out again.'

'That's not consistent with what happened,' I told him. 'He said we were about to land and started to reduce height. If what you say is true, how do you account for that?'

'I don't know the details because I wasn't there,' he reacted. 'The guy was crazy. Who knows what was in his mind? All I can say is that he was out to kill you to spite me. That's the way it's always been!'

'And what about the incidents in Crete? Tomar Duran, Commander Spring, our doubles! You know all about that!'

'I know only of the situation in Britain and Israel,' he insisted. 'Only those two countries! Crete is not within my jurisdiction!'

'All right. Then tell me where Jan is!'

'That's simple, Jason. When I saw her an hour ago, she was opening the front door of your house with her key.'

I leaned over the desk and took him by his shirt-front, pulling him towards me. 'Don't play games with me, Primar, or I'll knock the living daylights out of you! Remember, there's just you and me now!'

'I'm not kidding! She was going into your house!' I released him and sat back before ringing my home number but there was no reply. 'She may have left the house by now. Perhaps there's a note. You ought to find out.' I stood up and made for the door but he leapt from the chair to catch my arm. 'Hey! We still have a deal!'

I felt into my inside pocket and took out the envelope with the false microfilm handed to me by Menel. 'Here! Take the damn plans and leave me in peace! And for your sake, Jan had better be fit and well!'

He took the envelope, stuffed it into his pocket, bit deeper on the matchstick, and left without another word. I went to the outer office to face my secretary.

'I'm going home,' I told her. 'Primar tells me that Jan went to the house this morning. I have to check it out.'

It took me over half-an-hour to get home. I rushed inside shouting Jan's name but there was no answer. A note in her handwriting rested on the mantleshelf indicating that she might have come home, but anyone could have gained entry and placed it there. It merely told me she had returned to collect some of her clothes and she would be in touch with me in a few days' time. The situation was infuriating! I had never chased a woman so much in all my life!

CHAPTER NINE

The pundits who classify themselves as health experts claim that hot showers are refreshing while cold showers cool the blood. I tried both but their effect on me was practically negative. When I dried myself off and dressed, I lay on the settee in the lounge nursing a stiff whisky as I cogitated the fast-moving affairs of the past twenty-four hours. Gradually, my blood pressure subsided and I began to think clearly again. Someone wanted me to believe that Jan was moving itinerantly from place to place, as though she was being deliberately elusive. The other woman in my life was becoming even more enigmatic. She had killed Tomar Duran as I grappled with him on the ground, shooting him through the temple with his own revolver. I saw the effects of that incident with my own eyes. Therefore, how could he be alive and well, working at the weaponry division of Dandy Advanced Electronics as a research assistant? Number five! Suddenly, it occurred to me that Penny might have shot the wrong man by accident. For all I knew, I should have been the target. Now there was a thought! I picked up the telephone receiver and rang her.

'Penny!' I began sharply, trying to control the level of my voice. 'I saw Tomar Duran at the weaponry division today. It's a physical impossibility....seeing that you shot him through the head in Crete. There's no doubt about it because he's listed by that name at the plant. Can you explain that?'

There was a long pause at the other end of the line before she spoke. 'That's classified information! I can't talk about it at present. And definitely not over the telephone!'

'What do you mean it's "classified information"? I saw the man's body after you shot him!'

'I can't talk about it now. Let's meet tomorrow evening at seven-thirty at our usual restaurant.'

I began to lose my temper at her response. 'For heaven's sake, Penny! I want an answer now. Why can't we meet and talk about it? I don't want to wait until tomorrow evening!'

'You'll find out,' she replied. 'Goodbye!'

The line went dead and I replaced the receiver slowly. She was operating on her own account instead of running in tandem with me. I went back to the settee, picked up my drink, and dwelt on the matter. Eventually, my mind moved to the answering machine beside the telephone. I pressed the button on the instrument to listen to the recorded messages. The first was from Schmuel Musaphia.

'I've flown to London especially to see you,' he communicated in a wavering tone. 'Meet me at the Dorchester Hotel at eight o'clock this evening. I would prefer it if you came alone.... without your secretary.'

Schmuel Musaphia! The old man had come all this way especially to talk to me. What was that all about? The next recorded message followed swiftly. My back stiffened as I recognised Jan's voice.

'Jason! Sorry about the letter, darling. It wasn't my doing. They made me write it! I know you're worried about me but I'm all right. These people tell me they want certain things from you. They say they'll let me go if you help them. I don't know what happens if you don't. Anyway, I'm all right at the moment. Keep bidding those grand slams in hearts in bridge, especially with the one club system. I understand about your secretary. I love you, darling.'

I felt choked with emotion before anger raged through me. The bastards! Who was keeping my wife against her will? She said she was all right but was that the truth or did her captors force her to say it? Suddenly, I became sanguine and felt a surge of romanticism towards her, at the same time being frustrated at not be able to do anything to help her. I wanted to take her in my arms and kiss her; to have her with me by my side; to enjoy life just the way it had been in the past. I replayed her message on the tape, listening to every word. What did she mean when she said keep bidding those slams in hearts in bridge? And why mention the one club system? She knew very little about the game except for the odd phrases which cropped up occasionally. Yet here she was talking about bids and systems as though we discussed them regularly. In any case, how many times a year did one get a chance to bid grand slams in hearts? The jet lag began to overcome me and my thoughts turned into a jumble as I dozed off where I lay.

It was an hour-and-a-half later when I awoke. I felt dull and depressed. Life had painted me into a corner and I had no idea how to set myself free. A change of condition was required so I went to the local barber for a haircut and a shave, hoping that the shampoo would bring me back to life again. As the hot-towels were placed over my face, I lay back with the warmth spreading uniformly through every pore, feeling totally relaxed. If I could only fathom out Jan's message. Then the penny dropped. Of course! She was trying to tell me there was a slam in hearts. She had been abducted to Herts.... Hertfordshire. The one club system was one which I rarely used. She was either being held in a club or very close to one. What else? Keep bidding those grand slams in hearts in bridge! Why did she need to say "in bridge"? That was my game! She had mentioned it for a reason. The club was in Hertfordshire and it was close to a bridge. Well done, Jan! My problem now was whether to contact the police or undertake the research on my own account. When I returned home, I pored over a map of the county. It was then my troubles began. What kind of club were we talking about. A golf club, a football club, a scout club....or what?

At eight o'clock that evening, I put on my smartest suit and drove to the West End of London to meet Schmuel Musaphia. I had been to the Dorchester Hotel on one occasion only; for the reception of the wedding of a friend many years earlier. The prices there matched those of the King David Hotel in Tel Aviv. They were certainly out of my league. Musaphia was already there and he sat at one of the tables in the dining-room, puffing away at a large Havana cigar. He greeted me amiably, his eyes scanning the space behind me to make certain I had come alone.

'Why do you patronise a hotel which is owned by the Arabs?' I asked him as I sat down at the table.

'Tell me,' he countered. 'What's this obsession you have about Jews hating Arabs? Many of my friends are Jews and Arabs. I like them and respect them. The people we detest are the terrorists and religious fanatics who strive to die to become martyrs. To us, such people resemble the kamikaze cult of the Japanese in the Second World War. The Allied forces detested them too. Let me put it another way. Do you hate all Irish people because of the Provisional Irish Republican Army?'

I shrugged at the logic of his argument. The newspapers had conditioned the Western world for such a long time that everyone believed there was a fundamental root of hatred between the Israelis and the Arabs. Musaphia made it quite clear it was not so!

'There's work for you to do,' he went on. 'That's why I'm here. The problem is that your services are required in two places at once. We need you to obtain the plans of the laser gun. I understand you've already been to the weaponry division. We also need your participation in an international bridge congress in Istanbul.'

'Istanbul?' I echoed, in a loud voice, unable to contain my surprise. He made a sound to silence me so strongly that he almost lost the cigar from between his lips. I leaned forward to speak in a hushed voice. 'Why the hell do I have to go there?'

'After a great deal of research,' continued the old man, adjusting the cigar in his mouth, 'we've come to the conclusion that the rise of Islam will originate in Turkey. The surge of Islam will cause the most profound change in Western Europe, as great as anything emanating from the East. The biggest impact will come from Turkey which prides itself as Europe's bridge into Asia, and vice versa. Turkey's politicians believe the country is immune from the activities of the virulent Shias. After all, the Turks are the largest force in NATO after the United States. They are deeply mistaken! Turkey acts as a garrison between Soviet Asia, the Levant and the Persian Gulf. It also appears loyal to the rigid secularism of its founder, Kemal Ataturk. If that's what the leaders believe, they're wrong. The number of people wearing yashmak and chador....the new religious uniform....is increasing steadily. Forgive me if I use the word "steadily" euphemistically. By the end of the first quarter of the 21st century, the population of Turkey may reach a hundred million people who, more than likely, will seek recognition as the leading Islamic power. Turkey has become the leading light in the Islamic Conference already, while public observance of Islam grows every year. The focus has been the "cults" which are really divisions of the same religion. They derive their strength from the movement of population which has occurred as more people move permanently from the country to the towns. Some include groups such as the Naqshibendi, with roots in Egypt to influence people as far as Afghanistan, the Suliemanji, and the Rifai. At the strictest level, cults organise student adherents into segregated dormitories and prayer schools. Here the spiritual leader becomes the absolute authority on every aspect of life. There are signs that the strength in numbers is leading Turkey to form a non-Arab Islamic union across a huge area of Asia, through Afghanistan and Iran to Pakistan. A union of this magnitude will draw in Arab and non-Arab Moslems into its fold. Iraq, Syria, Lebanon, Saudi Arabia, large parts of India, Indonesia, and elements of many other countries will want to join. You see, the secular faiths have run out of steam. Those like Ba'athism in Iraq and Syria, Nasserism in Egypt, even Marxism in Algeria. In their place, mystical and fanatical religion have provided a way back to what the people believe was a golden age. In the forefront of this revival is the militant Shia with the ideal that if you want something done then fight for it. The concept is becoming more popular year by year and Turkey will be the nucleus when it all starts to come together. Its allegiance to

NATO will be swept aside like driftwood in the path of a tidal wave. The legacy of Kemal Ataturk is already in doubt. The army in Turkey would prefer Islam rather than any other way of life, which is not surprising when one considers that most of the population is Muslim. But there's another reason too. A reservoir of oil exists in Siberia which would dwarf that of the Middle East. Every nation wants to start drilling there but the Russians can't make up their minds how to proceed. If that reservoir is tapped by the Western world, especially by the United States through joint ventures with the Russians, the Arab states could become poverty-stricken in ten years or so. The price of oil would tumble and much of the West's supplies would be derived from Siberia. If that were to happen, the rise of Islam might be advanced by forty or fifty years. World War Three would be upon us very much quicker.'

'But how could a single country like Turkey affect a development of that nature?' I asked benignly.

'There are the republics of Uzbekistan, Turkmenistan, Kirghizia, and Kazakstan. With the break-up of the USSR, Turkey claims it has a responsibility for those republics. It sees a remarkable opportunity....one that relates to at least a share in the oil reservoir in Siberia. If Islam can set its plans into motion fast enough, it could accomplish control of that reservoir, and ultimately control the world. You see, it would own some eighty-five per cent of the world's oil resources. Within a few years Islam would become a threat to the stability of the West. Many millions of Russian Muslims, including millions of new converts, could be facing Istanbul instead of Moscow. Look at the debacle in Yugoslavia. Because someone jumped the gun there, Turkey may resort to a revival of the Ottomans, to recapture the old Ottoman lands in the Balkans. They were victorious in Kosovo in 1389 over the Serbs. They could do it again.'

'Well, Mr. Musaphia,' I told him. 'It's all very well for you to tell me these things but I'm not really impressed. For one thing, I'm not a member of the 21st Century Crusaders and I don't wish to be nominated. There are hundreds of major causes in the world. I'm not the slightest bit interested in getting involved with any of them. Call me selfish, if you like. I won't be offended. I became involved in this charade to protect my secretary and mistress. Now I find my wife was kidnapped and my secretary is behaving so suspiciously I can't trust her any more. I've no material interest in helping you.'

'Then why did you come here to meet me?'

'I came to plead my case. I want everyone to get off my back and leave me alone. But more importantly, I want them to return my wife!'

He puffed furiously on his cigar. 'The organisation hasn't got your wife. Whoever abducted her doesn't belong to us.'

'Well that's hard cheese!' I riposted. 'Perhaps it would be more practical if you found out how I could get her back!'

'Forgive me if we took too much for granted. It was assumed you were interested in helping us. We were told you were a humanist. At least that's what Primar said.'

'Primar!' I repeated. 'Now there's another thing. He's got the false microfilm of the plans Menel gave me. Who does he really work for? I haven't fathomed it yet. Only he plays pretty rough with a bodyguard called Kemal.'

A waiter came to take our order for dinner and then departed.

'I sympathise with you, Jason,' continued Musaphia, with candour. 'I like you for your honesty and resolve. However, we fight against the Jihad....the religious war....in the same way we fought against despots and tyrants in previous world wars. This is a replay of the first Crusades. The difference is translated by the technology of war and weaponry. We certainly need those plans.'

'Well, from my point of view, I'm taking all the risk and getting nothing in return. You're going to have to do something better if you want my co-operation.'

'Agreed. Your file states clearly you're a man seeking a cause to occupy your time and your mind. A man who searches for constant change and challenge. We have something in mind to solve your problem. Let's say you're serving a probationary period. We'll try to find your wife, wherever she might be.'

The waiter brought some drinks and we paused until he left. 'You're still offering me nothing, Musaphia,' I replied.

'It's already been given you,' came the response. His lips pressed even tighter on the cigar. 'In 732, Charles Martel led the Franks to Tours where he defeated the Muslim army. If he had not been successful, the interpretation of the Quran would now be taught at Oxford, and the pulpits of the City of Gleaming Spires might demonstrate the sanctity and truth of the revelation of Mohammed. The benefit has already been conferred upon you by others, nearly thirteen hundred years ago, who didn't hesitate to act in the face of adversity when they were called to arms. We're all indebted to them.'

'I'm sorry, that argument doesn't sway me to become a volunteer,' I told him bluntly. 'History is in the past. I don't hold that I owe anyone anything. I'm sure that others wouldn't hesitate to dedicate themselves to your cause but I'm too selfish, too cautious, too suspicious! In this case, I was caught with my pants down through those photographs and my wife's disappearance. But there are limits for everyone beyond which they refuse to go.'

Another waiter returned with the hors d'oeuvres and fussed around the table for a while.

'O.K.' returned my host. 'You've made it clear, but I feel there will be a turning point in your mind. When that happens we can talk about it again. In the meantime, we'll try to find your wife. But I will offer you a deal. If you co-operate, we'll arrange for you to play for your international bridge team for a whole season.'

Silence reigned between us for a few moments as I allowed the information to sink into my brain. 'How can you arrange something like that? It's not possible!'

'You'd be surprised what we can do. If you're willing to help us you'll be in the British team for one season. You can play for your country in Istanbul tomorrow. What do you say?'

'I'll agree to that!' I consented without hesitation, astonished to learn he was able to pull such powerful strings.

'But first, there's a small task I want you to perform while you're out there.'

'I knew there'd be a catch to it.'

'You'll be free to do as you wish when you're not playing bridge. I want you to visit a man called Mustapha Ozal at this address.' He put his hand into the inside pocket of his jacket and pulled out a slip of paper and a passport. Once in Turkey, you will adopt the identity of Mushtaq Hussein with this passport when you go on the mission. You're the editor of a new Islam newspaper in Britain, similar to Hurriyet, a Turkish journal.'

'What am I supposed to do?'

'Ask him how it feels to be the Mahdi....the man ready to assemble all of Islam to rise up against the evil infidels of the West. Tell him you want to write about him in your newspaper so that every Muslim in Britain will learn about his coming!'

'But how do you know this man is the Mahdi....a God-guided deliverer? Most religious sects grew popular after such "Mahdis" were dead.'

Musaphia drew deeply on his cigar and puffed out the smoke slowly. 'In the modern world, one cannot leave such matters to divine providence. If the oil ran out and no deliverer appeared, the people of Islam might lose momentum without a strong leader and drift to other religions, or create a new one themselves. So it's necessary to select people of outstanding qualities with superior leadership ability to be trained as Mahdis in advance. In that way, when the God-given time comes, someone will lead. To our knowledge, there are fourteen Mahdis being groomed at the present time. All outstanding personalities, with excellent leadership qualities, awaiting selection when the time comes.'

'That's crazy!' I told him. 'If what you say is true, it's like having fourteen Jesus Christs....all at the same time! You can't have so many people in the field doing the same thing!'

'I'll tell you how you can.' He flicked a speck of cigar ash off the lapel of his white jacket with his hand. 'Firstly, none of these men know of the existence of the others. Secondly, they all train in private so they're not known to the people. You'll understand a lot more when you meet him. After that, we'll arrange for a debriefing. It helps to know what goes on in the mind of a God-guided deliverer.'

'What happens if something goes wrong? What back-up do I get?'

He looked at me strangely. 'What could go wrong? You're a reporter for a new magazine on Islam in Britain.'

'That's just it!' I remonstrated. 'What do I know about Islam? He'll talk of esoteric religious matters of which I'm ignorant. He'd soon twig I'm an imposter.'

'You're a man of originality seeking challenge,' he responded. 'Normally you would go to your reference library to learn all there is to know about Islam. But as you'll be leaving by the eight o'clock plane tomorrow morning the opportunity is lost. You'll need to find a book on the subject at the airport. As far as your background goes, you're a British subject born of parents who emigrated to Britain from Beirut. You won't be expected to know everything about Islam.' He placed his hand in his pocket again and handed me an envelope. 'Here's your plane ticket. Remember, it leaves at eight o'clock in the morning. And good luck in the tournament.'

My mind was in a whirl. I hadn't played bridge for nearly three weeks which didn't bode well. A lapse of that time could cause a player to lose his edge. In addition, I had no idea who would partner me in the international team. It was essential we had an excellent understanding between us if we were to be successful at that level. There was also another matter which would have to wait. If I went to Turkey, I couldn't meet Penny at our usual restaurant. I wanted to hear her explanation about the incident with Tomar Duran in Crete, but it would have to wait.

Musaphia and I continued the meal, enjoying first-class cuisine and choosing our conversation carefully. He took care to avoid talking about the 21st Century Crusaders and Islam, while I chose to become more amiable. I still had no idea why such an elderly man needed to travel across the world ostensibly just to meet me. Although I tried craftily to ascertain the reason for his visit, he avoided any discussion of that kind. For the time being, his mission to London would remain a secret, but it had to be something important! I still couldn't understand how it was possible for anyone to arrange for me to become part of the international bridge team for a whole season. Bribery of that kind was out of the question. It was becoming clear that many elite people had been recruited to the ranks of the 21st Century Crusaders, or at least supported them. The other part of the deal was that they would try to locate Jan. Musaphia always boasted about contacts. But would they succeed? I reminded myself that Jan's abduction was another matter requiring urgent attention. If I was to be absent for a few days, playing bridge in Turkey, I wouldn't be able to follow up the clues she had given me. I had to take action immediately.

When I arrived home, I opened a large map to examine Hertfordshire in detail. A club and a bridge. My eyes scanned the map trying to unearth anything which might provide the solution. Potters Bar..... Hatfield....St.Albans....Welwyn Garden City....Stevenage... Hitchin. The task seemed impossible! There had to be hundreds of clubs; dozens of bridges! I poured myself a stiff whisky and sat back for a while trying to work out a solution. My approach to the problem then became clearer. If I couldn't follow it through myself I had an excellent assistant at Dandy Advanced Electronics who could do it for me. I sorted through the telephone diary and found his home number.

'Harry,' I began, 'I've got a job for you. It's personal and urgent. Will you have a go at it for me?'

'Of course,' he agreed unhesitatingly. 'What is it?'

'It's a matter of life and death but I won't go into the details. I want you to list all the clubs in Hertfordshire.... clubs of any description....and also all the bridges in the county. Do you think you can do that for me?'

'It's simple enough,' he returned. 'There's a large tome with an orange cover in the library listing all the clubs and associations in the country, but I'll do some double checking to make sure. As far as bridges are concerned, I can get them from an ordinance survey map. How urgent is it?'

I took the airline ticket and the foreign passport from my pocket and placed them on the telephone table with a wry expression on my face. 'I need the information as soon as you can get it. Unfortunately, I'll be away for a few days. If you list the details and drop them through my letter-box, I can go through them the moment I return.'

'This is about your wife, isn't it,' he ventured audaciously.

'Don't ask questions, Harry!' I cautioned. 'And don't be perceptive. Strange things are happening in the environment and I wouldn't like you to find yourself involved. But keep all this to yourself. I don't want anyone to know what you're doing. Do you understand?'

'Well, it's no sweat to do some research on a little old English county,' he added. 'Leave it with me. I'll get the information for you.'

I replaced the receiver with a sigh of relief. Harry was a magician when it came to research. He would produce all I needed within a very short time. I finished my drink and went into my study to browse. The walls sported many bookshelves, most of them reaching to the ceiling. Each shelf was stuffed full of books of all sizes which covered a wide range of subjects and works. Eventually, I discovered one relating to the religions of the world. For a while I read, and re-read, the chapter on Islam with interest. It wasn't long before the knowledge transferred itself from paper to mind, at which time I had learned a great deal about the Quran, the Five Pillars of Islam, the Islam calendar, and the variations within Islam, as well as its festivals. I began to feel that, under the identity of Mushtaq Hussein, I had a reasonable chance of passing muster with the Mahdi. Naturally, I would have to remember everything I had read and recall the information in the right order.

My suitcase was packed before I went to bed. According to airport regulations, I would have to arrive at the airport at about six-thirty in the morning to ensure my luggage was booked in and loaded on to the aircraft. There was little time for sleep that night. Not that I would fall asleep anyway. The vision of the weaponry division and the Brigadier kept spinning around in my mind all night threatening to become a nightmare but never quite instilling fear. The alarm went off as the first rays of light channelled through the space where the curtains failed to meet. I opened my eyes, awake and alert. Such conditions did not bode well for an international bridge player. It meant that my mental energy would seep away during the day. In the evening, when the competition at the bridge table intensified, I would feel drained and tired, have difficulty in concentrating, and become erratic when making important decisions in the game. It was not the best way to obtain good results in any match, let alone in an international tournament! I rose and went to the kitchen to make myself a cup of coffee. It was then I noticed a white envelope laying on the doormat. I picked it up and opened it slowly. Inside, there was a single sheet of paper with a message made from letters cut from a newspaper. It said simply: "Don't fly to Turkey if you value your life! Don't fly to Turkey if you value your wife!". I went to the telephone and dialled the Dorchester Hotel, asking for Schmuel Musaphia. It was unnecessary to wait for the answer. I knew exactly what they would say. He had paid his bill and left after we had finished our meal. Who every heard of a guest leaving a hotel at eleven o'clock at night? I stared at the letter again. There were no clues....nothing! I was up the creek without a paddle, not knowing what to do. Should I go to Turkey or should I stay at home? That was the question!

CHAPTER TEN

The flight from Heathrow to Istanbul took nearly four hours and it became apparent from the literature on the aircraft that the international airport was twenty-five kilometres from the city centre. After landing and passing through immigration, I gathered my suitcase from the luggage carousel and walked towards the exit. There were the usual group of people awaiting relatives or friends on arrival. However, one man stood out in the crowd. He was holding a placard with my name written on it in block letters. For a moment I was reminded of Chedda in a similar situation at Stansted Airport, recalling what had happened on that occasion. I made myself known to him and he threw the placard away, taking my free hand and shaking it furiously.

'Welcome to Turkey! Welcome to Istanbul!' he greeted enthusiastically. 'I'm Turgut. I've been appointed as your guide.'

'Appointed?' I asked suspiciously. 'Who appointed you?'

'I received a message on my answering machine the other day,' he explained. 'I was told you were coming here and the caller hired me to be your guide. I accepted the assignment and receive the fees in advance.'

'How did you accept the assignment?'

'They left a telephone number in England. I rang them and they paid the fees straight into my bank account. No problem!'

He took my suitcase and I stared at him closely. He was rather short, dark-haired, with incredibly dark eyes, dressed in an immaculate white shirt which was open at the neck, and he wore black trousers and smart black shoes. He had been blessed with a perfect set of white teeth, although he chose to exhibit a gold filling on one side. His smile was very engaging; at the same time his English was excellent.

'I have a car waiting for you,' he told me, clearly intending to care for every need. 'If you've been here before you'll notice many changes have taken place. Modernisation schemes include a new transport system combining an underground railway, a tram network, a railway and rail tunnel under the Bosphorus, and a World Trade Centre close to this airport. They've already begun to line the commercial suburb of Levent with Taksim, the business heart of the city, by means of an underground railway line.'

'This is my first visit,' I told him, as we walked out of the airport building. 'I've never been here before.'

He led me to a black car and motioned me into the back seat while he placed my suitcase in the boot. Then he climbed into the driver's seat and drove off. 'Never been here before, eh?' he repeated. 'Well, you have some real Turkish delights ahead of you. Perhaps I ought to tell you a few things about the place....other than the belly-dancing at the leading nightclubs. You can get a boat trip along the Bosphorus which is the best way to see the city. No hustle and bustle. The passenger ferries zig-zag all the way along the coast. The old imperial centre of Stamboul is a colourful place where you can find many of the main sightseeing attractions. The Ottoman Topkapi Palace and archaeological museum, the Sultan Ahmet mosque, the Blue mosque, and Aya Sofya, the Byzantine Church. The area is also famous for its covered bazaar. The world's biggest bazaar. Nearly five thousand shops covering ninety-two streets. If you get fed up with the minarets and mosques, you can always visit the sixteenth century tiled baths on Itfaiye Caddesi.'

'Thank you,' I replied, with little enthusiasm. I had business to attend to in the city. There would be no time for sight-seeing!

'You may be interested to know they elected Turkey's first woman Prime Minister. Tansu Ciller. An American-trained economist. The whole economy's gone screwy here over the past fifteen years. Crazy! Too much influence from the West. The government freed foreign exchange controls, floated the Turkish lira, reformed tax, and introduced Value Added Tax, but that didn't go down very well. Then they liberalised banking and started to privatise everything. Inflation's gone mad. About sixty per cent each year. It's hard to keep up with wages and prices these days. Unfortunately, seven of the ten top companies are still owned by the government and they're very inefficient. But....we survive!'

'Fascinating!' I returned, trying not to show my disinterest in the commentary.

'I've arranged for you to stay at the Istanbul Sheraton at Taksim. You'll like that. It's a really good hotel. The other bridge players are staying there too. They told me you play bridge. Practically everyone's a Muslim here. The religion forbids it. Only foreigners are allowed to play roulette or card games. It seems crazy that someone arranged for Istanbul to be the venue for an international bridge tournament. But then, everyone in the world is mad, except me and you....and I'm not so sure about you.' He laughed alone at his own joke.

'Who's paying for your services?'

'I told you. They paid the fees straight into my bank account. Some company in England called Dandy Advanced Electronics. Do you work for them?'

It was a clever move by someone to hide their tracks. They had contacted Turgut, pretending to be Dandy Advanced Electronics, and had paid him directly by remitting cash into his bank account. It was a means by which the 21st Century Crusaders could make the payment and remain undetected. As far as Turgut was concerned, he had been given an assignment and had been paid in advance. Any other details were of no consequence to him whatsoever.

It took him nearly half-an-hour to reach the hotel. It was a first class hotel. He took my suitcase to the reception desk, set it down, and stared at me flashing his white teeth.

'Well, thanks for the ride,' I said gratefully. 'You've done your part well. No doubt we shall meet again some time.'

He face registered surprise. 'You don't understand,' he explained. 'The arrangement was for me to do many things for you while you're in Turkey.'

'Such as what? What else do you have to do?'

'I was asked not to discuss the details. I shall wait for you here in the hotel lounge until you're ready to leave. My job is to be your chauffeur and guide at all times. That's what I was paid for.'

I snorted with frustration and collected my key at the desk before taking the lift to the fourth floor. The arrangement was for him to do many things for me. What did he mean by that? I shrugged my shoulders as I reached the door of my room. Turning the key in the lock, I entered and laid my suitcase on the bed. Before I could undo the zip, I had an uncanny feeling there was someone else in the room. I heard a slight rustle behind me and turned slowly to face a man in a white coat whom I presumed was a waiter at the hotel.

'I don't need anything at the moment,' I stated clearly, feeling uncomfortable by his presence.

His eyes blazed as he took a deep breath and then produced a small knife with a curved blade from the inside pocket of his coat.

'What the hell do you think you're doing?' I challenged, with fear welling up inside me.

He released a sharp sound, which could be described only as something between a battle-cry and a muffled scream, and charged at me with his arm raised, intending to bury the blade in a vital part of my body. The blood drained to my legs as fear raged through me rampantly. Who was this assassin? Why did he want to kill me? I was listed as an international bridge player, not a political spy! Then the adrenalin poured into my veins and I jerked into action. At first, I kept retreating as he made his way across the room slashing the space in front of me. On occasion, the blade missed by only a fraction of an inch; at other times, he was very wide of the mark. Fortunately, his lack of skill proved he was not a professional killer or I would not have lasted very long. After a number of near-misses, I managed to seize his arm and attempted to force him to drop the weapon, but he surprised me with a vicious kick to the abdomen, causing me to retreat and clutch my stomach in agony.

'For God's sake!' I shouted. 'Why are you doing this? Who paid you to assassinate me?' His eyelids flickered as I spoke but I doubted whether he understood English. 'Look, you've got to stop this nonsense at once! Do you understand?'

He hesitated for a few moments as though trying to interpret my words which gave me time to remove my wallet and flick it open to show him a wad of Turkish lira. He seemed surprised at my actions in the middle of a fight to the death and paused to think how he could benefit by my generosity. Then it occurred to him that if he killed me he could take all the money anyway, so he decided to complete the task. With a sudden thrust forward, he lunged at me with the knife. I assumed a low position and forced upwards the arm which held the weapon. This had the effect of keeping the blade from doing any damage and also impeded him from using his arm. He struggled for a while with my hand on his wrist which squeezed harder and harder as I tried to compel him to release the weapon. He soon realised he was about to lose the fight for he was not my equal in a wrestling match. Only five feet two inches in height, it was his misfortune to give me the benefit of about thirty pounds in weight. The only advantages on his side were the weapon and the element of surprise....the latter of which by now had been lost. He still maintained his hold on the knife, but after establishing my superiority I turned his arm sharply and thrust him forward intending to push his body into the settee in front of the window. However, he broke away from my grip and stepped back a couple of paces to put some space between us. Out of the corner of my eye, I noticed that, unwittingly, the maid had left an aerosol can of mosquito repellent on the coffee table. In an instant, I gathered the canister with one scoop, pointed the nozzle at the face of my assailant, and pressed the button firmly. A jet of spray squirted out at tremendous speed directly into the other man's eyes. He staggered back sharply and stepped on the settee which tipped over so that he fell backwards with great force. Before I could do anything to prevent it, he had fallen through the window which shattered on impact, and sailed through it, yelling at the top of his voice. There were screams from below and I hurried to the opening, staring past the jagged slivers of glass, expecting the man to be lying inert on a mass of concrete. But he had landed in the swimming pool and was climbing the ladder at the side of the pool to make his escape under cover of the hotel guests lazing in the sun. I sighed with relief that the man was still alive, with the ability to lose himself in the city. It meant that the police would not be involved. If he were caught, his story would probably be similar to that of Turgut ....that he had been employed by telephone with his fees paid directly into his bank account in advance. The hotel would imagine that a burglar, disguised as a waiter, had broken into the room and had jumped through the window when trapped. Drastic measures for crisis situations! There were advantages in hiding the fact that he had tried to stab me. It was all very strange! No one knew I had come to Turkey for any reason but to play bridge, except Schmuel Musaphia. Why should anyone be waiting here to kill me? I recalled it was the second time that death had come close after a meeting with Musaphia. The first time had been the incident with the grey car. Perhaps it was advisable to avoid the octogenarian in the future if I wanted to enjoy a longer life. Of course, Turgut knew of my arrival. Perhaps he had something to do with the attack, but such speculation was merely grasping at straws.

Suddenly, all hell broke loose in the room. People started to hammer on the door, shouting in Turkish, French and German in the corridor. After brushing down my clothes, I let them in and began to explain to the hotel manager that a burglar had been hiding in my room. He was appalled that such an event had happened at his hotel and ushered everyone out before making profuse apologies. Without delay, he telephoned the reception desk to make new arrangements. Ultimately, I found myself ushered gently to a different room with a page-boy carrying my suitcase. By this time, Turgut had heard the news and came looking for me.

'Tell me,' he whispered as we walked along the corridor. 'What are we into here? Why should anyone be in your room? This isn't the kind of hotel that has that sort of reputation. Have you done something very bad?'

I smiled at him. 'Turgut, it would be helpful if someone told me what was going on. I don't suppose for one moment you would admit you had a hand in it.'

'Me?' His black eyes widened like saucers. 'What do you take me for? I'm a simple guide in Istanbul. I never get involved in the affairs of my clients. In any case, how would I know which room had been allocated to you?'

'Oh, I don't think that's a problem,' I went on. 'Money can make all kinds of things happen. Anyone can bribe a desk clerk to reserve a certain room. And it would be easy to make sure an assailant was waiting in that room beforehand.'

'I don't do things like that, Mr. Scott,' he told me coolly. 'I like to sleep at night.' His white teeth flashed, showing the gold filling, and he returned to the hotel lounge.

I discovered which maid had cleaned the room I had just vacated and handed her a handsome tip. She was completely confused by my gesture. The woman would never know that but for the can of mosquito repellent she left in the room I might have been in very serious trouble....or extremely dead! When everyone had left, I closed the door and crept into the bathroom, looking in the wardrobe and under the bed. But there was no need to fear. I was completely alone. I telephoned the restaurant and asked for some sandwiches, fruit and coffee to be brought to the room. Time was speeding along and I wanted to visit the Mahdi as soon as possible. Ten minutes later, there was a knock at the door and I admitted a waiter bearing a silver-plated tray with a bowl of fruit. He put it down and picked up a knife. I froze like a block of ice. Not again! Not another man posing as a waiter with a contract to kill me! He stared at me with a menacing look in his dark eyes.

'If you wish,' he said slowly and subserviently, 'I will peel the fruit for you.'

I took the knife from his hand and ushered him out of the room, pressing a tip in his hand. I had had enough of knives and ostensible waiters for one day!

I ate lunch reading the notes I had written from the book in my study. 'The Mahdi, which meant the divinely guided one in Arabic, was the term for a messianic deliverer able to fill the Earth with justice and equity. He would restore true religion and herald a short golden age lasting between seven to nine years. Thereafter, the world would end.' One could almost say the same about Hitler. He claimed to be a kind of Mahdi, although the Reich that he predicted would last a thousand years ended within a very short time. He became President and Dictator of Germany in 1932, but his antics did not become serious until 1936. By mid-1945 his world had ended. The Islam religion was in contradiction about a divine deliverer. The sacred scriptures of Islam, the Quran, didn't mention anything about a Mahdi, nor did the Hadith, the sayings attributed to the Prophet Mohammad. It was the Shias who introduced the idea, while the orthodox Sunnis continued to question such beliefs. The Shias saw the Mahdi as a restorer of political power and the religious purity of Islam. The doctrine appeared to have gained ground during the confusion and insecurity of the religious and political upheavals of early Islam. The leader of a revolt of non-Arab Muslims in Iraq in the seventh century used the doctrine in respect of Mohammad's son-in-law. It was claimed that his body remained alive in the tomb in a state of occultation and would reappear to vanquish his enemies. The body was supposed to rise and return to the world, carrying a black banner. Every time a crisis arose in history, the Mahdi tended to receive new emphasis. After the battle of Las Navas de Tolosa in 1212, when Islam lost most of Spain, Muslims circulated prophesies ascribed to Mohammad foretelling a reconquest of Spain by the Mahdi. Over the centuries, the title was claimed by a number of social revolutionaries in the Islamic world. During the Napoleonic invasion of Egypt, someone claiming to be the Mahdi appeared for a while in Lower Egypt. North Africa had seen many self-styled Mahdis, including the founder of the Fatimid dynasty, the founder of the Almohad movement in Morocco, and the Mahdi of Sudan who besieged General Gordon in 1881 and overthrew Egyptian power in the Sudan. In essence, the Mahdi was a complete myth, devised by human beings for their own use. It was similar to the analogy of the large vicious-looking dog whose owner told a stranger that the animal was harmless. 'I know that, and you know that,' replied the stranger, 'but does the dog know it?' The Mahdi was no different. He was the divinely guided one, to administer justice and restore religion. I knew that, and everyone else knew that, but did the Mahdi know it? History had often proved otherwise!

After lunch, I pocketed my second passport to become Mushtaq Hussein, and went to the hotel lounge to find Turgut. 'I want to go to this address,' I told him, showing him the information Schmuel Musaphia had given me at the Dorchester Hotel.

'Ah,' he responded hesitantly. 'That's one of the things I've been asked to rearrange. This address is incorrect. I have a new one for you.'

'A new one?'

'Yes. They've probably done it for security reasons. In case someone steals the information on the way here. If they stole it, they will have the wrong address.' He led me out of the lounge to the car park and we got back into the vehicle. 'We have to travel to the old section of Istanbul. The walled city.' He started the engine and drove off. 'We leave this modern part, cross the Golden Horn on the Galata Bridge, and enter that part of the city which is still fairly free of bulldozers, although it won't be long before the developers get their way. The address I have is in the Stamboul section. A place where time seems to have stood still for centuries.'

It was only a short drive away from our destination and he stopped the car a few hundred yards past the Column of Arcadius. He pointed ahead with the index finger of his right hand. 'If you go down that street, you'll find it's the third house on the right. I daren't drive you to the door. There are thousands of watching eyes.'

I got out of the car and walked down the street with an uneasy feeling in my bones. This was yet another horrendous venture into the unknown, only this time I was carrying a false passport and assuming a new identity in relation to a religion of which I knew very little. I reached the third door on the right. It wasn't as miserable as Menel's house in Jaffa but it could have done with substantial repair and repainting. There was a small door-knocker which I used forcefully, to be welcomed by a man in Western clothes.

'I've come to interview Mustapha Ozal. I'm Mushtaq Hussein from the British Hurriyet newspaper.'

He bade me enter but as soon as I crossed the threshold he placed a hand on my shoulder to prevent me going further. Before I could speak, he had run his hands over my body and down my legs. 'Sorry about that,' he said insincerely, in a good English accent. 'It's just a formality. We all have a multitude of things to do in these troubled times. One of them is security. You can never be too careful. Please come with me.' I followed him down a short passage which had a number of doors. He opened one of them and ushered me inside. 'You'll be called shortly.' he said, closing the door behind him.

I sat down on a modern chair and looked round the room. There were three comfortable chairs and a round table made of mahogany. On a coffee-table lay a miscellany of Turkish newspapers and magazines. A few pictures adorned the walls but some were surrealistic and beyond my comprehension. In the far corner, on a small desk, sat a computer and monitor. I had imagined that the man and the place were going to be mystical and strange. I was in error. After five minutes passed by, just as my nerves were beginning to get the better of me as a result of the deception, the door opened and a man of medium height, dressed in a dark blue suit, entered the room.

'Sorry to have kept you,' he apologised politely. 'There are so many things to do these days, one gets bogged down in trivia.'

I stood up as though it was necessary to do so in the presence of a potential messianic deliverer but he motioned me to sit down with a wave of his hand.

'You are Mustapha Ozal, I presume,' I began with an element of surprise creeping into my voice. I had expected to find him swathed in Arab robes, with a turban, clutching a copy of the Quran in his hand and uttering phrases from it. The man before me was smart, dapper, well-dressed, and very Westernised, and he spoke as though he was a member of the aristocracy in Britain. I had seen pictures of the Mahdi of the Sudan, who fought General Gordon, depicting a wild, savage person on a horse, with evil eyes that pierced fiercely through the mortality of every individual. My subject was a far cry from that image.

'That's correct,' he replied. 'And you are Mushtaq Hussein from England. I applaud you for publishing a new magazine to provide information on Islam and for the Muslim people of Britain. The brotherhood has grown exceedingly quickly over the past fifty years, while the work of the Ayatollah Kumeini in establishing Iran as a totally secular state was a stroke of political genius. We need men like him in the world: we need men like you! It's communication that counts. In Turkey the spread of Islam has accelerated at the speed of light. The population balance between city and villages has been reversed. Sixty per cent of the people have become city dwellers compared with only forty-three per cent in 1980. Township immigration increases the numbers to the fold.' He paused for a moment. 'Forgive me. I'm chattering about matters of which you're already aware. Please ask any questions you feel appropriate. And perhaps you'll tell me all about your magazine.'

'Well,' I replied falteringly, 'the magazine will be glossy, in four colours, and consist of about thirty pages. It will be issued monthly, not only to our brothers but to everyone willing to read it. Hopefully, we shall attract many people to Islam over the next decade.'

'Good! Good!' he commented enthusiastically. At that moment the door opened and the other man entered with a tray bearing two cups of coffee which he set down on the small table.

'So that's the basic concept of the magazine,' I continued. 'There will be articles on Islam but also information on general matters of interest to everyone. It's necessary to be realistic in a modern world where people have so many diversions.

'Indeed!' he uttered solemnly, lifting one of the cups which he handed to me.

I decided to venture on to the main subject so that I could prepare some kind of report for the debriefing session with Schmuel Musaphia. 'If you'll allow me to cut to the chase,' I went on somewhat hesitantly. 'The Mahdi is a divinely guided one. How do you see yourself in that role?'

'It's not so much how I see myself as how others see me. There have been many self-styled Mahdis over the centuries. Some are not even recorded in history because they were so insignificant. In order to understand the arrival of the Mahdi, one needs to examine such a role in five different ways. Firstly, it's absolutely essential that Allah has endowed such a person with virtues of outstanding charisma....an aura which can be felt by his followers, and the capability of mesmerising people to the point at which they offer their total commitment. Added to this is the essence of leadership, which is often enhanced by the gift of speech or a silver tongue, and the ability to command. None of these attributes can be acquired by learning or training. One has to be born with them. Without authority which stems from these endowments of Allah, a man could not be a Mahdi. Secondly, the divinely guided one is likely to be a Shi'ite because of the militancy of the Shias compared with the jurisprudent Sunnis. This may not necessarily be the case, for if Allah deems that the Mahdi should rise from the ranks of the Sunnis, then it is the will of Allah, not of man. As you know, only one Muslim in seven is a Shi'ite. Thirdly, the Mahdi who once appeared carrying a black banner into battle would hardly survive in these times. He has to be well-educated and trained to a high degree in both politics and modern warfare. All the charisma and leadership in the world would be useless to a wild, uneducated warrior. Gone are the days when a man with the gift of speech could rouse an army into action and go charging at the enemy with such fanaticism that the battle would be won. Those activities are best left to the savagery and romanticism of the past. The modern Mahdi needs to read at a reputable college or university and be skilled in politics. He must understand every aspect of war and weaponry, because if he intends to use strength and might there will be retaliation equal to that he intends to exert. In fact, the technology is so advanced that a war could be ended in hours if operated at its ultimate. Before you came, you probably wondered how much mysticism there would be in the Mahdi. Forget it, my brother. There is no mysticism in this modern age. We have to learn facts and absorb vast quantities of information at colleges and universities. The fourth issue relates to timing. History has been remarkable at fitting people into the right slot at the right time....or failing to do so. For example, Sir Winston Churchill was much ignored in the 1930s and his political career was, at that time, largely elementary. However, the timing of the Second World War was perfect. It brought him directly into the limelight. History records he was an exceptional leader. Had the war begun thirty years earlier or thirty years later, he would have been relatively unknown in the annals of history. Therefore, it is timing that brings the Mahdi to life, rather than his sudden appearance on the horizon holding a black banner. It may well be I shall be too old when the true time arrives and someone else may have to take my place.'

'If that happens, do you think there will be another Mahdi?' I recalled that Schmuel Musaphia had told me there were fourteen Mahdis being prepared and trained.

'There will always be a Mahdi,' returned Ozal modestly. 'There will always be men of such quality. The problem is whether the time is right for the Jihad in their lifetime.'

'And what of the fifth issue?' I replaced the coffee cup on the table and began to jot down some notes on a pad.

'The fifth one. That's the one which really counts. Anyone with charisma and leadership qualities can become educated, politically inspired, and train for war, whether they are Shia or Sunni. The timing of the Jihad cannot be forecast. It is a matter of fate. However, the last element concerning the Mahdi is the most important one. According to the Quran, Allah created two parallel species of creatures....man and jinn. One was made of clay, the other from fire. The Quran says little about the jinn although it's implied that the jinn are endowed with reason and responsibility, but they are more prone to evil than man. What I'm saying is that the Mahdi cannot be a man: he has to be a jinn. It's necessary to be evil to be militant ....to want to destroy people and sack cities, seize power, and control continents.'

'And that's what makes the Mahdi,' I returned quietly.

'No, not at all!' he returned defiantly. 'The Mahdi has to be a jinn but he also has to hear the voice of Allah giving him instructions what he must do for the people of Islam.'

'And you hear his voice?'

'Of course. The Mahdi is the divinely guided one. He has to be guided divinely. That's both logical and reasonable, even if it sounds mystical. History is legion with similar occurrences. Joan of Arc. Bernadette of Lourdes. And many others. What more would your readers want to know?'

He sat as still as a statue and I took a long hard look at him. The man was arrogant but controlled, which I presumed would be two of the qualities required by a Mahdi. He was cool and concise, and he had an authority in his voice which made one obedient without wishing to be so. The most frightening part of the interview, however, was about to begin. He cast his eyes in my direction in a fixed stare and I could swear they turned yellow....as yellow as the fire of a jinn....while his body stiffened and he seemed to become mechanical in his delivery.

'When the time comes,' he declared, in a voice slightly louder than before, with a tone that became very sharp, 'and Allah tells me I have to lead the people in a Jihad, there will be a holy sound throughout the lands echoing death and destruction of such magnitude that every infidel will be destroyed by the mighty arm of Islam. It will be my task to purify the world so that religion will flow like the freshness of a stream....like the smell from the petals of the rose. Islam will be strong! Islam will be great! Islam will conquer the world!'

It was another ten minutes before I managed to escape from the building. I was terrified! When I returned to the car, Turgut scanned my face.

'You look very pale. What happened in there?'

I took a deep breath and sighed with relief as he drove back to the Sheraton. 'I think I heard the voice of Allah,' I told him cryptically.

'The voice of whom?'

'The voice of Allah!' I could see those yellow eyes searing through me as Ozal's words echoed repeatedly in my ears. "Islam will be strong! Islam will be great! Islam will conquer the world!" Maybe Primar, Penny, Commander Yasood and Schmuel Musaphia had a point. Perhaps there was a role in the world for an organisation like the 21st Century Crusaders!

CHAPTER ELEVEN

Turgut drove me back across the Galata Bridge to the hotel in silence. I believe he still nursed a slight grievance against me for the allegation I made that he knew the assailant in the hotel room. The moment I arrived back in the room I closed the door behind me. I took a small bottle of whisky from the cocktail cabinet and poured myself a drink. Then I lay back on the bed trying to relax. My experiences with the 21st Century Crusaders were successful in creating one traumatic experience after another, and it was likely there would be many more to come. As I held the glass in both hands I could see them shaking slightly. After visiting the Mahdi, it was going to take some time to calm my nerves. On reflection, my condition probably related more to delayed shock stemming from the surprise attack by the assailant earlier. Whatever happened, I had to steer clear of the police. If they discovered I had two passports in my possession with completely different identities, my position would be untenable. I had no reasonable explanation to satisfy them. I entertained the idea that someone may have planned it that way so that I would be tried and imprisoned as a spy. Why should anyone want to do that? But then everyone seemed to have good reasons for what they did, even if at first those reasons seemed illogical. I had to admit that adopting the role of Mushtaq Hussein had never failed to make me feel uneasy. The deceit, accompanied by the fear of being caught in an international incident weighed heavily, filling me with concern every moment I remained in Turkey. Yet such troubles were dwarfed by the fear instilled in me when the startling change took place in the Mahdi. He had turned from a man into a wild, ranting maniac in a matter of seconds. How could I describe something so fearful to Schmuel Musaphia at the debriefing session? Perhaps such intensity emerged from charisma and leadership. If so, I could understand why people were so much in awe of Adolf Hitler during his brief reign. Was it prudent to mention that the Mahdi believed he received his instructions directly from Allah? If anyone declared such thoughts from my neck of the woods he would be identified as a mental case and locked up in a padded cell in the nearest lunatic asylum!

The telephone rang to shatter my thoughts. It was Terence Wellby, the captain of the bridge team. 'I haven't seen you yet, Jason,' he commented diplomatically. 'Are you all right?'

'I'm fine!' I told him. 'Just fine!'

'We start at seven-thirty this evening in the large conference hall. You're all geared up and ready to go, I hope. The team is looking forward to beating the hell out of the opposition. And we can do it!'

'Sure,' I answered woodenly. 'All geared up. Ready to go!'

'Great! Tony Woodman will partner you. You've played with him before so there should be no problems.'

'Tell me,' I ventured. 'How did Istanbul happen to be chosen for this venue? I mean, no one's allowed to play cards here unless they're foreign.'

He chuckled at the other end of the line. 'Oh, that was a real cock-up. Some chap from the Swedish management assumed the mantle of administration because the Swedes insisted on running the venue this year. He was told that his role was a turnkey operation. Turnkey. Like when someone builds a complete computer system and the buyer has only to turn the key to make it work when he purchases it. In that sense they tried to impress upon him that all the arrangements had to be completed in total before we arrived. Well, he misinterpreted the instructions and thought that turnkey meant Turkey, so he booked it here. By the time everyone realised the mistake it was too much of a problem to change the venue. So here we are. As you know, we're playing Iceland tonight. I'll expect to see you at about ten past seven for a short briefing.'

'By the way,' I went on. 'did you select the team yourself?'

'Always do, old chap. With a little help from my friends. See you at ten past seven then.'

The line went dead and I returned the receiver to its cradle thoughtfully. Terence Wellby selected the team....with a little help from his friends. Was he trying to tell me something without actually saying anything? It didn't really matter. For one reason or another I was in the team. I fell asleep on the bed and awoke feeling extremely troubled. One thing was certain. I wasn't fit to play bridge at high level in my frame of mind and I felt sorry for Tony Woodman who would have to put up with some poor decisions during the evening. I ordered dinner from the hotel restaurant to be delivered to my room, preferring to eat alone. As someone had tried to assassinate me earlier and failed, they might not be able to resist the temptation to try again. I had to limit my exposure outside the hotel room as much as possible, even though I would be in public view in the conference hall the whole evening. Sliding off the bed drowsily, I stripped and stepped into a cool shower. By the time I had freshened up, there was a knock on the door and a waiter wheeled in a trolley with the dinner. But I wasn't hungry. For a while I played with the meal and then replaced it under the silver hood provided to keep it warm. In due course, I picked up the telephone receiver and asked reception to find Turgut. He rang shortly, like the good servant he was, asking me what I wanted.

'I need a gun, Turgut,' I told him. 'A revolver. Not just an air pistol. I want something that can kill if necessary. A weapon that can kill.'

There was a long pause at the other end of the line before he spoke. 'Mr. Scott, you're going to get yourself in deep trouble. I think you should think about it carefully before you ask me to do something like that.'

'Your instructions were to look after me at all times,' I reminded him. 'I need a gun for protection. I'm asking you to get me one. I'll pay the going rate.'

'Do you realise what would have happened if you'd shot the man in your room today? The police would have hauled you in for questioning and you would miss the tournament.'

His comments poured off me like water off a duck's back. 'I want you to get me a gun that can be split into two or three parts. Something that won't show up as a gun on the airport scanner. I want to be able to hide it in different places in my suitcase. Do you get the drift?'

He coughed and paused for a few moments. 'I reckon I could get you a nine millimetre semi-automatic Beretta for two hundred United States dollars. I'll have it for you in an hour, but first you've got to promise me something. My job is to look after you at all times. Don't leave the hotel when I'm gone.'

'Look, Turgut,' I countered. 'I've got to be at the tournament in less than an hour. There's no way I'm going to leave the hotel. Just come straight back here as soon as you've got it. Remember, it has to split into two or three parts.'

He was true to his word. In just over half-an-hour he was knocking on the door. When I opened it, he was beaming all over his face. 'Here it is!' he said proudly, as though he had achieved the impossible. 'Two hundred United States dollars. It's in three parts.' He laid the pieces on the bed and then began to assemble the pistol. This clips into here. That into there. And you need to use this bolt to secure all the parts of the gun together. It's a simple task.'

'And ammunition?' I asked, taking my wallet from my jacket to pay him.

'Two boxes!' He produced them like a magician pulling rabbits out of a hat.

'I haven't got dollars but you can have the equivalent in English money.' I passed the notes to him. 'This will cover the cost of the gun and leave some over for yourself. I'm very grateful to you.'

'Well you'd better be very careful,' he warned. 'You have two passports and a revolver. Those are risks I wouldn't take in a foreign country. Is there anything else.'

'I could do with a bottle of smelling salts. I need to be sharp when I sit at the bridge table.'

'It'll be waiting for you when you go to the conference hall,' he assured me. 'I would have made a good supply officer if I was in the army. Yes?'

He left the room and I lay on the bed motionless for a while. My mind and body felt so drained that I acted more on instinct than purpose. Before I realised what was happening, I had dressed, taken the lift downstairs, and stood with Terence Wellby in the conference hall waiting to be briefed.

'Some of them play the Iceland one club system,' he informed me. 'They open on less than seven points and have responses which identify the shape of their hands. Don't let them fool you out of a game or a slam! And watch the one with glasses and a strange bow-tie. He's the captain and a very fine player. Well, you'd better go off and talk to Tony about your plan of campaign this evening. Just keep it tight, that's all.'

I went over to Tony Woodman and sat opposite him.

'You made it into the team then,' he commented rhetorically. 'There was a lot of speculation.'

'Yes,' I told him. 'Someone up there likes me.'

'I hear you threw a burglar though the window of your hotel room earlier today,' he went on. 'Let's hope there's just as much excitement in the game tonight.'

We continued our discussion until a gong sounded and the Swedish controller stood on the podium. He made a short speech to herald the opening of the tournament. The competition would last for a few days so that all the teams could play each other. Shortly, the cards were shuffled and dealt at each table to find their way into the duplicate shoes. Tony was an excellent player; a credit to his country. He was a permanent fixture in the English team, having played for them for over five years, and he could be brilliant when he put his mind to it. On occasion, during the play, I felt he was doing so well that he was working for the pair of us. Slowly and steadily we made headway, hoping our partners, who would play the hands held by our opponents, accomplished excellent results. The match had progressed about an hour when the heat started to overcome me. At the end of one game, I excused myself and went to the mens' room to pour cold water over my face and wrists. I was drying myself with a towel when I felt a tap on my shoulder. Slowly, I turned and felt a shock jolt through me as though I touched with an electric prod. Standing before me was a man who looked exactly like me; my double! In an instant, I began to experience the same horror felt in Crete when Penny and I met our doubles out there.

'We'd better go into a cubicle in case someone comes in, old man,' he suggested. 'They might get confused. I've something for you.'

I rued the fact that the nine millimetre semi-automatic Beretta I had just purchased lay idly in piece in my hotel room. It should have been resting in my pocket now, ready to protect me. 'Are you the same chap who had trouble with his contact lenses in Crete?' I asked.

'That's right,' he replied, handing me an envelope. 'Here, you'd better take it. I've been told it contains an airline ticket back to London and a message. The plane leaves in an hour-and-a-half. You must collect your luggage and get off to the airport right away.'

'Tell me, how come you're still alive? The woman I was with shot you through the head.'

'There's no time for that now!' he said sharply, pressing the envelope into my hand.

'But I can't leave!' I remonstrated. 'I'm in the middle of an international bridge tournament!'

'Forget all that! You must leave immediately! Commander Spring's orders. By the way, the Commander told me to remind you we're on your side, and Mr. Musaphia also sends his compliments. I'm going to take your place at the table with Tony Woodman. You'll be leaving the hotel by the rear. Don't worry about the bill. I'll take care of that. And whatever you do, on no account return to the conference hall. We don't want anyone to know there are two of us!'

'There are some questions I have to ask you!'

'No time, Jason! No time! You'll need to get your skates on if you're going to catch that plane. Now hurry!'

He pushed me out of the cubicle to start me on my way. I was in a complete state of confusion. Leave the tournament! I had only just started to play. Was he any good at the game in practice? Of all things sacred to my pride was my reputation at bridge. I didn't want my double substituting for me to ruin it. Suspicion welled up inside me but the fact that he had mentioned Schmuel Musaphia gave me some comfort that he was telling the truth. I had avoided succumbing to the malady of paranoia so far but the position was becoming marginal. Yet there was a silver lining after all. If he was taking my place, any potential assassin would be aiming at him instead of me.

I emerged from the cubicle at speed and collided with a man who had just entered the mens' room. He was a tourist, probably a guest at the hotel, who had been drinking far too much. He scanned my face and muttered a mild expletive when the impact took place. As I opened the door of the room to depart, my double came out of the cubicle. The inebriate stared at him momentarily and then looked at me, his eyes widening as he reeled back in amazement.

'Bloody hell!' he shouted fearfully. 'I've got delirium tremens! I'm seeing everything double! Double!'

I beckoned to Turgut urgently in the hall and we hurried to my room. I opened the envelope to find the airline ticket and a small slip of paper in Schmuel Musaphia's handwriting which said: "Return immediately. Plans have greater priority!" I packed my suitcase quickly and Turgut distributed the parts of the Beretta into different locations within it. Then we left swiftly by the rear exit and he drove me quickly to the airport. We made our brief farewells and I was sorry to see him go. He gave me confidence and it was clear he had done everything in his power to take good care of me. I needed a minder of that quality with me all the time, but destiny and location insisted we had to part.

My double misled me entirely with regard to the time the plane was scheduled to leave the airport at Istanbul. In truth, I could have played in the bridge tournament almost to the end of the evening. Perhaps he wanted to savour the thrill of playing in the team, but then he had a few more days at his mercy. I was also concerned about the matter of identity. He was substituting for me but his attitude was far more flamboyant than mine. I feared that Tony Woodman would recognise the difference before the evening was out. But that was hardly my problem. I slept quite well on the plane back to Heathrow. It was as though I was leaving most of my troubles behind, although such ideas were fanciful. After landing, I returned home to determine the timing of three major issues. Firstly, there was an urgent need to obtain answers from Penny Smith concerning Tomar Duran and my double. Secondly, I had to choose a time when Chris Devon and myself could assault the weaponry division to secure the plans of the laser weapon. And thirdly, with the highest level of priority, was the information which my assistant would have produced in relation to Jan's location. Sadly, I was overwhelmed by Murphy's Law....the law which states that if anything can go wrong it will go wrong. As I entered the house, it was evident that the place was a wreck. Someone had broken in during my absence and turned everything upside down. Primar! No doubt he had learned that the microfilm I gave him was false and he burgled the place to look for the real plans. The intruder had made certain to make his presence felt. The rooms were strewn with broken furniture laying idly in strange sculptured shapes after being smashed or splintered by force. Upholstery had been cut and ripped in a crude fashion, destroying expensive seating throughout the house. Fittings had been torn roughly from their sockets in the walls and ceilings in an indiscriminate fashion. Slivers of glass littered the floor everywhere. Most of this was caused by shattering the doors of elegantly designed cabinets, in addition to the glass from every framed photograph, whether hanging from the walls or not. Papers and books had been pulled off shelves to be thrown aside haphazardly, and there was also evidence that many carpets had been pulled up in an attempt to find where the laser plans might have been hidden. The damage was considerable. It had been conducted wantonly, achieving nothing. I found Harry's note in a envelope by the collapsed telephone table in the hallway. It had been ripped open by the intruder in the hope it contained what he wanted. Harry had done a good job in a very short time. The list identified all the clubs in Hertfordshire and their locations, as well as all the bridges in the county. There were six football clubs, of which two were professional, three golf clubs, three scout clubs, five nightclubs, five bridge clubs, three cricket clubs and four youth clubs. There were also eight bridges but three of them were very small and situated at such obscure locations it was reasonable to discount them. I picked up the telephone which was still working and rang him.

'You've got a helluva job on there,' he began, in a troubled voice. 'There were dozens of little clubs but I eliminated them. You know the ones. Pigeon racers, bingo, amateur dramatics, writers' groups, and all that. I concentrated only on those which had premises of their own rather than those which rent rooms weekly or monthly. So I have to tell you that if the place you're looking for happens to be one of those little obscure clubs I may have missed the net. If that's the case, you would never have found it anyway. When you put the whole thing together, you've got twenty-nine clubs and five main bridges, so the odds of finding the right one is about a hundred and forty-five to one. Naturally, you might go to one place and hit the jackpot straight away if you were very lucky, but it could take many weeks to cover all of them. I mean to say, your wife could be hidden in a cellar or a back room. A visit to a club wouldn't be sufficient on its own. You really need more information. Something to narrow down the odds, but how you do that I've no idea.'

My heart sank at his words. He was absolutely right. It would take a lot of time to check out even one single club to find out whether Jan was being held there. How could I get further information to narrow the odds? Poor Jan! She probably thought her cryptic message was all that I needed to find her. How little she knew! I went to the dining room and sat on the only unbroken chair in the house. There was no point in trying to pour myself a drink because every bottle inside the cocktail cabinet had been smashed. Whoever had broken in was a particularly spiteful character, destroying everything in his path whether it had anything to do with his mission or not. It annoyed me that I had such good clues from Jan and yet I was stumped. I went back into the lounge to find out whether it was possible to rest on the ripped settee. The room was a debacle. Nothing had been left intact. The television sported a large hole in the screen and it lay where it was tossed in the hearth. The video-recorder had been dashed to floor with great force to ensure it would never work again. The telephone answering machine had been pulled from it socket to suffer the same fate, while its recording tape lay inert in the middle of the floor. Each of the standard lamps had been snapped into two pieces. What a mess! And then a thought crept into my mind which had the touch of genius! The recording tape from the telephone answering machine! It was sitting in the middle of the floor trying to tell me something! The only link with Jan was the message on that tape. It might be possible to establish other information from it such as background noises, familiar sounds, or something which could introduce new clues in addition to those she had given me....and shorten the odds! But in order to develop the idea I needed the services of someone who had the equipment and the expertise to be able to put my inspiration into practice. And I required those services urgently! Chris Devon! The name sprang at me like the string of a bow returning to its position after the arrow had been fired. Of course, Chris Devon! If anyone could do it he had to be the man! I picked up the tape and drove to the hovel where he lived. I knocked several times on the front door and my heart sank when there was no answer. As I was about to walk away in disappointment I heard the sound of footsteps on the stairs. Within a few moments, the door opened and, to my jubilation, his ugly face came into view.

'Thank God you're home!' I exclaimed with relief.

'Oh, it's you,' he replied. 'You want me to do that gig now. O.K. If you hang on, I'll be ready in five minutes.'

'No, no!' I stressed. 'Not yet! This is something quite different. It's personal. I need your help.'

'Well come inside, man!' he invited. 'I hate standing in doorways talking to people. Come inside!'

I followed him upstairs to his room and produced the recording tape from my pocket. 'I know the definition on these tapes is pretty poor but it's very important for me to try to find out the background noises on it. It's a matter of life and death. Can you bring up the background noise on your equipment? Is it possible to amplify it? I want to find out something from the second message. The woman's voice.'

'No sweat, man!' he returned. 'Do it all the time. In my spare moments I'm also a radio ham. Didn't you see the aerial on the roof? Here....let me have the tape!'

He placed the tape in a machine, donned a pair of headphones, and played it through once. 'Hey, that's heavy, man!' he commented, taking off the headphones. 'Sounds as though she's been kidnapped. What's all the stuff about bridge?'

'Never mind that now,' I told him. 'Can you reduce the foreground and enhance the background. I want to hear what's going on in the background.'

He scratched his unkempt hair and I imagined him turning his lips into a pout underneath the frothy beard as the wheels of his mind began to churn. He put on the headphones again and played with the equipment for a while before removing them. 'The definition is lousy. Those telephone answering machines are designed to give you a message....nothing more. But I think I might have something.'

He handed the headphones to me and I wiped them thoroughly before placing them over my ears, nodding to him to start the machine. There was a lot of white noise and some static as Jan delivered her message and I listened intently. Eventually, I removed the headphones and shook my head slowly. 'There's something there but it's impossible to make it out. I need more than that.'

He chewed on his lower lip for a while and then turned to me. 'What I can do is to make a copy of the tape which you can keep for record purposes. Then I can play around with the main tape in a number of ways to bring up that background. The trouble is there's a chance the main tape could be destroyed if I push it too far.'

'Can't you take a copy and play around with it instead of the original?'

'Not really. Every copy loses definition. I want to give the main tape the full works.' I consented and he made a copy which he handed to me, before setting to work on the main tape. 'Help yourself to some coffee,' he suggested, setting the headphones back on his head.

I surveyed a number of unwashed cups on the table and decided not to accept his invitation. He devoted his attention to the machine and started to perform a number of activities. The tape fizzed forwards and backwards, shunting to a violent halt one way and then the other. I watched him as he played with the machine for a considerable amount of time. There was no way I could assess his ability but I could only hope he knew what he was doing. Eventually, he sat upright and offered the headphones to me again.

'I've wiped out practically all the white noise, eliminated the static, and reversed the foreground and background. But let me say this. The quality is poor but at least you'll be able to hear the background with reasonable decibel value. There's a chance I might be able to raise part of the tape volume but such action could destroy it. Here, man! Listen in!'

I put on the headphones and listened intently. Jan's message could be heard but it was very faint. Suddenly, I could hear the sound of music although it wasn't possible to identify the tune. It appeared to be right at the end of a song. As the music finished, there was a voice which was only just audible. 'Stop it there!' I ordered sharply. 'I heard the last few bars of a tune and the sound of a voice. Can you bring up that voice?'

'If I do it might destroy the tape,' he reiterated.

'Then do it!' I commanded. 'Play it! As loud as you can!'

He pressed a number of buttons on the machine and returned to the exact point where the music had finished. "Ladies and gentlemen!" related the voice of a man, and then the tape ended. Chris Devon shook his head sadly. 'I'm afraid that's it, man! It's kaputsville. We stretched the elastic too far! I just hope you got what you wanted.'

Music, and a man saying: "Ladies and gentlemen!" It was all I needed. At a stroke, I had narrowed the clubs down to five, for there were five nightclubs in the county and Jan was being held in one of them. I thanked Chris Devon profusely for his efforts, paying him handsomely for the result, and raced home again to contact my assistant.

'Harry,' I began, with an edge of excitement in my voice. 'How many nightclubs are there close to any one of the bridges you identified?'

'Give me a moment, will you?' he replied, and disappeared to check and double-check the maps before returning to the telephone. 'I think this must be your lucky day,' he chuckled, as though we had won a prize. 'There's only one nightclub close to a bridge. The bridge is there because there's a lake just beyond it. It's called The Golden Peacock near Welwyn Garden City. How did you work out that the place had to be a nightclub?'

'Thank's Harry,' I said gratefully. 'I'll tell you all about it when I see you.'

The Golden Peacock near Welwyn Garden City! At last I knew where she was! I thought about contacting the police. It would have been the right thing to do but there were certain to be complications. As soon as I told them the exact location where she was being held they would ask me how I got hold of that information. My only proof was the copy of a tape taken by Chris Devon and that was of little value because the original, with all the real information, was corrupt and useless. In addition, I would draw attention to myself which could affect the assault on the weaponry division when Chris Devon and myself set out to steal the plans. No....finding Jan was something I had to do alone! I decided to contact Penny to obtain answers to the questions that kept nagging me but there was no reply. She was now becoming extremely elusive. I had felt certain our intimate relationship took us beyond the reach of the 21st Century Crusaders but it seemed I was wrong on that point too. I replaced the receiver and sought an answer by reflecting our last conversation. 'It's best if I meet you tomorrow evening at seven-thirty at our usual restaurant,' she had insisted. Unfortunately, I had been in Turkey and it wasn't possible for me to be there. Where was she now? Why was she avoiding me?

On the following morning, I started clearing up the house to make it more habitable. It was noon when I finished and lay back on the settee to rest when the telephone rang. I hurried to answer it, hoping it was Penny, but the voice was that of Schmuel Musaphia.

'Meet me at the Savoy Hotel tomorrow morning at nine o'clock,' he insisted.

'I have other plans,' I responded, without revealing that I intended to visit The Golden Peacock at Welwyn Garden City.

'Cancel them!' he continued bluntly. 'Nine o'clock at the Savoy Hotel. We have a lot to talk about! You'll be interested in what I have to say!'

Before I had the chance to reply the line went dead. What did Schmuel Musaphia have to tell me that was so important? I felt like a small pawn in a very large chess game. Everyone was searing across the board at different angles and jumping all over the place. All I could do was to take one step forward at a time. In the meantime, not only was I extremely vulnerable but I was also at everyone's mercy!

CHAPTER TWELVE

On the following morning I got up and took another look around the house. It was still a wreck despite my efforts to return it to a reasonable condition. Although most of the debris had been shifted to the back garden, all the furniture in the rooms appeared incongruous. Nothing seemed to fit properly in the right place. Cabinets and cupboards leaned unstably to port or starboard, sometimes rocking in their locations to the slightest movement. Grey plaster gaped like eye-sores from walls where the wall-lights had been wrenched out. Ceilings no longer portrayed the embellishments of expensive lamps or chandeliers which had been ripped violently from their sockets and dashed to the floor. Even the carpets failed to resume their original positions where they had been raised. If the burglar had intended to lower my morale by means of vandalism, he had succeeded well. I made myself some breakfast, even though Schmuel Musaphia had probably arranged for me to eat at the Savoy Hotel. I dressed smartly for the occasion and did the best possible when shaving and combing my hair for no mirrors had survived the burglary. Just before I left, I fitted the pieces of the Beretta together and tested the empty revolver by pulling the trigger several times to make sure it worked properly. Then I loaded it with ammunition, keeping some spare bullets in my pocket in case I needed to reload. I felt more prepared to face the world with the pistol in my pocket. I had never fired a gun before so I had no idea whether I was capable of hitting a target even at close range. The only other time in my life I had held a gun was in Crete when I had wrested it away from Penny, but that didn't count because I hadn't fired it. In any case, that gun had been loaded with blanks otherwise Tomar Duran and my double would have been dead. But the weapon brought its own problems. Firstly, it became impossible to button up my jacket with the gun in my pocket. Secondly, it made a large bulge when my jacket was open, causing the garment to become misshapen through its bulk and weight. I needed a gun holster. Nonetheless, I felt safer with the weapon than without it.

    I arrived at the Savoy Hotel on the stroke of nine o'clock. Punctuality in my book was a priority in terms of respect for other people. Not even the events of the past few days could shake off that element of my character. As expected, Schmuel Musaphia was waiting there for me. He looked immaculate in his white suit and bow-tie which I was surprised to see him wearing at this time of the morning. Perhaps it was the only suit he took with him when travelling, or maybe he had half-a-dozen of the same suits because he liked them. As usual, he held a large Havana cigar fixed firmly in his mouth.

'Sit down,' Jason!' he greeted. 'We have a lot to talk about. I want to know all about the Mahdi. What he told you, how he spoke, what you felt about him. Everything!' He stared at my face with a bewildered expression on his face. 'What happened to your hair?'

'My hair?' I laughed, with an element of chagrin. 'Someone broke into my house while I was in Turkey and smashed every piece of furniture, pulling all the lights out of the walls and ceilings. There isn't a mirror left in the house. Some bastard really took care of the place while I was away!'

His eyes narrowed slightly. 'Is that so?' he uttered softly.

'I tried to get you at the Dorchester Hotel when we last met but you checked out after we had our meal. Couldn't you afford the prices?'

A small smile crept into the corners of his mouth as he puffed on his cigar. 'I'm an itinerant. Can't help it. You know what an itinerant is, don't you? It's a person who travels from place to place. Funny, I used to move around a lot when I was young and burnt the midnight oil. The pundits warned me that if I didn't take it easy I would burn myself out before I was thirty years old. Now they're dead and I'm still moving from place to place and burning the midnight oil. So tell me, who's the pundit?'

'All I can say is that you must have a lot of enemies to have to shift about at such speed.'

He laughed loudly. 'Jason,' he told me philosophically, 'let me tell you something. I owe a great deal to my friends but all things considered I owe even more to my enemies. You see, the real person springs to life under a threat much better than under an embrace. Why did you try to get hold of me?'

'I received a note which said: "Don't fly to Turkey if you value your life! Don't fly to Turkey if you value your wife!" Have you any idea who might have sent that message? Or any reason for it?'

'None at all. But I'm the bearer of very good tidings. I have some good news for you. We've found out where your wife's been taken. It's a place called The Golden Peacock near Welwyn Garden City.'

I felt a wave of pain float through my mind in frustration. It had taken so much effort to find out Jan's location and here was this man handing it to me on a plate. 'How did you manage to get that information,' I asked with interest.

'The most important fact is that we found her for you. The question is what are you going to do about it?'

'Well, as it happens, I learned about The Golden Peacock yesterday, and I would have gone there if someone hadn't smashed up the house. But I'll be off the moment I leave you. I don't suppose any of your crowd is willing to give me a hand.'

'Jason, Jason! You tell me you don't want to become part of the organisation....that you're not interested in any causes, or the fate of the world, or the people in it. One doesn't catch flies with vinegar. Give me a good reason why we should consider helping you.'

'I'll give you one. You recalled me from Turkey because you need the plans very quickly. That's why I'm here this morning. If I get into trouble at The Golden Peacock I won't be able to get the plans. You need to protect me at all times. In the long run, it would be better for your people to recover Jan than to let me thresh about like an amateur into the unknown.'

He puffed on his cigar, allowing the smoke to drift to the ceiling. 'Looking closely at your face with these tired eyes,' he told me, changing the subject quickly, 'I can see you're in need of rest. You know, for a young man you're getting bags under your eyes.' The waiter arrived at the table and we ordered a Continental breakfast. Musaphia drew once more on his cigar and stared directly at me with cold unrelenting eyes. 'You've drifted off the subject,' he chided. 'I want to know all about the Mahdi.'

'I wrote a report on our meeting yesterday. You'll find some of the words a little quaint. The bastard who smashed up my home also damaged my computer printer. It's a comprehensive report.' I took an envelope from my pocket and placed it on the table in front of him.

'Tell me about him....in your own words,' he persisted, puffing smoke to the ceiling again.

'For the most part he seemed to be a normal person, educated in the West, wearing Western clothing. Then, as the rhetoric proceeded, he assumed the mantle of the Mahdi. He suddenly became strange, drifting off into a mystic trance which scared the hell out of me. He claimed he was a jinn rather than a man. Do you know what a jinn is?'

He nodded sagely without showing any emotion. 'I should do, being a Muslim.'

His words came at me like a tsunami, enveloping me in a tidal wave from which I could hardly breathe. I was so surprised by his declaration I almost became lost for words. 'You're a Muslim?'

'I know all about the Quran and jinns. I was born in Teheran, the capital of Iran. It use to be Persia then.'

'I don't believe it!' I gasped. 'Then what are you doing with the 21st Century Crusaders?'

'I'm an ardent support of the cause. Tell me, did you vote at the last General Election in this country.'

'Of course,' I replied slowly, wondering where the conversation was leading.

'Did the party you voted for succeed in becoming the government?'

'They did.'

'And do you agree with everything they say or do in respect of the important policies relating to your country and its people?'

'Not necessarily. But I don't join the opposition because of any differences of opinion.'

'Would you still support them if they pursued a policy of civil war, or a war of aggression against another country whom you considered to be innocent?'

I shrugged my shoulders. 'It would never come to that. Not with the British government.'

'All right,' he continued. 'What about Islam, now that you've met the Mahdi?'

I had to admit he had a point there. If I hadn't met the Mahdi I might have stuck to my argument, refusing to accept he was a Muslim fighting for a cause against his own religion. But the words of the Mahdi still echoed in my ears: "It will be my task to purify the world so that religion will flow like the freshness of a stream. Islam will be strong! Islam will be great! Islam will conquer the world!"

'You see, I'm a Sunni,' he informed me, breaking into my thoughts abruptly. 'One of the intellectuals. We don't believe in the Jihad, the Holy War, or the Mahdi. They were the inventions of the mystics many centuries ago. In the modern world, we have the problem of logistics. The Shias make up fifteen per cent of all Muslims. If the number of all Islam totals two billion in fifty years time, we're talking of three hundred million militants, many of whom believe in terrorism, torture and martyrdom. Hitler had less than one-sixth of that total when he took on all of Europe. Not only that, but I'm certain that at the commencement of the Jihad many Sunnis will be converted to militancy, perhaps doubling the Shia figures. Just imagine it. An army exceeding half a billion servicemen setting out to conquer the world. It's formidable! I couldn't support such a policy.'

I shook my head in disbelief. 'You never fail to amaze me,' I told him, 'in everything you do.'

'I assure you there's more to come,' he advised, puffing on his cigar again. 'Life can be very exciting if you're willing to take the risks. But be warned. Taking risks doesn't mean you'll necessarily win.'

'The Mahdi believes he takes his instructions directly from Allah. I suppose that's one step nearer to sanity than believing he's Allah himself.'

'You shouldn't mock a holy man!' warned Musaphia, with a serious expression on his face. 'We know so little of paranormal activity. There have been cases recorded in history where such messages were conveyed to mortals. In order to prove he's the Mahdi it's essential for him to receive divine messages. Otherwise he will be regarded as an ordinary man making decisions on his own account.' He placed the envelope into a pocket of his white jacket. 'I'll read this report with interest. But now we must get to the matter of the laser plans. For reasons I cannot divulge they're required extremely urgently. In fact, immediately. So much so that we had to substitute you at the bridge congress in Turkey to get you back here. We need them tonight.'

'Tonight?' I echoed, not relishing the idea of breaking into the weaponry division. It was one thing to plan an assault and musing about the operation: it was another thing to carry it out in reality.

'There's something I ought to mention, if you don't mind me saying so,' he went on. 'That gun in your pocket is sticking out like a sore thumb. If you want to carry a pistol, get yourself a holster. If I can recognise that you carry a gun so can every thug in the area.'

He was right of course. I was very green in these matters. It was important to listen to people like Musaphia who had managed to survive to a grand old age as a result of their knowledge and experience. 'I'd like to know why there's such a rush to get the plans. A few days ago it was a task which had to be completed at a reasonable future date. Now it's so urgent I have to get them tonight. Why?'

'All in good time,' he said quietly. 'there are things happening in the environment I can't tell you about at present. All I can say is that you must get the plans now. After that you'll learn the answers to many questions.'

We continued our breakfast in harmony and I listened to some of his exploits in earlier years. He was a great teller of tales. There were many good reasons why I should have disliked him, however I considered him to be an honest, kindly man at heart and I liked him for his directness. His revelation that he was a Muslim floored me for a while, but I could see the sense of his argument and recognised the trust place in him by the organisation. After we had finished breakfast, he reiterated his message to make certain there was no misunderstanding.

'Tonight! It must be tonight! He handed me a small slip of paper. 'I want you to commit this telephone number to your memory. Read it as many times as you wish, and remember it. The number was chosen specifically for its simplicity. When you have the plans you must contact me immediately at this number. Immediately! I'll then tell you what to do. Is that clear?' I stared at the number and memorised it before passing it back to him. He produced a book of matches from his pocket, lit one, and then burned the paper in the ash-tray. 'Walls have ears and waiters have eyes. We don't want any problems. And like I said last time, something good is going to happen to you soon.'

'The best that could happen to me is a good night's sleep and peace of mind,' I confided. 'But I won't get that until I've found my wife and Penny Smith.'

He prodded the burned slip of paper in the ash-tray with the end of his cigar so that it broke into many fragments. 'I've never known anyone so fervent on a wife and mistress at the same time,' he commented.

I ignored the remark. 'By the way, do you know where Penny Smith could be? I can't seem to contact her anywhere.'

His face took on a thoughtful expression as though he had the same problem, but he declined to answer. 'Goodbye, Jason!' he said, with a wave of his hand, as though ready to be rid of me. 'Contact me on that telephone number the moment you get the plans!'

After leaving the Savoy Hotel, I visited an upholstery shop a short distance down the road. It took them less than fifteen minutes to fit me with a shoulder holster. The gun still felt bulky as it rested against my body but it was now contained and no longer caused an ugly bulge in my pocket. I telephoned my office in an attempt to contact Penny only to be told that she was still absent. Persistently, I rang her flat but no one answered the telephone. Even Schmuel Musaphia had looked blank when I asked him about her. She had vanished off the face of the earth! But it was essential to focus my mind on Jan. It seemed that everyone knew where she was now. Musaphia gave me her location without difficulty. How could he have found out unless the organisation had taken her? Or was his intelligence system so exclusive that he was able to find out about anyone at any time? Well, one thing was certain. He had confirmed that Jan was at the nightclub. Unfortunately, when I asked for help to rescue her he quickly changed the subject.

I drove nearly half a mile past The Golden Peacock, parked the car, and walked back at a steady pace. It was not my intention to alert anyone to my presence. The nightclub was a triumph of modern architecture. Shaped like a mediaeval castle, with towers and turrets on each side, it comprised a complex of offices, a dance hall, a conference room, a gaming room, a number of ante rooms, a high-grade restaurant, and numerous hotel rooms. It was owned by an international conglomerate whose principal activities related to hotel management and gambling. The facade reflected layer upon layer of blocks of stone designed to make the location resemble an authentic piece of history. There was even a dummy frieze surrounding the turrets, adorned with stone gargoyles and grotesques. Several people were waiting at the reception desk as I entered. Casually, I sat down on one of the comfortable seats to read a leaflet on the hotel and its accommodation.

"The castle stands in its own extensive grounds. With ninety-five bedrooms, this 4-star hotel ensures its service is maintained at the highest level by over one hundred professional staff. The restaurant is acknowledged to be the finest in the county boasting French, Italian and English cuisine. The classic menus and silver service are perfectly complemented by its own superb and high-individual surroundings. The Forum Room caters for every type of function and can be quickly adapted for conferences, trade show, banquets or wedding receptions. Guest rooms are appointed to a high standard offering single or double accommodation with bath/shower facilities en suite. Rooms have colour television, direct dial telephones, controllable central heating, and tea/coffee-making facilities. Executive rooms include trouser-presses and hair-dryers. Suites are also available offering one or two bedrooms, some with separate lounge, patio and private gardens. The Health and Leisure Spa offers an all-the-year round centrally-heated pool, and guests can also enjoy a sauna, jacuzzi or a range of health treatments. The pool bar serves refreshments and food at the poolside. There is also a Gaming Room where guests can play roulette, blackjack, and enjoy themselves on a miscellany of amusement machines."

There was no doubt that The Golden Peacock was a first-class hotel, although I was concerned that it employed a hundred professional staff. Hopefully, most of them were instructed to come on duty in the evening rather than during the daytime. I had to maintain a low profile at all times. I rose slowly and made my way casually to the Gaming Room. I opened the door slowly to find it was vacant and in darkness. However, some natural light filtered through the few high windows in the room which was sufficient for my purpose. I went to the roulette wheel and allowed my eyes to scan the room, listening for any noises which might assist me in finding Jan. It was practically silent. The only sounds I could hear were the occasional clatter of cups rattling on trolleys as they travelled down the adjoining hallway to the restaurant. I was particularly comforted by the gun in the holster, adopting a nervous habit of touching it now and again to check it was still there.

After a while, I realised I had to cease random activities and embark on a proper plan of campaign. Jan was probably a prisoner in one of the hotel bedrooms. If so, the room was likely to be near the roof where any noise she made would go unnoticed. Alternatively, the other place was the basement. I decided to advance to the top floor and work downwards. As I left through a side door, I discovered a cupboard with a number of white coats. Donning one of them, I took the stairs to the top floor and began to knock on each door systematically pretending to be a waiter calling to take an order for a meal. There were ninety-five bedrooms on five floors. It could have been worse! I listened carefully at each door before knocking, but many of them were unoccupied. It took twenty minutes to deal with the top floor and I was disappointed at the end of it. I believed that if Jan had been in any of the rooms she would have made sounds to attract my attention after I had knocked on the door. I stopped at an open window in the hallway and looked outside. A window cleaner's cradle, secured by ropes attached to the roof, hung idly in the breeze. It was as though fate had prepared the vacant vehicle for my use. I climbed through the window, leaning out dangerously to catch the rope of the cradle, and swung on to the platform. The search turned distinctively in my favour from the new vantage point. Within a short while, I learned how to manoeuvre the craft and removed a handkerchief from my pocket, pretending to clean the windows. If I couldn't gain access from the hallway, I would search from the cradle by looking in through the windows of each room. I inched my way across the facade of the castle but jubilation soon turned to disappointment. There was nothing to be seen of Jan. One didn't need to be Sherlock Holmes to realise she was not being held on the top floor. There was also little point on searching the rooms on the lower floors. It would be folly for her captors to keep her in a room surrounded by hotel guests!

Following that logic, I presumed it was more than likely she was being held in the basement. I made my way back towards the window and swung the cradle so that I could climb back into the hallway. As I scrambled through the window, a chambermaid carrying an armful of linen came round the corner and almost screamed with fright as I landed on my feet in the hallway. I managed to silence her by placing the index finger of my right hand to my lips.

'Don't take any notice of me, young lady,' I lied. 'I'm a kissogram man....come to sing a rhyme to a woman in Room 412. She's was going to bump into me in the hallway and I didn't want her to see me so I dodged out here.'

The chambermaid walked away in disgust muttering expletives about kissogram people, and I sighed with relief as she entered a room and started changing the bedclothes without calling the hotel security. I made my way down the back stairs until I reached the ground floor. The white coat was unnecessary so I discarded it and descended a flight of steps to the basement door. It was a large room of which three-quarters was filled with furniture and junk. Jan wasn't being held there but I noticed four doors leading off the area. The first led back to the stairs from which I had just come. The second bore the sign "Bar", which made it the most unlikely place in the hotel for anyone to be kept a prisoner. The third was the Gaming Room, while the fourth related to the kitchen. There had to be somewhere else! I tried each door in turn to make sure they were authentic. After all, a sign on a door could be an excellent deception. The bar was the main bar to the hotel with a mezzanine cellar where the barrels were kept. I recognised the Gaming Room having been there earlier. The kitchen could not be mistaken for any other room but there was no space to hide a person. I sat on a stool in the basement and let my thoughts drift through my mind for a while, undecided on the next step. There was little point in returning upstairs to search to the hotel rooms. There could be secret passages in parts of the structure, but to find such entrances or exits was beyond my power. The sound of footsteps echoed a short distance away and I crept into one of the murky corners of the room, pressing myself against a wall. A man descended the concrete steps and walked through to the kitchen, closing the door behind him. It was then I discovered an awkward piece of metal sticking into my back and turned to find I was leaning against a fifth door. It was faced with a shield of steel that had been painted black to hide its identity. There were no signs or markings although I knew, even before I opened it, that it led to a cellar. I pulled the handle, opening it slowly and listened carefully, but all was silent. The entrance heralded a set of steps, leading to another door which sported a chink of light at the bottom. I went down the steps and stood outside the door. Taking my gun from its holster, I inhaled deeply, and rushed into the room brandishing the weapon dangerously.

'O.K.' I shouted fiercely. 'Everyone stay exactly where you are!' I blinked twice in the light to adjust my vision. The room was an ordinary office. There was nothing to cause an eyebrow to be raised in suspicion. Two men inside the room sat in comfortable armchairs and they froze in the middle of their discussion as a result of my rude interruption. One looked as though he was the manager of the hotel: the other may have been his assistant or an accountant. They stared at me blankly as I took up a menacing position.

'May I help you?' began the manager, in a situation which certainly had never been included in his training manual.

'Where's my wife?' I snarled, determined to make my presence felt. 'I know she's here! Where is she!'

'Your wife,' replied the man coolly, although his eyes never left the wavering barrel of the Beretta. He obviously considered me to be an enraged husband. 'What's her name?'

'Janice Scott. I want to know where she is and I want to know now! Do you hear me? Now!'

He opened the book in front of him. 'This is the hotel register. I was just checking it.' His eyes ran down the columns and then he looked up. 'Yes, she was in Room 418 but she checked out of the hotel early this morning.'

'Was she on her own?' I demanded.

'Room 418 is a single room,' he replied calmly. 'I suggest you hire a private detective if you want further information.'

'Did she leave a forwarding address?'

'Guests do not leave forwarding addresses!'

I lowered the gun, much to the relief of the two men, and replaced it in its holster with some difficulty. 'Can I get out of the hotel through this door?' I asked sheepishly, pointing to another door.

'You can,' related the manager. 'Walk up the slope to the fire-door ahead. It leads to reception.'

On leaving the hotel, I felt an absolute chump. I had made a complete mess of it. From the start I should have approached the reception desk and asked whether Jan was staying there. How stupid to knock on doors disguised as a waiter and swinging to and fro in a window cleaner's cradle frightening young chambermaids. So Jan had stayed there but she had left early that morning. What was she doing in a hotel room by herself, if indeed she had been staying there by herself? Someone was using me as a pawn again and I didn't like it!

I returned to London and went to the restaurant where Penny and I had enjoyed many precious evenings. This time it was different. I sat alone at our favourite table working out a plan of campaign on a serviette. I didn't want to repeat the farce which had taken place at The Golden Peacock. The weaponry division at Dandy Advanced Electronics would allow no quarter in terms of its security system. Any mistake there would end in disaster!

CHAPTER THIRTEEN

It was evening when I visited Chris Devon for the assault on the weaponry division. There was a strange feeling of malaise in my bones and it could hardly be said I was filled with enthusiasm for the task. In my opinion, Devon was an unshaven, unkempt, filthy individual with a special talent for electronics which, as far as I was concerned, was as yet unproven. I had already discounted his efforts in relation to Jan's message on the recording tape from the answering machine, especially as he had caused the original tape to become corrupt. I parked the car outside his house and paused to allow the events of the past few days to filter through my mind. I didn't really have to go through with this caper, although I could imagine what might happen if I didn't. Schmuel Musaphia would set the wolves on me. That much was certain! I had a job to do and it had to be done. I had a gut feeling that the heavens would fall in on me if I took fright and ran. But why had the theft of the plans suddenly become so urgent? It was a pity someone didn't trust me enough to tell me. An early drunk staggered past the car singing the song "Into each life some rain must fall, but too much is falling in mine". If that were really true then we both had something in common.

I hammered on Devon's door and waited impatiently before the sound of his footsteps could be heard on the stairs.

'Oh, it's you, man!' he greeted casually as he opened the door. 'I can see by your face this is the moment.'

'Yes,' I repeated. 'This is the moment.' I followed him up to his room. 'You'd better get your things together. I'll tell you about it on the way to the plant.'

'Not in a million years!' he snapped, taking a stance which intimated he was refusing to go. 'What do you think this is, man? Boy's Own magazine? We're going to break into a place bristling with the latest security equipment and armed guards and you want to tell me about it on the way there in the car! How do I know what equipment we need? If we cut this caper on your say-so we'd have to break off every few minutes to come back here for more gear. If you think I'm going with you on that kind of deal you must come from Mars!'

'All right, all right!' I conceded. 'You don't have to get excited! I'll brief you on the layout of the place.' I took some drawings and information provided by Penny from my pocket and handed them to him. He surprised me by sitting down at the table, laying out the papers, and examining every detail with great interest. 'The first hurdle is the electrified fence. We'll have to short-circuit a part of it and cut our way through.'

'Are you crazy, man?' he returned, with a shocked expression appearing above the top level of his beard. 'You've been seeing too many films about World War Two! The moment you short-circuit that fence, everyone on duty in security is going to know you're trying to break in. The faults show up on a circuit system. Monitors will show the exact point of the short-circuit at the second it occurs. Within two minutes, the place will be crawling with security officers. You'd be caught in no time!'

I was stunned at his revelation and annoyed at my own ignorance. 'Then how do we get into the compound?'

'We fly there, man!' he riposted. 'Haven't you heard of trampolines?'

'Trampolines? The kind you jump on?'

'There's no other kind to my knowledge. We take two miniature trampolines. One of us jumps over the fence; the other man throws his trampoline over the top so that one of them is on the right side when we want to get out. Then the second man makes the jump.'

'You realise this is a ten-foot fence! And it's electrified!'

'You'll just have to make sure you jump high enough!' he said insolently.

'Where do we get these trampolines? My principal advises me he wants those plans tonight!'

'I've got two of them in the garage downstairs,' replied Devon casually. 'They always come in handy. Providing you get your arse high enough we shouldn't have any problem with the fence.'

'Then we have the scanner at the sentry station. After they checked my pass, the guard lifted the barrier manually to let my car through.'

Devon chewed thoughtfully on his beard, pressing the hair into the corners of his mouth. 'I think we might have trouble there. We won't need a plastic card for identification but the security system will operate a whole range of electronic beams at night. You can't see them. They're invisible to the naked eye. If you cut across any one of them, the alarm system will go crazy.'

'How do we overcome that?'

'Leave it to me. I'll sort it out.'

'After that, I drove to a small building and was taken by jeep to the research area about a mile south.'

'Jesus!' exclaimed Devon, with anguish showing in his face. 'A mile south! Do you realise what that does?'

I racked my brains unsuccessfully. 'What does it do?'

'It reduces our chances of escape if anything goes wrong. If we trip one of the alarms, we have to run a mile northwards to get back to the trampoline. We'd be shot down or captured before we got that far. Did you notice whether the electrified fence was close to the research area a mile south?'

I thought hard for a moment. 'I think so. I really can't remember.'

'You'd better remember, man! You life may depend on it!'

'What difference does it make?' I asked innocently.

'If the fence runs along there, we take the trampoline with us. If we trigger the alarm, we can exit quickly. I'd rather chase the mile to the car outside the plant than try to outpace the security guards on the inside! It's a pity you don't know where the research area is located because it might be possible to park nearby and trampoline straight to it.'

'Well, can't we work it out?' I asked, pointing to the map. 'If that's the entrance, then there's the building I drove to. The jeep took me along this route to here. Look, there's the fence. About two hundred yards away. We could park the car outside the fence here so we wouldn't have to chase back to the entrance if something went wrong.'

'That's providing they have no cameras on the perimeter. If they do, the infra red rays will pick up a parked car.'

I had always considered Chris Devon to be the lowest form of life. However, his review of the situation was so concise and so expertly assessed I was forced to revise my opinion of him. I knew one thing for certain. Without his assistance the security guards would have caught me within two minutes of cutting the wire fence.

'O.K., man! Read me what happens next!' he continued.

'The weaponry research area is guarded by a computer. It has to be fed a plastic card before the door will open. The door, by the way, is made of solid steel. Once you've used the pass-card, it's useless for at least twenty-four hours. They do that to ensure maximum security so that people can't walk in and out at random.'

'No sweat,' he commented, tugging at his beard.

'Then we went down a corridor with a sloping floor until we came to a dead end. By the side of the wall was another computer terminal. It operated by means of handprints. The only handprints it recognises are those of John Packman and his supervisor.'

'Oh, that's bad news!' returned the computer genius. 'Bad news!' 'I thought the handprint would floor you.'

'No, it's not the handprint! That's easy enough! The bad news is the sloping floor and the dead end. I came across something like that once before. As soon as that door opens the joint will be jumping. I have a suspicion it has a built-in electronic beam operating from the base of the door into a sensitive eye fitted in the floor below it. When the door opens, the beam breaks and the alarm goes off. It's a fail-safe method designed to beat burglars.'

'Does that mean we can never get into the research room without triggering the alarm?'

'By normal standards, that's right.' He bent forward slightly, resting his face in his hands, as he concentrated on the problem. I stood by idly, looking round the room at the miscellany of equipment scattered there. It took him over a minute to come to a conclusion. Then he released a long sigh and allowed his hands to fall to the table. 'There might be a way, man. I don't like it but it could be done if we can find an electric point in that corridor. I don't suppose you noticed if one was there.'

I shook my head sadly. 'No, I'm afraid I didn't.'

'Man!' he shouted in frustration. 'I've never known anyone to look over a place and not see anything. You're really something. Do you know that!'

'The laser gun is located in the middle of the room.'

He moved back away from the table and stared at me coldly. 'Now you just hold on a minute! That laser gun is connected to so many alarms that if you breathe on it from ten yards away the whole of the country will know what's going on. You told me we only had to steal the plans from the computer system, not the laser gun itself!'

'Yes, yes!' I confirmed, ignoring his animated actions. 'It's only the plans we want. As soon as we take a copy off the printer, we can............'

''Oh, no!' he interrupted sharply. 'We're not taking any copies off printers! Every time you press a switch or a button you risk being detected. If we're going to get the plans, we need a microfilm camera to photograph the designs and details on the computer screen. Let me guess, man. You don't have a camera of that kind either!'

'I haven't,' I told him humbly.

'How could Penny team me up with a rookie like you?' he complained bitterly. 'O.K. It's no sweat. I've got a camera that can take microfilm. Is there anything else you want to tell me. I don't care whether you think it's important or unimportant. I'd rather know now than later! Do they have security guards patrolling the perimeter fence?'

'I don't think so.'

'You don't think so. Man, they could have your balls and you'd still be in dreamland! When you're out on one of these gigs you have to know all the details. Else you're running blind!'

'My information is that they rely on an electronic alarm system at night. The only other thing I can think of are the boys in Block "B".'

'The boys in Block "B"!' he returned contemptuously. 'Who the hell are they?'

'The security men who act as the television crew. They sit in front of a series of monitors watching every part of the plant.'

'I know what a television crew does!' he snapped angrily. 'Do you have a diagram of the camera locations throughout the building?'

'As it happens I do,' I replied, causing him to look rather relieved. 'Penny managed to get one. Here it is!'

He pored over the diagram for a long time and then released a painful sigh. 'O.K.,' he said finally. 'I'll take this along with us. But first, I need a whole range of equipment if we're going to have any chance of getting those plans.'

'How are you going to get equipment over the electrified fence?'

'Throw it over, of course. It won't walk on its own! You make yourself a cup of coffee while I get to work. And while we're on the subject, man, I don't want you moving a muscle tonight without asking my permission. Not a muscle, do you hear! That plant is alive with electronics. If you sneeze you'll bring the security crew down on your neck like a ton of bricks. You do nothing without my agreement, and you go nowhere without me. Do I make myself clear?'

'You're the boss,' I told him unconditionally. 'You run the show. I won't do anything without your agreement! You have my promise on that.'

He left the room and went down to his garage to sort out the equipment. Once again I decided against making myself a cup of coffee and sat back with my eyes closed. In normal times, Devon was a complete mess. But when the chips were down, he was an expert in his field of operation. It was fifteen minutes before he returned to the room.

'O.K., man!' he said, as he entered. 'It's all downstairs packed in four canvas bags, and there's two trampolines.' He looked at the map and pointed to an area on it. 'This is how I see it. We don't go to the main gate. Our target is the place where the weapons are stored....the research area. That's the computer I want to tap. We park outside the perimeter fence here. If all is well, we go over the top and walk about a hundred yards to the unit. It makes sense to be able to get in and out as quickly as we can.' With that, he folded the map, put it in his pocket, and walked out.

I followed him as he left and helped him put the equipment in the boot of the car. Then we drove off to the weaponry division. Having been there before I directed Devon to the appointed place outside the perimeter fence. He got out of the car and walked up and down the deserted road for three hundred yards in each direction before returning.

'No cameras to identify cars on this road,' he declared happily. 'We can park here and they won't know anything about it.'

We removed the bags and the trampolines from the boot of the car and set them down by the side of the road. Devon tested one of the trampolines and motioned me towards it.

'How the hell am I going to clear that fence on this stupid thing?' I asked with dismay. 'I'll never do it!'

'Negative thoughts!' he countered. 'You must get rid of negative thoughts! The trampoline is specially designed for this purpose. The surface isn't flat. It has an angle of forty-five degrees to give you short-distance momentum.'

I tried to stand on the contraption but it was too steep, causing me to fall forward at each attempt. As I picked myself up from the ground for the fourth time, my colleague clapped his hands together in frustration, encouraging me to act more positively.

'Come on, man! We haven't got time to stand around!' he hissed angrily. 'It's all systems go! Get your act together and jump! You come in from behind with a run of about fifteen yards, but make sure you get your timing right. Your feet must hit the surface of the trampoline together and at speed. It's simple really. A run, a jump, and whoom, you're over! Lean your body forward a little, but not too far forward! If you do it right, you'll shoot over the top like a missile!'

There was nothing more I could do than put my trust in his words. If I failed, I would end up on the fence like a human barbecue with no more worries in this world. I paced back about fifteen yards and started my run. It was too late to stop now! My feet hit the trampoline together and, before I knew it, I had catapulted over the top of the fence, clearing it by at least a foot. But Devon hadn't advised me about the landing. I hit the ground hard. Very hard! Fortunately, I had the sense to somersault forward to break the fall. I could hardly believe I was inside the compound! As I turned jubilantly towards my colleague, a trampoline came flying over the fence to land beside me. This was followed by the four canvas bags containing the equipment. Devon had been careful to balance the weight in each bag so that they could be despatched into the compound. Within seconds, he was standing beside me, undoing the bags so that we could proceed as planned.

He put his hand into his pocket and drew out a pair of spectacles that looked familiarly like sunglasses. Then he put them on and peered in all directions. 'Stay exactly where you are!' he commanded, swivelling in a semi-circle on his haunches with an electronic detector in his hand. 'I'm defining the location of electronic beams scanning this area. If you're concerned about the glasses, don't worry about it. They designed to help me see them.' After a short pause, he stood up and started walking towards the target building. 'Follow me!' he continued. 'But take it slow in case they operate a revolving beam that sweeps in an arc. We don't want to get caught by an old trick like that! We'll take these two bags and leave these two here. I'll take this one; you carry the other.'

We approached the building slowly until he motioned me to stop with a wave of his hand. 'Lucky we didn't have to come in by the main gate down the road. I detect about fifty beams over there.' He stiffened as we reached the building. 'Careful!' he warned. 'There are three steps in front of you leading to the pavement in the foreground of the building. The first is clear. The second is clear, but the third step has a beam across it. When you get to the second step, jump as high as you can to the pavement. Do not use the third step! I repeat. You must not use the third step! Is that clear?'

I followed his instructions carefully and he came alongside me to place a plastic card into the slot of the computer terminal.

'How can you be sure it will work?' I whispered.

'If you go to a hotel, the manager has a master key which can be used to open any door of the hotel. Let's say this card is a kind of master key for computers. It has characteristics which ask what's required from the computer and then establishes them itself. I think of it as an aunt saying to her young nephew: "I'll give you a kiss if you smile." He smiles and she kisses him.'

At that moment the steel door opened and I was about to move forward when he placed a firm hand on my shoulder. 'No!' he cautioned. 'Not until I tell you!' He waved the electronic device forwards and backwards in front of him before pointing to an imaginary line across the doorway about twelve inches high. 'There's a beam about a foot high off the floor. It stretches right across the doorway. You'll have to step over it. Be very careful!'

We entered the building and made our way cautiously down the sloping hallway. We had reached the half-way point when Devon warned me to duck below another beam located at waist-high level. As we approached the terminal requiring an authorised handprint, he removed his spectacles and delved into the bag he had been carrying.

'What are you going to do?' I asked in a hushed voice.

'Whoever used this terminal last had to leave an imprint of his hand on the glass. Fingerprints. Thumbprints. Palmprints. The lot. My task is to take a copy of that handprint from the glass. Then it can be translated on to a plastic glove and re-used to open the door.

'Very clever!' I commended.

'The problem is that the door probably has an in-built sensor device at its base which continues into the floor below....like having a nail inside your shoe with the sharp end pointing through the sole, so that when you tread on a wooden floor it sticks to it. As soon as I lay that handprint on the machine, the door will open cutting off the beam to the sensor device so that it sets off the alarm. I have to prevent that from happening.'

'Such as what?' I was intrigued to learn his solution.

'Hold on!' he muttered, stiffening like a cat with its back arched. 'There's a camera right above us facing that door. When it opens, even if the alarm doesn't go off, the boys in Block "B" will be able to see us. In your bag there are hoods designed to fit over camera lens. Let me have the one marked "Hall".' I fished into the bag under the guidance of his torch and found it. 'Get down on all fours!' he ordered. I did so and he stepped on my back to reach the camera. Within a few seconds he had fitted the device over the lens. 'It's a special kind of lens cap,' he explained, noticing the inquisitive look on my face. 'Inside the cap is a photograph with its own reflected light of a corridor. The boys in Block "B" are looking at that fixed picture on their screen. They can't see us any more. Now, see if you can find an electric socket!' He flashed the torch on the walls and located one on the wall opposite the handprint machine. 'I'm going to create a triangle rather than a direct beam,' he went on, although I had no idea what he was talking about. He took a piece of glass in the shape of an ice-hockey puck from his bag and placed it on the other side of the corridor. 'If I can attract the beam at the base of the door, and also the sensor in the floor below it, into this glass puck, the beam will shoot from the door into the glass puck and bounce back to the sensor. In that way, the beam will not be broken when the door opens, although contact will be triangular rather than direct. At the end of the day, it should prevent the alarm from going off.'

He removed a small machine from his bag and plugged it into the electric socket on the wall. After putting on the spectacles again, he began to dig into the floor carefully with a metal tool to expose the sensor located in the floor. After ten minutes, with the aid of another piece of equipment, he heaved a sigh and pressed a switch on the unit. Then he removed the spectacles and handed them to me so that I could witness the electronic triangle he had created. A beam fired from the bottom of the door into the glass puck was directed back into the sensor below the door and sent back to the original alarm unit at the bottom of the door. 'That should do the trick!' he said with a degree of satisfaction. He delved into the bag to retrieve a machine which looked like a toaster with one side missing and rested it on the glass screen of the security machine. After sixty seconds, he lifted it off and placed a plastic glove on the surface of the screen, rubbing his hands over it a number of times. Then he pushed his fingers into the glove until it fitted his hand perfectly and place his palm on the glass screen. The triangular beam remained constant as the door opened.

'Don't go anywhere near that triangle!' commanded Devon. 'And give me back those goggles!' He put them on and looked round the research room. 'Great!' he exclaimed joyfully. 'No beams across our path to the computer but dozens around the laser weapon. We've got to kill two cameras. One is near the computer in a clear region. I'll have to duck and dive to reach the other one. Stay where you are while I do it!' He took two television caps from my bag and advanced swiftly to the wall behind the computer. Then he jumped on a chair and placed the hood over the lens. For the other camera, he crept slowly along the wall, ducking under, or stepping over, scanner beams which obstructed his path. When he had completed that task, he made his way back to the computer terminal with great care, beckoning me inside and indicating I shouldn't forget to bring the bag entrusted to my care. 'Don't speak unless you have to,' he whispered. 'There may be audio alarms, or the boys in Block "B" may have audio access.' He sat at the computer terminal and switched it on, arriving at a point where it stated "Access denied". He reached into the bag and brought out another device which he connected to a socket in the computer.

'What does that do?' I asked softly.

'When a peterman....a safe cracker....wants to open a safe he uses a machine similar to this. It runs through the codes, finds them, and opens the safe for him. It's the same with this little wizard. The only reason it exists is to find a way through the computer maze when access is denied.' The screen flashed at that moment to display the word "Passwords".

'I forgot to tell you,' I whispered tardily. 'There are two passwords of five letters each.'

He glared at me for the late information and delved into the back to bring out yet another appliance. He plugged it into a socket before setting it in motion. Suddenly, the two passwords appeared on the screen. "JPACK" and "RNOON".

'Do these words ring any bells, man?'

JPACK stands for John Packman, the director of the weaponry division. I don't know the other one.'

'Then we're on the right track,' he returned, becoming absorbed in his task. He began to tap the keys at an incredibly fast rate. As an executive in the computer division of Dandy Advanced Electronics I had seen some good computer programmers at work but I had never seen anyone capable of using the keys at such speed. 'How old is this laser weapon?' he asked without taking his eyes off the monitor.

'No longer than four years from initiation, I should imagine. Why do you ask?'

'All the plans and sequences are in date order. I'm racing through the files from eighteen months ago backwards. Damn! I have to look at each file because all the research projects are given code names. For example, an electronic guidance system in the nose of a fighter aircraft is called "Visor". An electronic communication system is called "Lino"....someone had a sense of humour there. Ah, what about Red Rum? That was the name of a horse which won the Grand National three times. I get it! When reversed it reads "Murder".' He paused as the file came to the screen. 'Bingo!' He pressed some buttons on the keyboard to move the pages of the file forwards. 'Look at that! Sixty-two pages of information, details and illustrations. What more could anyone want?' He moved the file back to the beginning.

'Well let's start filming!' I suggested strongly, nurturing the idea of leaving the complex as quickly as possible.

'Get to work then,' he encouraged. 'You've got the camera!'

The blood drained slowly from my face. 'I haven't got it,' I told him meekly, believing we had taken all this risk only to discover that the camera had been lost or left behind at Devon's house.

He felt in his pocket and laughed. 'Here it is! Just my little joke! He handed the camera to me. 'You take the photographs. I'll turn the pages.'

It took a short while to complete the operation and I held on to the camera to make certain the plans stayed in my possession. After he had switched off the computer terminal, he told me to make my way back to the sloping corridor while he removed the caps on the television cameras. Then he set to work on the door, removing his apparatus, the glass puck, and the cap from the television lens. After that, we made our way carefully back to the perimeter fence.

'Why did you bring four bags,' I asked, 'when we only needed two?'

He opened the third bag which sported two machine-guns. 'The other bag has ammunition, grenades, and a few surprises. I never intend to get caught on these missions....one way or the other!'

Chris Devon had risen very highly in my estimation. I recognised him to be a true professional. He threw the bags over the fence and placed the trampoline in the appropriate position, indicating to me to go first. I had more confidence this time. In addition, leaving the complex enthused me to take the leap. Devon joined me a few seconds later. We placed the bags in the boot of the car with the single trampoline used initially when, suddenly, there was a tremendous howl like the wail of a banshee penetrating the night air.

'Someone's set off the alarm!' shouted Devon. He thought hard for a moment. 'Would you believe it! Someone else is trying to get those plans!'

I realised why Schmuel Musaphia had recalled me from Turkey so quickly to raid the weaponry division. There was competition! All hell broke loose in the compound as security guards raced out of their huts brandishing weapons, while some of them fetched the dogs. Eight of them jumped into two jeeps and drove off towards the research laboratory. Before they could get anywhere near the building, a solitary figure raced towards the fence in the darkness to the point where our car was parked. As he reached the fence, on the inside, he shouted to us in desperation.

'You've got to help me!' he pleaded. 'You must help me!'

It was Tomar Duran with fear written all over his face.

'Use the trampoline over there to get you over the top,' Devon called out, with an element of mercy showing through the careless facade he portrayed.

Tomar Duran stared at the trampoline for a few moments in confusion and then looked over his shoulder at the two jeeps approaching the area. Realising what he had to do, he took a number of paces backwards and raced forward at speed. However, only one of his feet hit the surface of the trampoline and he lost height from the start. To his credit, he almost made it but a miss was as good as a mile when the stakes were at their highest. His body struck the fence near the top and the flashes emanating from contact with the electrified fence lit up the night sky. Tomar Duran may have escaped death in Crete, but this time it was for keeps! We drove away from the area before the security guards arrived without leaving a trace of our presence behind. They would believe that Duran had brought the trampoline with him. It was inconceivable that two robberies had take place at the weaponry division at the same time. They would never realise we had stolen the plans and vanished without trace!

CHAPTER FOURTEEN

The sweet smell of success was exceptionally good for morale. To achieve entry into the weaponry division and secure the plans of the advanced laser gun undetected, amid a wealth of technology employed in the security system, was a remarkable achievement. All my concern about the competence of Chris Devon for the task was unnecessary. He had proved himself more than capable, showing skills and ingenuity surpassing all my expectations. Not even the barbecued body of Tomar Duran on that electrified fence could smother my jubilation. I drove Devon back to his home and helped to return the equipment to his garage. Then we went upstairs to unwind and he took a bottle of brandy out of the cupboard.

'I keep this for special occasions only,' he told me, pouring the drink into two stained goblets. 'Here!' he went on, passing one of them to me. 'I think we deserve it. Don't you?'

'You deserve it!' I replied, not wishing to pretend I had contributed anything to the success of the operation. 'I don't know what financial arrangements were made but I hope you're going to be paid well.'

He rocked his head gently from side to side in a thoughtful fashion. 'They're pretty good when it comes to pay day. Enough to set me up for a year or so. I'm not a spendthrift as you can see. In fact, if I'd been poorer I'd still have my teeth. I've got a sweet tooth so whenever I earn any money I buy lots of sweets and chocolate. My teeth have worn away.'

'If I ask you a sensitive question would you answer it honestly?' He shrugged his shoulders aimlessly so I continued. 'Would you have actually used the weapons you took with you? To kill innocent security guards so that you could escape if the alarm went off.'

'Man' he laughed, 'you really are something! Do you think I carried two bags of weapons and ammunition all the way out there just for fun? No way! A few years ago I went to prison for something much less important than what we did tonight. The judge was a bastard. He must have woken up on the wrong side of the bed that day and he threw the book at me. I made myself a promise that if I was ever caught again I'd fight my way out of it and do whatever was needed. I don't intend to go to jail again.'

It was my turn to shrug as I visualised the two of us facing a dozen security guards jumping out of jeeps as we distributed death with machine-guns and grenades in the middle of the night. 'Who actually hired you for this job?' I enquired. 'Who's going to pay you?'

'Is this some kind of trick question or are you just double-checking?' He observed the quizzical expression on my face before he continued. 'Oh, come on, man! What's all the cloak-and-dagger stuff? You know your wife booked me for the job!'

'No, you're mistaken,' I returned. 'Penny's not my wife. She's my secretary.'

'I know that!' he spat. 'I don't mean Penny. I'm talking about your wife....Janice. The first time I met her was when she defended me in court a few years ago.'

I stared at him in disbelief. 'Jan's the one who's going to pay you?' The hair at the back of my neck stood on end.

'Well, not out of her own money, man. The organisation will pay. But she's the one I'm dealing with.'

I swallowed the whole glass of brandy in one gulp and took a deep breath. Jan was a solicitor. That much was correct. But how did she come to be involved with the 21st Century Crusaders, if indeed she was working for them? But why didn't she confide in me?

I left the house and made my way to the nearest telephone booth. The revelation by Devon had sickened me and I was more confused than ever. It came to mind that something awful had happened to Jan. Perhaps the organisation had arranged for her to be duplicated....the same way they had duplicated Penny and myself. I was beginning to lose track of which people were the originals and which were the duplicates. I rang Schmuel Musaphia on the number he made me memorise and he answered as though he had been sitting by the telephone waiting for it to ring.

'I've got it!' I boasted. 'I've got it on microfilm!'

'Good!' he congratulated, with a token of excitement in his voice. 'Good! I must have that film tonight.'

'At this time of night?'

'Listen to me carefully,' he muttered into the telephone. 'Drive straight to Leytonstone underground station. I'll meet you there in about twenty minutes. I must have that film tonight!'

The line went dead and I sat in the car for a while. My destination was only a short distance away so there was no urgency on my part to get there. The question was now one of morality. Should I give Musaphia the plans or not? After all, I had met him only three times at high-class hotels. I really knew nothing about him. For all intents and purposes he might be a very evil man. Someone who wanted to do something awful to this world before he passed on to the next one. Some people harboured grudges or tried to fulfil their lifetime ideals before their demise. Perhaps this man was using everyone else for his own purpose. I now understood how Atlas felt with the weight of the world on his shoulders. Oh, for the wisdom of Solomon....or a crystal ball to allow me to see what was going to happen to the world in the future!

Schmuel Musaphia was as good as his word, arriving just before the twenty minutes had expired. He had been driven through the night by a chauffeur, and I climbed into the back seat of his car to sit beside the old man. The vehicle was filled with cigar smoke which had issued from a large Havana cigar fixed firmly between his lips.

'You really pulled it off!' he said, his eyes shining with admiration. 'I don't know why but I never thought you'd go through with it, let alone achieve it!'

'You don't think I went there to fail, did you?' I boasted.

'I'll take the plans,' he said in a casual manner.

'Not so fast!' I countered, unwilling to hand them over without an explanation. 'Chris Devon tells me he's been dealing with Jan directly to get these plans. He's getting paid handsomely for his efforts.'

The octogenarian paused for a few seconds. 'Oh, I see!' he returned. 'He's getting paid handsomely and you want to know how much you're going to receive. Is that it?'

'No, that's not it!' I snapped, starting to become angry. 'I don't want money! I want my wife! If she's dealing with Devon then she's not been kidnapped or abducted!'

'Who said she was abducted? Let me think! Ah, yes. It was you! You told me that!'

'I said that because of the messages I received.'

'Well, I have some good news for you, Jason. I can assure you you'll be with your wife within the next forty-eight hours. I have it on good authority she's alive and well, and looking forward to seeing you again.'

'Forty-eight hours?'

'It's been arranged. I'll have the details tomorrow. I'll let you know then.'

'By the way,' I added, offering an extra tid-bit of information. 'Tomar

Duran was incinerated on an electrified fence at the weaponry division tonight. I presume you already know that.'

'If I didn't know it before then I do now.'

'What are you going to do with the plans?'

'What does anyone do with plans? They build on them. Now, if you'll let me have the microfilm.'

'I suppose once I give you the plans it'll be the last time we see each other.'

'How wrong you are,' he said, holding out his hand. I gave the microfilm to him which he placed in his pocket. 'I'll have this developed tonight,' he concluded. 'I want to see you at noon tomorrow in the lobby of the Tower Hotel at St. Katherine's Dock in the East End of London. Noon! Then I'll give you details about meeting your wife.'

I returned to my car and drove home certain I had done the wrong thing. I had robbed my employer to give a man, whom I never really knew, sensitive information of national, or perhaps international, importance. But it was too late to do anything about it now. He had the film and all I had was hope....that I would be with Jan shortly. Although I should have been delighted to get the 21st Century Crusaders off my back, I slept uneasily. Grotesque forms came into my dreams and went, almost in nightmare fashion, but I managed to get through the night. My prime task was to locate Penny and the first place to start looking was at her apartment.

The place was very familiar to me. I had visited it many times before and had slept there on numerous occasions. It had always given me a sense of warmth and excitement. Now it appeared cold and unrelenting. I knocked on the door but no one answered. I knew that something was terribly wrong. I had to get inside. Removing a plastic credit card from my wallet, I attempted to slip it between the lock and the door in the hope of gaining entry. My lack of talent in such matters ensured I was unsuccessful. I mused that people who broke into houses in the "movies" never seemed to have any trouble when they tried to unlock doors in this fashion. In real life, it didn't always happen that way. Eventually, I committed my badly-damaged credit card to my wallet and searched for an alternative method. The crudest means of entry would be to smash a hole in the window and undo the latch inside so that I could climb in. However, the noise would probably alert the neighbours and they would call the police. I searched under the mat outside the door and above the window lintel for a spare key. In that I was successful. Unlocking the door, I opened it slowly and called out her name. The sound of my voice echoed through the apartment and there remained an eerie silence. I recalled the black and white two-toned shoes I had seen there some days earlier. They were the same as those which belonged to Jan and were size five. Penny had told me they belonged to her but I refused to believe it. The coincidence was too great and I had to check it out. Entering the bedroom, I opened the wardrobe and examined Penny's shoes. They were all size five-and-a-half. She had lied to me! Not only that, but Jan's shoes were no longer there. Perhaps they had found their way back to their owner. I felt that the case relating to Jan's shoes was proven. It meant that Penny was involved with her disappearance.

I stood outside the lounge with a deep sense of foreboding. I was never one to indulge in the science of the paranormal but I had the feeling that something awful had happened. Penny had disappeared off the face of the earth without any warning whatsoever. No messages. No communication. It was almost uncanny! She would never treat me that way and she wouldn't avoid making contact....unless something had happened which was beyond her control. It was that reason which made me so fearful. Slowly, I opened the door of the lounge and peered inside. A strange unpleasant odour drifted towards me which I failed to recognise. For a moment it looked as though everything was in order. Then I saw her body. She was laying on the settee, apparently asleep, but her condition was far worse. She had been shot through the right temple; a neat bullet hole was evident. She had been murdered in cold blood! Her eyes stared blankly at the ceiling but her face was serene and it looked as though she had leaned back on the settee to rest for a while. From the odour in the room, I gathered she must have been killed on the day before I left for Turkey. If that was the case, she didn't have to wait for me in vain at our favourite restaurant. By then, she was already dead. I could only hope her soul would rest in peace!

I went back to the bedroom and returned with a blanket which I placed over her body. I uttered a short prayer, ran my fingers over her eyelids to close all sight of the world for ever, and pulled the blanket over her head. For a moment I was overwhelmed with anguish and sorrow. Then tears welled up in my eyes and saliva collected in my throat as though it wanted to choke me. She had been extremely close to me and very precious. She had been part of me for longer than I cared to admit. I had embraced her, caressed her, adored her, admired her, slept with her and, above all, I had loved her. She was someone special who had turned my life upside down, changing the rain into sunshine and tears into laughter. I would do anything for her which was the reason I had gone on this assignment in such uncharacteristic and rampant manner. She made me feel good, wholesome....a man! Now she was gone! That beautiful, wonderful, desirable young woman who had so much to offer....so much to live for. What a waste! No longer would we share the passion, the emotion, the sensitivity, the glory of a simple touch, the conversation in which we knew what we wanted to say without ever having to speak, the intimacy, and the warm feeling of satisfaction together. My life was shattered and, when I looked at her, I was staring at the pieces! It was the end of an era....of a relationship between two people who loved each other. An idyll which became a reality and was now committed only to the world of memory. Someone had taken her life and savaged mine. My immediate reaction was to seek revenge, for bitterness grew within me at a very rapid rate. But from whom did I seek revenge? Who was the assassin who had killed so unmercifully? In the complex world in which I now moved, it was possible I would never find out!

I heard a rustle behind me and turned sharply fearing it might be the police. Primar stood there looking at me with an enigmatic expression on his face.

'I see you found the spare key above the window,' he remarked smoothly, apparently oblivious of Penny's death.

'What are you doing here,' I demanded.

'I could ask the same of you,' he returned coldly. 'From the look of it I would say you're trying to hide a body.'

'As if you didn't know!' I snarled. 'Did you kill her?'

He walked past me and lifted the blanket. 'Pity! She was a beautiful woman.'

'And you know nothing about her death!'

'Why should I?'

I turned him round to face me. 'I suppose you came here because you happened to be passing by!'

He pulled a matchstick from his pocket and began to chew on the end of it. 'I came here because we work for the same organisation and she hadn't contacted me for two days.'

'I didn't know you had to keep such close contact with members of the 21st Century Crusaders,' I challenged. 'I don't believe you!'

'Don't be ridiculous!' he retorted. 'I'm not talking about the 21st Century Crusaders. I'm talking of MOSSAD.'

'MOSSAD? Who the hell is MOSSAD?'

He seemed to thrive on my ignorance and treated me like a spider whose legs were being pulled of systematically by a mischievous schoolboy. 'The Israeli intelligence agency. The equivalent to the CIA, MI5, the KGB, and the SDECE in France. MOSSAD is an abbreviation for Hebrew words meaning Institution for Intelligence and Special Assignments. It's responsible mainly for overseas espionage.'

'Are you saying that you and Penny both work for Israeli intelligence....for MOSSAD?'

'We worked in tandem.'

'What about your relationship with the 21st Century Crusaders?'

'It interweaves beautifully. The Arab states make up most of the Middle East and a large number of Muslims. If a Holy War took place, Israel would be one of the first targets of Islam. We have a right to defend our country and its people in the best way we can. I don't think even you would deny us that right.' He chewed a little harder on the matchstick.

'And you know nothing about Penny's death.'

'Why should I?' He placed his right hand over the area of his heart. 'I'm as shocked as you are. I don't know who could have done this terrible thing. Especially in a country like Britain.'

I was in two minds whether to believe him or not when I heard footsteps approaching the front door. Primar tried to move quickly towards the exit but I barred his way. A few seconds later, a man appeared in the doorway holding a stretcher.

'O.K. Primar,' he began. 'Where's the body?'

'You bastard!' I shouted at Primar, who let the matchstick drop from his fingers. 'You knew she was here all the time! You were the one who killed her!'

He reached into his pocket and produced a gun. He would have to kill me now to cover his tracks. However, he didn't know I carried a Beretta in a holster. Penny would have warned him if she had given me a gun, but he had no contact with Turgut in Turkey so he was unaware I was armed. Before I realised what was happening, a pistol was pointed directly at my head and I was staring down the hole into the barrel. The man with the stretcher took fright at the sudden change of plan and he ran off as fast as his legs would carry him. He knew that other people would hear the shot and the police would arrive shortly.

Primar smiled as he faced me. 'I got to like you, Jason,' he admitted. 'More than you'll ever know. It's a pity it has to end this way. A pity! By the way, I saved your life in Turkey, you know.'

'What are you talking about?' I managed to say, as I began to seize up with fear.

'Kemal was a staunch follower of Islam. In fact he was a member of their intelligence, although he'd be the first to admit their agency doesn't work very well. When he learned you were going to visit the Mahdi in Istanbul, he could hardly contain himself. They're very sensitive about foreigners meddling with their people, their customs, politics and religion, you know. He was right behind you when you crossed the Galata Bridge. His aim was to kill you before you saw the great man because he felt that 'your infidel eyes should never gaze on a person of such greatness'. His words, not mine. He was useful to me in a number of ways but I thought you had a higher value. So I killed him, just before he picked you off, with a Kalashnikoff rifle.'

'Am I supposed to be grateful for that?' I snapped, realising I was about to face death without so much as moving a muscle to resist.

At that moment, the sound of a telephone rang inside his jacket. He laughed loudly, highly amused at the incident. 'What a time to receive a telephone call?' he said, removing a portable telephone from his inside pocket.

For a few seconds his concentration lapsed as he extended the aerial and pressed a button on the instrument to receive the call. It was just the time I needed. Drawing a deep breath, I thrust my hand inside my jacket, produced the Beretta and shot him in the chest. It was over so quickly! In the fraction of a second before he died I could see the surprise register on his face. But it was of little satisfaction to me to gain such revenge, and no advantage to Penny whatsoever.

I closed the door of the apartment and hurried away from the place. It would be difficult to explain my role to the police if I had reported the incident and stayed there with the two corpses. In effect, leaving them there would not allow me to wash my hands of the affair. Penny was my secretary. The police would soon start to link up facts and there would be a lot of explaining to do. It was possible I might never be able to satisfy them with their enquiries. The consequences thereafter were unthinkable!

I went to a restaurant and spent over an hour there mulling over the dreadful situation before driving to the East End of London. Schmuel Musaphia was already in the lobby of the Tower Hotel even though it was well before noon. His face was very serious when I met him but his expression mollified as I arrived.

'I'm very impressed, Jason!' he commended, like a general trying to upgrade the morale of his troops. 'You've done a lot in less than a week and I'm proud of you! Now, follow me and I think you'll find something that will interest you.'

We walked away from the hotel slowly. I was rather surprised when he led me to St. Katherine's Dock to the maze of ancient warehouses. It was familiar to me as I had been there recently to follow up the clue given to me by Menel's daughter. The air was still polluted with wisps of wool and the aroma of coffee, musk and other spices. We went down a lane to one of the warehouses and he bade me enter. It was the same one I had visited before. The same place I had found Jan's coat filled with two bundles of hay. I hesitated outside the large doors reluctant to enter.

'What's the matter?' he asked.

'I've been here before. Quite recently. But it was vacant.'

'It was never vacant. Never!'

'Oh yes it was!' I insisted. 'I found Jan's coat in there filled with two small bales of hay to make it look as though it was her body!'

'Nonsense!' he laughed. 'Come inside and I'll show you what you failed to see!'

We entered and he waved his hand inviting me to follow him to another door behind some bales of hay. In the room there was a trap-door. He raised the flap and motioned me to descend some stone steps to a cellar into the bowels of the earth. He followed behind, allowing the trap-door to fall back into place. The room was well lit with fluorescent lights. It was an underground factory comprised of many kinds of lathes and machinery, with a large model of the laser gun located at the far end of the room. I recognised it immediately from the actual gun in the weaponry division.

'We managed to put a pretty good laser weapon together of our own design,' said the old man. 'You see, there's not much difference between any of them in terms of design and operation. It's the laser beam that counts. Most powerful laser beams can be produced only in short bursts. Continuous streams of laser light are necessarily weak because of the intense heat generated by the flash tubes which would be destroyed if the beam was too powerful. No one has yet been able to overcome that difficulty successfully. Today, we hope to combine experience, expertise, and magic to make a weapon capable of establishing world peace.'

'I don't understand what you're getting at,' I told him honestly.

He took me to a work bench on which there was a model of the core of a crystal laser. 'A crystal laser has a fluorescent crystal such as a ruby as its light-amplifying substance. The power for a ruby laser comes from a flash tube which is usually coiled around a crystal. The flash tube produces a brilliant flash of light which excites a large number of chromium ions, or electrically-charged atoms, in the ruby. The process is called optical pumping. You can see how that works from this model. At each end of the ruby rod is a mirrored surface. Coiled round that rod is a tube which creates the flash and drives the laser beam through the rod to emerge at one end. The technical operation is much more complicated.'

'What are you trying to tell me?' I asked meekly.

He drew on his cigar and puffed smoke to the ceiling. 'The most advanced nations have laser guns but the technology is too weak to support an offensive weapon that could be used as a deterrent. The Americans have played with it for two decades to make only small advances. The plans of Dandy Advanced Electronics are hardly any better. They're ahead of the Yanks but not by very much. So what we're going to do today is the culmination of five years of research by some of the best brains in the business. We're going to turn base metal into gold!'

'Base metal into gold?' I repeated innocently. 'But I thought your main directive was to produce a capable laser gun.'

He laughed so loudly he was forced to remove the cigar from between his lips. 'I'm talking metaphorically about the alchemists' dream,' he went on. My comment must have amused him greatly for it was the first time I could remember seeing him without a cigar sticking out of his mouth. 'We've combined the resources of three ruby rods and three flash tubes. The secret is that the flash tubes are twice as large as usual and the mirrored surfaces are much bigger. Also, instead of a single mirror at one end we've produced two angled mirrors to reflect the light from two different points. It's never been tried before. This is the first time. O.K. Joe!' he called out to one of the men. 'Let's get the show on the road!'

The man wheeled a unit on a trolley across the room. It carried a triplicated core which he placed carefully into the laser gun. At the far end of the room rested a steel sheet about the size of an ordinary door except that it was two feet thick. He waved his hand to Musaphia to indicate that the weapon was ready and put on a protective visor. The octogenarian nodded and the man squeezed the trigger. There was a short pause and a loud buzzing noise before the flash tubes exploded. Joe leapt backwards with his clothes on fire. The other man in the room rushed forward to put out the flames and we stared at the burned-out core with dismay.

'Only two of the flash tubes started to work,' claimed Joe, who seemed undaunted at having been set alight. 'There must have been a fault in the third one.'

'Pretty dangerous stuff!' I commented. 'Are you all right?'

'Fine,' he replied. 'Just as well I'm wearing protective clothing and a visor. But we never concern ourselves with the negative aspects of research here. People are only interested in winners, not losers. And don't worry about the loss of the core unit. We have others.'

The second man opened a cupboard and removed another triplicated core which he wheeled to the laser gun. The old man gave me a wry smile. 'In research, it's a case of try, try, try again. We'll get it in the end. Maybe sooner rather than later.'

Joe wiped the laser gun with a cloth to remove marks caused by the explosion and aimed it at the target. I admired him for his courage. If we had changed places and the equipment had exploded in my face, causing my clothes to catch fire, I wouldn't be in any hurry to try the test again. But this man appeared to be fearless to the point of becoming a martyr to the cause. He pointed the weapon at the steel sheet without any qualms whatsoever and squeezed the trigger, keeping his finger pressed back to engage a long burst of energy. The core unit buzzed and hummed inside the laser gun but the beam was not visible. However, within twenty seconds, a large hole appeared in the metal door.

'Enough!' shouted Musaphia, clearly overjoyed with the result. 'Enough!' Joe released the trigger and the core unit ceased to function. 'I want Menel to identify the reason why this laser unit functions so well. It'll be the embryo for other experiments. What it's done is to prove that we've worked the oracle!'

We walked over to the metal sheet which was still steaming. Then Joe pointed to the wall behind it in which there was a hole large enough for a man to walk through. 'Look!' he shouted excitedly. 'The wall is almost demolished as well. The beam treats, steel, bricks and mortar like a hot knife cutting through butter!'

The old man puffed fiercely on his cigar and put his arm round my shoulder. 'What you've seen here today, Jason, is a piece of history. This is the place where the laser beam deterrent was born! By the way, I want you to go to Stansted Airport in the morning, at about eight o'clock. A man will be waiting for you with a placard with the number twenty-one. A plane will take you to the Gaza Strip. There will be a debriefing session with Commander Yasood, and you'll meet your wife there.'

'In the Gaza Strip?' I echoed with little enthusiasm.

'And I can tell you that your team is doing well at the bridge tournament. Apparently, Tony Woodman is playing a blinder. Isn't that what you say? A blinder? It seems that everyone is having success today.'

I left the warehouse with a hollow feeling inside me. I wasn't sure whether to laugh or cry. Penny was dead: I would be reunited with Jan tomorrow. I had no idea which direction my life would take from this point. But then I had always believed that each man's destiny was written in heaven. I could only hope that mine would be favourable!

CHAPTER FIFTEEN

The sky was heavy with rain the next morning as I drove to Stansted Airport. I found a thickset man waiting there for me as arranged. He stood alone in the entrance hall holding a placard which read "21". I approached him and introduced myself.

'My name's Bross,' he informed me. 'I'm the pilot to take you to the Gaza Strip. The aircraft is ready for take-off.'

I followed him to the plane and boarded, ensuring that the door between the cockpit and the passenger compartment was unlocked.

'You have some kind of problem?' he asked, watching my actions. 'Maybe you don't like to sit with your back to the engine or something. Never mind. Sit with me if you like.'

His words comforted me and I consented to sit beside him in the front of the aircraft. He started the engine, contacted the control tower, and we were soon in the air. However, it was an erratic take-off and I fostered the suspicion that he was extremely short of experience.

'How long did it take you to get a pilot's licence?' I asked.

'Pilot's licence?' he replied, as though it was unnecessary to obtain one. 'We all learn from experience. My cousin used to take me up when he flew people to other destinations. He used to show me what to do.'

'Well how did you learn to read all these instruments?' I continued with some concern.

'I don't read the instruments,' he admitted frankly. 'Most of them hardly matter anyway. I just need to know the speed and altitude.'

I sat back in my seat expecting a bumpy ride but my fears for this part of the journey were unfounded as he switched on the automatic pilot to carry us across Europe. We continued our conversation, talking of generalities for well over an hour, then I was overcome by sleep due to the early hour of rising and the monotonous drone of the engine. I woke momentarily on a number of occasions but it was two hours more before I regained consciousness. There was a violent jerk as the plane seemed to hit turbulence on a grand scale. At the same time, a loud noise reverberated through the cockpit. As I sat up in my chair and yawned, I noticed that Bross was not in the pilot's seat. I went into the passenger cabin to discover he was not there either. Before I returned to the cockpit, I looked out of the port window. There he was, some distance below, swaying forwards and backwards at the end of the parachute. The aircraft had reacted violently when he opened the cabin door and jumped out. The loud noise was the door slamming back into place. I shook my head to make sure I wasn't dreaming and the returned to the cockpit to stare at the controls. What did I know about flying a plane? Nothing! I pressed a switch which I believed to be the microphone for transmitting messages and kept repeating "May Day! May Day!" but there was no reply. I didn't even know whether I was transmitting properly. I opened a panel at the left-hand side of the pilot's seat and found the operating manual. The aircraft possessed dual control yokes with vertical grips....one for each hand. Extended from the base of the instrument panel, there were two buttons: one to open the microphone for transmitting, the other to activate the positive control system....the automatic pilot. I pressed the communication button and continued to broadcast for assistance. Eventually, a radio ham replied to say that he had received the message and had passed it on to the authorities. For a moment I was overwhelmed with relief. But that hardly altered my situation. I was in deeply trouble!

'This is Air Traffic Control at Ben Gurion Airport,' came a voice over the intercom in due course. 'What kind of aircraft are you and what's your destination?'

'I don't know,' I replied, trying to keep my voice on an even keel. 'It's a light aircraft capable of carrying four passengers. We left Stansted Airport and were headed for the Gaza Strip when the pilot baled out. I have no idea why. I've never flown a plane before. All I can say is that we've been flying for well over three hours and there's lot of sea below but no land.'

'You're too low to show up on our radar screen,' continued the voice, 'but I can still talk you down. For Gaza, on your course from Stansted, your vector should be three hundred and five degrees. There's a gyro in front of you which should register that number.'

'The gyro reads three hundred and sixty.'

'O.K.,' he replied. 'Remove the automatic pilot control and move the yoke slightly to your left.'

I obeyed the instruction and the plane lost altitude quickly and veered sharply. For a few seconds it was totally out of control but somehow I managed to compensate and sat back after switching on the automatic pilot control again. 'Three hundred and five degrees,' I confirmed with a sigh of relief. My hands were shaking and my knees felt like they were made of rubber.

'Good! Now there's no point in continuing this dialogue until you reach land. When that happens I want you to call me. Roger and out!'

I sat in the pilot's seat without moving for a long time that then decided to return the manual to its locker. As I was about to thrust it back where I had found it, I stared at a device with a clock dial jammed into the space which had been hidden by the manual. Flashes of the wrecked plane in Crete returned to me as I recalled the place where the bomb had been lodged. The dial was already on zero which meant it was either about to go off or it wasn't working. I had no idea how long I had before the bomb exploded. Pray, I thought to myself. Pray! There was no point in advising Air Traffic Control and I couldn't remove the device for fear of setting it off. It was fifteen minutes before land came into sight. I resumed communication with Air Traffic Control and told them about the bomb. There was nothing either of us could do about it.

'As soon as you cross to land we'll get you down fast,' the voice went on. 'What you're going to have to do is called a sideslip movement. You'll need to turn the yoke to the left and simultaneously jam your foot against the right rudder pedal. The ailerons on the edges of the wings will respond immediately. The left aileron will be up; the right one will drop. The opposing forces created by the crossed control will make the aircraft turn sharply to its left side, putting the plane into distress and creating severe drag. It will drop precipitously in both air speed and altitude. You'll find the plane will lurch to a precarious angle and you'll experience the sensation of falling very fast. There'll be a lot of shaking, bouncing and rattling but you've got to sideslip firmly. If you fall too fast, be careful your wingtips don't touch the ground or you'll crash. When you're about forty feet from your chosen runway, ease up on the controls and level off. Then brace yourself for impact. As there's a suspected bomb on board, I suggest you take action as soon as possible. I'll keep this channel open in the meantime.'

The moment the aircraft crossed the threshold between sea and land I performed the sideslip manoeuvre. The plane reacted exactly as I had been advised, but it was one thing to talk about it and another to experience it. The controls almost wrenched themselves out from under my grip and the blood rushed to my head as I dropped like a stone. Then every piece of metal around me seemed to groan and whine as it bent and curved angrily. I was extremely worried about the angle of the aircraft for one wingtip faced the ground and the other reached up to the sky. The controls juddered fiercely, trying to wrest themselves out of my hands, but I held on for all I was worth. The altimeter sped round the clock much faster than I had expected, and when I calculated the magic figure of forty feet I levelled off unsteadily, gradually pushing the yoke forward so that the nose pointed downwards. The ground came up at me at a tremendous rate. As the aircraft touched down, it lurched heavily on the uneven surface. I jammed my heels on the rudder pedals causing the tyres to burst, and the plane skidded all over the place in a shower of sparks. When it came to a halt, I leapt out of the cockpit and sprinted as far as I could before collapsing on the ground about two hundred yards away. The threat of the bomb created greater fear than the dilemma of having to land the machine. It had been a reaction which suited the situation well.

I walked slowly to put more distance between myself and the aircraft, shading my eyes from the blistering sun and looked into the distance. There was desert all round. Paradoxically, it was possible that I had survived the landing but would die of thirst and dehydration. I had to find civilisation but it was necessary to choose a direction. The sea was behind me. I could follow the coast. I scanned the horizon for a clue and then noticed a jeep in the distance moving towards me. I waited patiently for it to arrive. When it stopped, the driver alighted and called out.

'Jason Scott?' he shouted. I nodded hesitantly, wondering whether he was friend or foe. 'Commander Yasood sent me to fetch you. You're a few miles off course. We picked up your communication with Air Traffic Control. It seems you were the victim of a vendetta.'

'Vendetta? Me?'

'We understand Bross was your pilot. He's a cousin of Chedda. He must have thought you had a hand in Chedda's death and decided to take his revenge.'

'Well,' I returned, 'I thought there was a bomb located next to the pilot's seat but it seems I was mistaken. I feel embarrassed at having caused a lot of fuss about nothing.'

At that moment, as if on cue, there was the sound of a tremendous explosion a short distance away and the aircraft collapsed in a cloud of smoke, falling forward in a heap before our eyes, as flames began to engulf it. We watched it blaze for a short while without speaking.

'You're very lucky, Mr. Scott,' suggested the driver. 'We need lucky people on our side. Climb aboard. I'll take you to the Commander.'

I got into the jeep and he drove off across the desert, well versed in following tracks I could hardly see. It was twenty minutes before we reached the rock in the desert with the interior redesigned by the 21st Century Crusaders. The driver produced a small remote control unit from his pocket and there was a smooth humming sound as the door in the rock slid open. He went directly to the underground car park and we walked along the corridor graced with flagstone floors.

'I think everyone is here already,' commented the driver, putting a little extra pace in his step. 'The car park is almost full.'

We walked through the double doors into the large auditorium. It was filled to capacity but this time there were faces which were familiar to me. Commander Yasood stood on the podium, about to address the audience. Commander Spring was seated in the front row. A few seats away sat Menel. And, as expected, there in the front row was Schmuel Musaphia.

'Welcome, Commander Scott!' greeted Yasood amiably. 'If you would please take your seat we shall start.'

I was stunned at the greeting but failed to comment in front of the audience.

'Good!' said Yasood, facing the audience from the front edge of the podium. 'Thank you for coming here today. We gather to celebrate a milestone in our master plan and I'm delighted to tell you that the second phase has now been completed. You will recall that the first was "formation", the second was "development", and the third will be "full operation". In the second phase, we recruited some fine people and established ourselves in many key countries in Europe. Currently, we're developing a weapon to give us superiority in terms of warfare ....far greater and more controllable than nuclear powered rockets. At the same time, our intelligence system is becoming equal to all others known in the Western world. Before I continue with the details of our development, it is well to report it's likely that the caucus of Islam will find its seeds in Turkey. Islam in the middle of the sixteenth century was at its all-conquering zenith. Its spearhead, the military empire of the Ottoman Turks, threatened to engulf Christendom. The might of the Ottoman Empire, under the rule of Suleiman the Magnificent, was ruthless, trained to inflict savage cruelty on all those who opposed it. As a matter of interest, I read to you his titles. "Sultan of the Ottomans, Allah's Deputy on Earth, Lord of the Lords of this World, King of Believers and Unbelievers, Shadow of the Almighty Dispensing Quiet in the Earth". We don't wish to have Lord of the Lords of this World governing us in the future. However, danger exists in the wake of the break-up of the Soviet Union. In Siberia lies the greatest oil reservoir the world has ever known. In previous assumptions, it was believed that Islam would rise within the next fifty years as the oil began to run out in the Middle East. But if Western countries undertake joint ventures with Russian states, the Arab countries in the Middle East will find their markets diminishing within the next ten years. The dependency for oil on Kuwait, Iran, Iraq, Saudi Arabia and Libya will almost vanish. The price of oil will fall substantially. As a result of this, World War Three is likely to approach much earlier than expected. Such news is not encouraging. It means we must act and react faster than planned. We must be ready to meet the rising tide of Islam!

He droned on for some time outlining details about the countries where the 21st Century Crusaders had become established, the weaponry soon to be in their possession, and the plans for full operation. When his delivery came to an end, he received outstanding applause and then the audience stood up and milled around the auditorium in discussion. My heart started to beat faster as I looked round to search for Jan but she was nowhere to be seen. Commander Yasood headed in my direction and drew me to one side.

'I hope you weren't shocked when I introduced you as Commander Scott,' he said apologetically. 'That's the good thing Schmuel Musaphia suggested would be coming your way. We want to recruit you as our Commander in the United Kingdom.'

'Is that what it was all about? The blackmail, facing death, those trips overseas, the abduction of my wife! All because you wanted to recruit me!'

'Tell me, Jason,' he went on. 'If you were the Chief Executive of, say, Dandy Advanced Electronics and you wanted the best deputy that money could buy to handle the weaponry division, what would you do?'

'I'd get in touch with the best executive personnel recruitment agencies and let them handle the selection for me,' I replied smartly.

'And then, when you received the curriculum vitae and completed the interviews, narrowing down the field, what would you do? You must bear in mind that the weaponry division is something very secret, very confidential, and ultimately special.'

'I'd check the person out thoroughly by means of a private detective. Every past record would be investigated.'

'But how could you be certain that everything that the private detective said was absolutely authentic. Would you know, for example, how the new recruit would react under certain kinds of pressure or crisis? Or how loyal they would be to the organisation over an extensive period of time?'

'Impossible to tell!' I told him flatly. 'Firstly, it's hoped the new executive would have a track record in the field of operation proving that he or she could take such pressures and handle crises without difficulty. With regard to loyalty, people respond to promotion, remuneration and rewards. Executives switch from one organisation to another if they can achieve something better.'

'Exactly,' he concurred. 'You see, we selected you for recruitment some years ago. Your background, temperament, obstinacy and analytical mind made you a prime choice for the role that needed to be filled. For a long time we required a senior executive to run the British end. We've had many people look you over and check you out in the past five years. Penny Smith was one; Primar another. We had checked you out in terms of credentials but we had no idea whether you had any zeal, audacity or spirit. So we set you difficult tasks but the plans went wrong through the ambitions of certain individuals within our ranks. But that is the way of the world! It was by the grace of God you weren't killed. Apparently, Primar and Chedda were waging some kind of a vendetta against each other. You were caught in the cross-fire. Chedda, believing you to be important to Primar, tried to kill Penny Smith and yourself. He intended to parachute to safety over Crete leaving a bomb on board the aircraft. No one would ever know what happened. But he was no munitions expert. This caused problems because his colleague, Tomar Duran, was waiting for him in Crete. Penny Smith was working for us and she used all her ingenuity to have you moved to safety by getting you arrested. However, you're still wanted by the police in Crete for questioning.'

'But there were no bodies,' I exclaimed. 'No one was killed. The duplicate Jason Scott turned up in Turkey. Tomar Duran continued working in the weaponry division of Dandy Advanced Electronics.'

'Not Tomar Duran. Miss Smith shot him with his own gun but substituted blanks for the real cartridges later on. The man you thought was Tomar Duran, who ended up on the electrified fence, was actually his brother trying to get the laser gun plans for his Muslim colleagues. In due course, Schmuel Musaphia, our strategist and adviser, insisted he met you. Unfortunately, Primar wanted to go independent. He worked for MOSSAD, the Israeli intelligence agency, as did Penny Smith, but he wanted to sell the plans of the laser gun to the highest bidder. He used you as he did Kemal whom he killed in Istanbul when the man was about to shoot you outside the home of the Mahdi. It was arranged for you to see the Mahdi and then steal the laser gun plans. You succeeded extremely well. Most commendable! For that effort, we're awarding you the Purple Ribbon of Valour, The highest honour of the 21st Century Crusaders, for audacity.'

'Are you saying that everything I did was solely a test of my courage and ability?' I asked, feeling my temper rising as I thought of all the pain and anguish I had suffered. 'And that my wife was never abducted but merely kept in the background as a blackmail threat in case I wouldn't play!'

'Well, that's a rather simplified way of looking at it but fairly accurate,' he replied coolly.

I stared at him angrily, gritting my teeth. 'When I think what I went through to get the plans of that laser gun and you didn't really need them, did you?'

'Our intelligence is very extensive,' he boasted.

'Well let me tell you a thing or two. Penny Smith is dead! She was murdered by Primar! And there's more! I killed Primar myself yesterday!'

'Oh we know all about that. Normally we remove the bodies so that they vanish without trace. On this occasion, however, we simply removed everything relating to Primar's identity and left a letter written by you to suggest that you discovered that Miss Smith was two-timing you with another man and that you would kill her if you caught her with him. The police will be looking for you to answer a number of questions, with a warrant for your arrest. You're going to have a rough time if they catch you.'

'I see!' I suddenly realised the game plan. 'You made sure I was wanted for murder by the police in Britain and Crete to force me into your organisation. I suppose you intend to set me up with a new name, a new passport and a new home. More blackmail! Who smashed up my house? You or Primar?'

'We did that,' he said smoothly. 'We wanted to make sure you had no papers, documents or material relating to any other organisation or agency. We can't afford double agents in this enterprise, not when one mistake could lead to a world war. We had to check you out very thoroughly.'

'And the function of the doubles?'

'They were brought in to fill your place whenever you needed to be somewhere else. The bridge tournament in Turkey was a typical example. There was nothing sinister in finding and training doubles. We had to focus your mind on breaking into the weaponry division and, ultimately, made it a rush job.'

'But what if I'd been caught at the plant? All your work to recruit me would have come to nothing.'

'I don't think so. Mr. Devon is not the man you think he is. He's a hardened criminal with a brilliant mind in the field of electronics. He would no sooner shoot the whole of the security team at Dandy Advanced Electronics than eat his lunch. Your only danger was the electrified fence. But then it's only ten feet high!'

'You bastard!' I swore angrily. 'You had no right to set me up like that!'

'I disagree,' he returned firmly. 'We simply investigated you thoroughly. Now, when you accept your appointment, you'll want to check out recruits of your own. Think hard on how you'll do that before you start criticising me.'

'Who wrote the note: "Don't fly to Turkey if you value your life! Don't fly to Turkey if you value your wife!"'

'We did that to test your resolve. Some people would have backed out in the face of such a threat. We had to find out what you would do. You ignored the threat and went. We were delighted to recognise your commitment.'

'What about the man who attacked me in my hotel room?'

'Nothing to do with us. He was a genuine thief and you caught him in the act.'

'I suppose I made a real fool of myself at The Golden Peacock, showing up there like an idiot when Jan was merely a hotel guest.'

'I liked the touch where your wife gave you three clues and you managed to find the solution. Then Schmuel told you the answer knowing you had already solved it.' He paused for a moment and smiled. 'So how about it, Jason? Enlist with the 21st Century Crusaders at a handsome salary, a new name, a new address in England, a good car, and everything provided. Surely that's compensation enough for what you've been through! And then there's the cause. An important cause to prevent the occurrence of World War Three. Doesn't any of that grab you?'

'To tell you the truth,' I ventured, 'I'm extremely angry. I risked my life many times for nothing, and people are dead all about me.'

'Sometimes it's necessary to help those who won't help themselves. You'll thrive on this appointment and contribute in a major way. It's a two-way thing. We need each other. Destiny calls you! I'd like your permission to nominate you to the committee as Commander Jason Scott. How about it?' He noticed my reluctance but chose to smile.

'If I don't agree you'll report me to the authorities for the murder of Tomar Duran, Penny Smith and Primar. Then when I start ranting about the 21st Century Crusaders, Islam and World War Three they'll lock me up in a padded cell in a mental institution and throw away the key.'

'That's about the drift of it,' he replied casually. 'If you haven't made up your mind yet, we'll talk later on.' He moved off and I had the feeling he was going to speak to someone else who had also run the gauntlet like myself.

I suddenly realised I hadn't asked him about Jan when she appeared in the doorway of the refectory. She was dressed in a brown uniform similar to the one Penny had worn in Crete. She moved towards me steadily, making her way through the throng. Our eyes met and I scanned her face. She looked extremely well and showed no traces of stress or duress but that was to be expected as her welfare had never been threatened. My attitude crystallised to one of cautious coldness as she approached, but she took my hands warmly into her own, hoping for a reciprocal response.

'So this is what it came down to in the end,' I began. 'The 21st Century Crusaders! Why couldn't you tell me?'

'I was under orders not to do so, darling,' she replied.

'What about the holy orders? The vows you made in church when you became my wife?'

'Those vows have been kept. I haven't broken them. You're the one who had a mistress. I hear that she's dead.'

I gave a wry smile. 'Bad news travels fast. Why all the deceit, Jan. Why couldn't you tell me?'

'That's not the way it's done, Jason. We're making history here. Protecting the world. I don't want to go through life gardening and watching television. Most people are interested only in themselves. That's not me. I want to contribute. To do something for mankind! And now you've been offered a marvellous appointment as Commander for the United Kingdom, we can be together and I can assist you. We have the opportunity of a wonderful future together.'

'What about the note you wrote. Did you mean it?'

'They asked me to offend.'

'So you wrote it....under orders.' I paused and heaved a sigh. 'What do we do now?'

'That depends on whether you still love me.'

'I wouldn't have married you if I didn't love you. Let's say there was a crossed line in my life which no longer exists. I don't know how you feel about it.'

'Life is for giving and for forgiving,' she responded. 'Perhaps we can try a little harder together. Are you willing to do that, Commander Scott?' She placed her arms round my neck and kissed me gently on the lips. 'No, don't say anything,' she continued as I was about to tell her I hadn't made a decision on the appointment. She took my hand and led me out of the auditorium, across the flagstoned corridor to the car park, and pointed to a black saloon. We got inside and she smiled at me charmingly.

'It's nice to have you back,' I told her, showing some emotion for the first time. 'I missed you. I missed you a lot!'

'I know,' she laughed. 'You missed me at St. Katherine's Dock. At The Golden Peacock. At our house. At Penny Smith's apartment. I had to keep moving to stay ahead of you.' She opened the glove compartment in the dashboard and took out two passports and a set of keys. 'You are now William Grover and I'm Selina Grover. These are our passports. The keys will open the door to our new address in England. So, we have new identities and a new home. You no longer work for Dandy Advanced Electronics. A letter has been sent to the Chairman advising him of your resignation on the grounds that you've accepted an immediate appointment in Kuwait with an international oil company.'

'That's taking a lot for granted, isn't it?' I returned, feeling my temper rising again at the liberties being taken with my life and future.

'Trust me!' she told me. 'Just trust me!'

I felt that if anyone else asked me to trust them again I would explode. She drove slowly through the exit of the great rock hide-out, closing the door behind her. Outside, a caravan of camels moved smoothly across the desert. All was peaceful, but that was the moment when the world was most vulnerable. At the root of civilisation was the essence of change. The only thing that remained stable was nature!